# THE BEAST OF LITTLETON WOODS

# THE BEAST OF LITTLETON WOODS

A Lady Hardcastle Mystery

T E KINSEY

THOMAS & MERCER

Text copyright © 2025 by T E Kinsey
All rights reserved.

Published by Thomas & Mercer, Seattle

www.apub.com

Amazon, the Amazon logo, and Thomas & Mercer are trademarks of Amazon.com, Inc., or its affiliates.

EU Product Safety contact:
Amazon Publishing, Amazon Media EU S.à r.l.
38, avenue John F. Kennedy, L-1855 Luxembourg
amazonpublishing-gpsr@amazon.com

ISBN-13: 9781662521621
eISBN: 9781662521614

Cover design by Tom Sanderson
Cover illustration by Jelly London

Printed in the United States of America

# The Beast of Littleton Woods

# Chapter One

'. . . and then I said, "But that's what I wanted the parsnip for in the first place."'

Daisy was in fine form, and the regulars at the Dog and Duck roared with laughter at their favourite barmaid's latest anecdote.

Still basking in their admiration, she looked over at my empty glass. 'Another one in there, Miss Florence?'

I made a brief show of indecision. 'Oh, go on then.' I looked up at Lady Hardcastle. 'Another for you?'

'I think so, dear, yes,' said Lady Hardcastle. 'But it's my round, I believe, so put your purse away.'

I knew it was her round and my hand was nowhere near my purse.

'Two brandies, please, Daisy,' she said. 'And one for yourself.'

'That's very kind of you, Lady H. I'll have a small Mattick's if you don't mind.'

While Daisy fussed with the brandies and her own glass of cider, I looked around at our fellow pubgoers. It was the usual crowd of farmers, farmhands and shopkeepers, with a scattering of wives and sweethearts, as well as a small group of young women out on their own. Their infectious, uninhibited laughter made a delightful contrast to the bellowing guffaws of the farmhands, and

I reflected once more on how lucky we were to have been accepted into the bustling village of Littleton Cotterell.

September had decided to make an impressive exit and we'd all been stuck inside for a week while terrible storms battered our little village. The wind had blasted the house, driving raindrops the size of dormice into the windows, and it had seemed for a while that we might never again know peace. Or be able to get to the shops without being blown away. Or drowned. Or battered by flying dormice.

But eventually the weather had eased and, as if at some subliminal signal, the whole village had descended on the pub to celebrate our survival. Or our freedom from blustery drenchings and whimsically airborne rodents, at any rate.

Initial conversations this Sunday night had been about little other than the storms. Some confidently said they were the worst the area had ever known. Others asserted, just as confidently, that the Great Storm of '98 had been worse. Meanwhile, Jagruti Bland – the vicar's wife – quietly pointed out that no one had experienced rain unless they'd been in her home village in Bengal during the monsoon.

After a while, a consensus formed that they had been *among* the worst storms the area had ever known and that we were all jolly glad it was all over.

Reverend Bland had accompanied his wife, and the two of them were chatting amiably to the local physician, Dr Fitzsimmons. Jag's ludicrous Great Dane, Hamlet, stood by her side, his huge head swivelling excitedly back and forth at each new sound. He was also on the lookout for discarded food. Ever the entrepreneur, landlord 'Old' Joe Arnold was selling his famous doorstop sandwiches from the bar, and Hamlet was alert to the possibility of carelessly dropped scraps.

Dr Fitzsimmons's head was swivelling almost as much as the dog's.

'We don't see you in here very often,' said Lady Hardcastle.

'You're right,' said the doctor. 'To my shame I seldom venture out these days. I feel I ought to socialize more – it's exactly the sort of thing I prescribe to my patients – but by the end of a long day, all I want to do is settle in my favourite armchair with an entertaining book. But after the week we've all had I thought, "Hang the book," and put on my hat and came over. I'm jolly glad I did.'

The vicar smiled. 'There's always a friendly crowd in here. Especially after Evensong, I find. I often wonder if they need a stiff drink to get over it.'

'Nonsense, darling,' said Jagruti. 'Your services are beautiful. But you're right: the pub is always busy afterwards. I like to think you've raised their spirits so much that they have to go out and celebrate life. Hamlet! Leave it!'

The Great Dane had nearly pulled her over in his attempt to reach a fallen crust but, unusually, had obeyed his owner. He'd be unstoppable if he decided to break free of her, but I liked to imagine he had reasoned that his obedience might be rewarded later.

The vicar laughed, and patted the dopey dog's head affectionately.

'Are you regular visitors to our local hostelry, my lady?' asked the doctor.

Lady Hardcastle nodded. 'We like to drop in when we can, don't we, Flo?'

'We do,' I said. 'Daisy is a good friend of mine, so it's a good opportunity to catch up.'

'Ah, dear Daisy,' said Dr Fitzsimmons. 'Are . . . are any of her tales actually true?'

I shook my head. 'Fewer than half, I should say.'

He laughed. 'And how does one tell truth from fiction?'

3

'I find that a good rule of thumb is that the more thoroughly improbable the story, the more likely it is to be true. Daisy's life is a chaotically exotic one for an apparently simple country girl.'

The doctor laughed again. 'I see a very different side of the villagers. They only seek me out when they're sick, and everyone is so serious and proper when they're poorly.'

'You've never seen serious and proper until you've been a country parson,' said the vicar. 'If I had a ha'penny every time someone said something they thought they oughtn't and then followed it up with "Begging your pardon, Vicar", I could retire.'

'Another reason you should join us here more often,' said Lady Hardcastle. 'This is their world and they're much more relaxed here. You'd enjoy it. And they'd enjoy seeing you both letting your hair down a little.'

Dr Fitzsimmons patted his balding head. 'Chance would be a fine thing. But you're right. And I shall. But for now, I think I ought to get home to my book before my housekeeper sends out a search party.'

'We should be getting back as well,' said the vicar. 'It's been a delightful evening, but our housekeeper will be having kittens, too. It's funny how we seem to be so much in thrall to our servants, isn't it?'

Lady Hardcastle laughed and gestured towards me.

I shrugged. 'As if I have *any* power or influence.'

Still chuckling, the three said their goodbyes and made their way across the room together. Jag used Hamlet to clear a path for them, and was somehow looking in the opposite direction as his great head swung to one side and took half a round of beef sandwiches from a plate on a table near the door. They didn't hear the "'Ere, who's 'ad my sandwich?' as the door closed behind them.

Lady Hardcastle and I looked over to the bar, but Daisy was busy so we stood with our backs to it and surveyed the room, seeking out fresh conversation.

At that moment, Sid Hyde approached the bar clutching his empty glass and tried to attract Daisy's attention. We had known him for a few years – he had bought Top Farm from Audrey Caradine and her son not long after Spencer Caradine was murdered – and with his friendly disposition and ready smile he was a popular figure in the village.

His smile didn't seem quite so ready this evening, though.

'You look troubled, Mr Hyde,' I said. 'Is everything all right?'

He gave a sad smile. 'I've been better, Miss Armstrong. I've been better.'

Lady Hardcastle took the glass from his unresisting hand. 'Daisy! Another cider for Mr Hyde, if you please.'

There was some special quality to her voice that not only cut through the general babble of a busy pub, but also commanded instant attention and obedience wherever she was, even when her tone, as now, was at its friendliest. Shopkeepers and waiters fell at her feet, eager to do her bidding, and even cheeky West Country barmaids cheerfully did as she asked without demur.

The drink arrived and she gently pressed Hyde's coins back into his hand, offering Daisy some of her own instead. 'Allow me.' She raised her glass. 'Your good health, Mr Hyde.'

'Ta, Lady H. That's very good of you. Bottoms up.'

'Chin chin.'

They clinked glasses and we all took a sip of our drinks.

'But Flo's right, dear,' said Lady Hardcastle. 'You do look out of sorts. What troubles you?'

'Oh, 'ti'n't nothin', not in the big scheme of things. Just a bit of bother at the farm.'

'You're quite exposed up there on the hill. Did you suffer much damage in the storms?'

'Not too much. Lost a bit of the barn roof but that was easily fixed. There's branches and other rubbish everywhere, and the old elm tree took a batterin' – that'll need fellin' afore it falls on the road by itself. But we can cope with all that.'

Lady Hardcastle nodded. 'Nevertheless, one could do without it. If we've learned anything since we retired out here it's that farmers' lives are precarious enough, even before one considers the random damage caused by Mother Nature.'

'You gets used to it. Nature causes most of our worries, to tell the truth. Not enough rain, too much rain, not enough sun, too much sun, too many pests – it all goes with the job. But sometimes somethin' comes along that don't seem like it's part of the natural way of things.' He sipped his cider. 'We got through last week's tempests with no losses. We had that little bit of damage, of course, but the sheep were all safe. We checked them all afore the storms, and they're all ready for tupping over the next few weeks.' He took another sip. He was clearly quite upset. 'But this mornin' I goes out and finds one of my best ewes ripped to bits down by the spinney. Never seen carnage like it.'

'Ripped to bits?' I said.

'Torn open like a Christmas parcel. Somethin' fierce and wild done that. Somethin' I shouldn't like to meet unarmed.'

'Good gracious,' said Lady Hardcastle. 'A stray dog, perhaps?'

'Perhaps. But it's like no dog attack I've ever seen. Most dogs just chase them for a bit. They might bite if they gets overexcited, but they don't do what I saw this mornin'. Somethin' feasted on that ewe.'

One of the farmhands sitting with a group of his friends nearby had overheard Hyde's account and turned towards us.

'I don't reckon it were no dog,' he said. 'I seen a big cat down by the stream this mornin'.'

His friends guffawed.

'A big cat?' said one. 'Like our ma's tabby?'

'No,' said the first, indignantly. 'A proper big cat.'

'Tiddles is quite a size, mind. You'd know if she jumped on you from the top of the kitchen dresser.'

The men laughed again.

The first man wasn't backing down. 'I knows a moggy when I sees one. What I saw weren't nothin' like your ma's Tiddles.'

One of the men sniggered, then stopped and blushed when he noticed Lady Hardcastle and me looking at him.

'What exactly did you see?' asked Lady Hardcastle.

'Like I said, m'lady. A big cat.'

'How big?'

'It were some way off so I couldn't see clearly. Four foot long, maybe? With at least another two foot of tail. It were drinkin' from the stream, then sommat spooked it and it slinked off up a tree.'

The friend with the family tabby was still unconvinced. 'There i'n't no cats six foot long.'

'This one was. Easy. I seen a panther at the zoo once. Like that it was.'

'So it was black?' I said.

'Could-a been,' said the farmhand. 'Risin' sun was behind it, so I couldn't be sure. But if Sid's sheep is gettin' attacked, I reckon it's more likely sommat like a panther than any dog from round here.'

'The vicar's wife's dog could take a sheep,' said his friend.

'Hamlet might exhaust a sheep with his exuberant play,' said Lady Hardcastle, 'but I doubt it would ever occur to him to deliberately harm it.'

Hamlet was an affable idiot of a dog whose size and playfulness caused no end of trouble but, as Lady Hardcastle suggested, he had never deliberately harmed anyone or anything.

The farmhand shrugged and turned back to his friends.

'What do you think, Mr Hyde?' I said. 'Could the lad be right? Could it be a big cat?'

Hyde shrugged. 'I got no way to know. I a'n't never seen no panther on my land. I a'n't never seen no panther nowhere, tell the truth. I'm not even sure I knows what one is, never mind where I might find one or what it would look like when I did. Where'd they come from?'

Lady Hardcastle grinned, relishing the chance to show off a little. 'Actually, they're leopards, but they have an excess of melanin, and instead of having lots of small spots they're completely black – it's as if they have just one giant spot. So they come from wherever one finds leopards and jaguars: Africa, Asia and South America.'

'Not Gloucestershire, then.'

'Hardly.'

'So no, m'lady, I don't reckon it were no panther, no matter what young Billy says. I'm stickin' with dog. I'll take a good look round tonight afore I goes to bed.'

'You be careful,' I said. 'Even if it is just a dog, you've seen what it can do.'

'I appreciates your concern, Miss Armstrong, but me and my twelve-bore is a match for any hound. I'll be fine.'

'Just see you are,' said Lady Hardcastle.

He smiled and raised his empty glass. 'Now we've talked about it, I reckon I ought to go and check my boundary like I said. Thank you very much for the drink – you mustn't let me forget to buy you one the next time we're in here.'

'My pleasure, Mr Hyde. Good hunting.'

With a cheery wave, Hyde walked to the door and we turned our attention back to Daisy and her barely believable tales.

◆　◆　◆

We left the pub before closing time and walked the short distance home. The sky was clear but the moon had yet to rise, so it was dark as we walked around the village green and up the lane towards the house.

'We could do with some gas lamps out here,' said Lady Hardcastle as we made our way slowly and carefully between the hedgerows.

'We'd have to have a gas main first,' I said. 'Or, better yet, electricity.'

'Wouldn't that be a boon? It's only when we go to London that I forget how cut off we are out here.'

Work for the Secret Service Bureau over the summer had required us to spend quite a while in a rented flat in London, and we had both grown accustomed to having gas and electricity.

She gave a little chuckle. 'Let's hope we don't meet any dangerous animals in the blackness.'

'We'll be fine,' I said. 'The worst of them will all be in bed by now.'

She paused thoughtfully for a moment. 'You're talking about cows, aren't you?'

'You know how I feel about cows. The deadliest of all creatures.'

'I doubt Sid Hyde's sheep was ripped apart by cows.'

'I wouldn't put it past them.'

She laughed. 'I think we – and the district's livestock – are quite safe from the likes of Clarabelle and Buttercup.'

'But imagine if they got their hands on weapons.'

'Their hooves on weapons, you mean.'

'Metaphorical hands. Obviously they'd have to wield their deadly blades in their terrifying, slobbery mouths.'

'You paint a genuinely disturbing picture, but I still say we're safe. Wait . . . what's that?'

We stopped dead a little way short of our front gate and listened to a rustling in the hedgerow. The rustling, accompanied by a low grunting, stopped. My eyes had become somewhat accustomed to the darkness, but still I couldn't make out any details of the activity ahead of us.

I thought I heard claws on the road. Quite a lot of claws.

I felt Lady Hardcastle's hand on my arm.

'Badgers,' she whispered delightedly. 'Two of them. Oh, they're beautiful.'

Lady Hardcastle had many wonderful gifts – she was a scientist, an artist, a musician, a linguist, a crack shot, the best and most generous friend – but one of her most astonishing natural talents was that she needed only the faintest glimmer of light to be able to discern things that others of us might barely manage to see in bright sunshine. In this case it was the dim light from a lamp I'd left on in our drawing room that gave her the necessary illumination.

At the sound of her whisper, the badgers – I was in no position to question her meline assertion – scampered back into the hedge with yet more rustling and grunting.

Lady Hardcastle took my arm and led the rest of the way to the gate.

Once inside, and with our coats and hats hung up, I made us some cocoa and we settled down in the drawing room to drink it before bed.

Lady Hardcastle bent and unbuttoned her boots. 'The bovine menace aside, what did you make of poor Sid's story?'

With a tut, I picked up her boots and carried them out to the hall while I considered my response.

'He's a reliable chap,' I said as I sat back down. 'So I don't doubt that he found one of his sheep badly mutilated this morning.'

'Agreed. But I'm not sure I give any credence to young whatshisname's claims—'

'Hyde called him Billy.'

'Oh, I say, well remembered. But Billy's panther claims are just a little too far-fetched for my taste.'

'Mine, too, if I'm honest.'

'Says the woman who not ten minutes ago was speculating on the possibility of cows carrying knives in their teeth like eighteenth-century pirates.'

'By the powers, but they'd be a proper menace if they did, Jim lad.'

She laughed. 'They would, indeed. Do we have any biscuits?'

'That's it for sheep mutilation, then, is it?'

'I'm not sure I have more to add. And I fancy a biscuit. Rich Tea if we have any. And can you bring the post back in with you, please? I was so busy today I completely neglected to look at it.'

I got up and went to see if Miss Jones – our cook, and a noted biscuit aficionado – had stashed any Rich Teas in the hiding place in the pantry that she thought I didn't know about.

She had.

On my way back with the tin I stopped in the hall to remove my own boots and pick up the post.

I presented the biscuit tin.

Lady Hardcastle's hand paused in mid-air on the way to the biscuits. 'What, no plate?'

'You know where we keep the plates if you're that desperate. But do we really need one? I thought we might save a bit of washing up.'

'Well, I'm not sure about dropping our standards like this. I—'

I sighed. 'Do you want a biscuit or not?'

'Yes, please.'

'Then shut up and take one.'

'Two. I'll take two.'

'You do that.'

I sorted through the post and handed over the ones addressed to her.

From the postmark on my own letter, I could see that my dear American friend, Ellie Wilson, had written to me, and I was disappointed I hadn't thought to look earlier. Still, it would be a delightful pleasure to read it before bed.

Life in Annapolis was as frustrating as ever for young Ellie. She was eighteen now, and her family – wealthy Marylanders – were becoming increasingly impatient in their demands that she settle down as soon as possible and marry someone 'appropriate to her station'. Their ideal partner for her was a young man from a good family, preferably one with whom the Wilsons could form a useful political alliance. The problem was that Ellie was already deeply in love with a charming drummer she'd met one evening in a hotel at Weston-super-Mare. And Skins Maloney – for it was he – was from a perfectly ordinary London family with no political connections and even less money. Her own family knew nothing of the epistolary romance between the two young lovers, hence the nagging about appropriate Maryland men. Although, if they had known, the nagging would have been even more aggressive – Skins was absolutely not the sort of man they had in mind for Eleanora Wilson.

The advantage for me in all this intrigue was that Ellie and Skins had been conducting a regular transatlantic correspondence; and so I, in turn, was able to keep up to date with Skins's news through Ellie's letters. He was absolutely hopeless at writing to me, but she wrote at least once a month, sometimes more often if she was bored.

'Skins and Barty have a regular engagement at a club in the West End,' I said.

'Skins has written to you? How delightful. How is he?'

'It's from Ellie. She says he's well.'

Lady Hardcastle laughed. 'Young love, eh? I hope those two find a way.'

'I can't quite see how, given the distance between them – social as well as physical. But I hope so, too.'

She held up one of her own letters. 'I, meanwhile, have heard from dear George Dawlish.'

'I do love Colonel Dawlish. Is he well?'

'He's having a fine old time. The circus is thriving, and they're just getting ready to lay up for the winter at their place in Dorset. "Time for all those maintenance jobs we've been putting off all season," he says. There's lots of news of the troupe. You should read it – he addresses it to you, too.'

'I'd like that, thank you. More cocoa?'

'I'm tempted, but I'd better not. I'm quite sleepy after all the excitement – I think I'll retire.'

'Right you are. I'll just tidy up – I don't like leaving dirty dishes for Edna and Miss Jones.'

And so I washed the cups, replaced the biscuit tin in Miss Jones's not-so-secret hiding place, and turned out the lamps before heading upstairs myself.

I rose early on Monday and got a start on what Lady Hardcastle had taken to calling my 'morning faffing'. For many years while we were working together as spies for Queen – and then King – and country, I had been her only servant and I had grown used to the routine of taking care of things about the home.

When we moved to Littleton Cotterell, Lady Hardcastle had immediately employed a part-time housekeeper, Edna Gibson, and a part-time cook, Blodwen Jones. Edna insisted on being referred to as a housemaid, in part so that it meant she wouldn't be formally responsible for all the duties of a housekeeper (which she undertook anyway, with impressive efficiency) and in part so that she wouldn't be called Mrs Gibson – a name, she insisted, better suited to her formidable mother-in-law. As cook, protocol dictated that my good friend Blodwen ought to be known as Mrs Jones despite being unmarried, but it didn't suit her so she was always Miss Jones while she was working.

Between the three of us we kept the household running smoothly. As lady's maid I shouldn't have been faffing at all and, in truth, the other two could take care of things very well without me, even working only half-days. But I liked to do a bit of tidying after my morning exercise and I enjoyed being responsible for Lady Hardcastle's 'starter breakfast'. Named by Lady Hardcastle's good friend Horatia, it had started out as a cup of tea and a round of buttered toast, but had lately become coffee and toast for reasons neither of us could recall.

With my t'ai chi done and my faffing faffed, I got changed into something a little more presentable than my Chinese exercise garb, and returned to the kitchen to put the kettle on and make some toast.

I was just spreading the butter and trying to decide whether Herself might like some honey as well, when I heard a key in the side door and knew Edna and Miss Jones had arrived. I put the kettle on again to make them a pot of tea.

'Mornin', Miss Armstrong,' said Edna. 'Is the kettle on? We needs it this mornin'.'

I waited until she and Miss Jones had removed their coats before asking why.

'You'll never believe it,' said Miss Jones. 'Actually, maybe you might. Sid Hyde—'

'Sid Hyde's dead,' interrupted Edna, keen as always to be the main source of village news and gossip.

'Dead?' I said. 'But we were talking to him only last night at the pub. He seemed fine.'

Miss Jones nodded. 'I saw him there, too, but it wasn't natural causes. He—'

'He was killed by that same wild animal as took one of his best ewes,' said Edna. 'Torn to pieces, he was.'

I caught Miss Jones's exasperated expression and couldn't help but smile, despite the terrible news.

'His lead farmhand found him this morning,' she said. 'He—'

Edna was oblivious to Miss Jones's efforts to tell the story. 'Louis Finch said he found him with his shotgun beside him. Still loaded. Never 'ad a chance to defend hisself, poor beggar.'

Miss Jones shrugged and rolled her eyes. It was a struggle not to laugh.

'That's terrible,' I said. 'Terrible. Poor Doreen.'

Sid Hyde had been walking out with a widow from Woodworthy and we'd all been expecting him to propose marriage at any moment.

Edna shook her head. 'She'll be devastated, the poor love. I a'n't never known nothin' like it. Lived round 'ere all my life, I 'ave, and I never seen no wild animal attacks. It was bad enough when it was his sheep, but now a lovely man like Sid's been killed . . . Well . . . someone's gotta do sommat.'

'But what?' I asked. 'Whose responsibility is it?'

'Wally Dobson and Sam Hancock,' she said, confidently.

Sergeant Dobson and Constable Hancock were our village policemen.

'I'm not sure it's up to the police to deal with wild animals,' I said. 'It's probably a matter for the Board of Agriculture. Don't they have a representative out here?'

'Some bloke from up Gloucester comes round once in a while to "help" and "advise". Poke his nose in, more like. Useless article. And what's he gonna do, anyway? Issue it a summons for not fillin' in the proper government forms? Fine it for gorin' folk to death without a licence?'

She had a point, but what would the police do? Hyde had a shotgun and hadn't been able to save himself; Dobson and Hancock were fine fellows, but they were unarmed and probably no match for the sort of wild dog we were all imagining.

Miss Jones spoke up. 'Wally and Sam'll know who to talk to, at least. And they've got to make sure people don't go lookin' for it themselves. More could die.'

'Actually, that's a very good point,' I said. 'And not by the fangs and claws of this wild dog, either. There are few things more dangerous than gangs of armed men roaming the countryside looking for something to kill. If the dog doesn't get them, they might easily shoot each other.'

'Lady H'll know what to do,' said Miss Jones.

Her faith in her employer was touching – I wasn't confident Lady Hardcastle would have the first idea what to do, myself. But perhaps it was worth asking, at least.

'I'll take up her starter breakfast and find out.'

# Chapter Two

To the uninitiated, it might appear that the bed was unoccupied. A little rumpled, perhaps, but entirely free of forty-four-year-old widows.

Those in the know, on the other hand, would remember that among the many eccentricities of one particular widow of that age was her penchant for sleeping with her head under the covers.

The coffee cup rattled in its saucer as I put it down on the bedside table, and the covers twitched. A bear grunted resentfully. Or a forty-four-year-old widow – it was difficult to tell the difference some mornings. The sheet flicked down, revealing a blearily blinking face surrounded by a halo of dark hair.

'What time is it?' croaked the bear.

'A quarter past seven,' I said, brightly.

She groaned. 'Do get out, then, there's a love. I have forty-five minutes' more snoozing to do before I can properly cope with your matutinal cheeriness.'

'Would that I could, o somnolent one, would that I could. But I come bearing news which can't really wait.'

'Bad news? Who's died?'

'I sense you're half joking there, but actually—'

She struggled upright. 'Who?'

'Sid Hyde. His lead farmhand found him mauled to death this morning.'

'How utterly awful. The poor man. Poor both men. Imagine coming to work and finding your employer mauled to death.'

I grinned.

'Oh, don't give me that,' she said. 'You'd be devastated. Was it the wild animal again?'

'That's the prevailing assumption. Edna and Miss Jones brought the news – it's all over the village. They think something should be done, but don't know what. I said I'd ask you.'

'I'm touched by your confidence in me, but I'm blowed if I know. Can't the rozzers handle it? The Board of Agriculture?'

'Those were the options we came up with, certainly. Oh, and a mob of angry villagers with torches and pitchforks.'

She smiled. 'The Frankenstein solution. But we have to try to prevent that sort of thing. There's more chance of someone being killed by a frightened mob than by a wild animal.'

It was gratifying to have my own opinions reflected back at me, but it didn't get us anywhere nearer to a preferred course of action.

'Miss Jones favours letting the police handle it,' I said, 'and I think Sergeant Dobson must be aware of what's going on by now. So perhaps we should just leave it to him.'

'I honestly can't think of anything better. Pass me that delicious-smelling toast, would you, dear? I ought to have some sustenance before I get up.'

I gave her the toast and made sure the coffee was within reach.

'I'll leave you to it,' I said, 'while I go and try to reassure Edna and Miss Jones.'

◆　◆　◆

Edna and Miss Jones calmed down somewhat once Lady Hardcastle came downstairs and dispensed her wisdom. It didn't seem to bother them that she was only saying what they'd said themselves – somehow the fact that someone as well educated as she was saying it gave it more weight. I sometimes envied her easy charm and authority – I certainly admired it. It had got us out of a number of sticky situations in the past when my own instinctive response – a swift and decisive smack in the chops – might just have made matters worse.

I'd never once considered smacking my colleagues in the chops, but they were still less likely to have confidence in their own problem-solving abilities – or mine – than in Lady Hardcastle's, so I happily relied on her to set their minds at ease when the situation warranted it.

Having restored order to the household, Lady Hardcastle retired to her study after breakfast to catch up with her correspondence while I got on with some mending and alterations. She was still no better at keeping her clothes free of rips and tears – hence the repairs. She had also put on a little extra weight lately – hence the discreet alterations.

I interrupted her mighty labours at eleven to invite her to the drawing room for tea and biscuits. Miss Jones made up a tray for us and I was on my way through the hall with it when the post clattered on to the doormat. I hovered for a moment, undecided whether I would prefer to make two trips or try to find a way of taking the post and elevenses through in one go. I decided that a single delivery would be more impressive and maid-like, but then hovered for a few moments more while I tried to work out the most efficient way of picking it all up. The most obvious solution was to put the tray on the hall table, pick up the letters, then carry the whole lot through. But what if I balanced the tray in one hand, crouched to get the post, and then—

'Are you all right out there, Flo?' called Lady Hardcastle from the drawing room. 'You've been aaaages.'

'On my way,' I said, and plumped for the hall table option.

I arrived with the tray of letters, tea and biscuits, and plonked it down before flopping into my usual chair. So much for appearing impressive and maid-like.

Lady Hardcastle grabbed the letters and started riffling through them.

She tutted. 'Well, this one's not for us . . . nor this . . . nor this.' She sorted the rest. 'Only one of the six is for us. The rest are for people all over the village.'

'Odd,' I said. 'It's late, too. First post is usually here by eight.'

'I shall have to pop over to the post office to take them back.'

'I can do that for you.'

'You're kind. But I need to post some letters and I could do with the exercise. I'm sure some of my dresses are getting a little tight. We can do it on the way.'

'On the way where?'

'Did I not mention that we've been invited to The Grange for lunch?'

'You did not.'

'Oh, I'm sorry. We've been invited to The Grange for lunch.'

'So I gather.'

'Gertie and Hector are back from France and seem desperate to share details of their new grandchild.'

'How lovely. We can drop in to the post office on the way.'

'That, tiny servant, is a splendid idea.'

'I have my moments.'

'I don't imagine there's anything especially wrong at the post office, though. I suspect the Talbots are still getting used to things.'

The village postmaster, 'Old' Mr Porlock – the people of Littleton Cotterell were charming and friendly, but not terribly imaginative when it came to descriptive soubriquets – had retired, and the post office had been taken over by a delightful couple of newcomers to the village, Jimmy and Bessie Talbot.

They were a lovely couple of indeterminate age, but were probably in their forties to judge from their appearance and worldliness. They were too young to be grey, but not so young as to be irritatingly naive about the world.

We'd had few direct dealings with Mr Porlock, who had run the post office since long before we moved to Littleton Cotterell. He enjoyed administration and organization, but wasn't so keen on people, whom he found, for the most part, to be chaotic and difficult to understand. The post office under Porlock had been a place where letters and telegrams were received and dispatched with pleasing efficiency, but not a place where villagers would gather for gossip. Spratt the butcher was the best place for that, though Holman the baker and Weakley the greengrocer were sometimes up on the latest news, especially if our own Edna had already been in to share it with them.

The Talbots were still too newly arrived to be fully trusted with gossip, and too unfamiliar with the principal players to be able to properly understand it anyway. But they were warm and friendly, and I predicted that it wouldn't be long before they, too, were a valuable source of news and chit-chat.

If they lasted. Warmth, friendliness and a willingness to gossip were fine qualities in any shopkeeper, but sending the morning post to random addresses throughout the village did not mark them as a potentially outstanding postmaster and wife.

'I imagine postmastering takes a while to master,' I said. 'Shall we go as soon as we've finished this?'

'As soon as I've changed into something a little less constricting.'

I pointed to her favourite blue dress. 'I've just mended this one.'

'Oh, thank you. I don't know how I keep ripping them.'

I knew: she was clumsy and careless. But it didn't do to say so. Instead, I said: 'It's as well we're going together – I can protect you from wild dogs.'

'And panthers.'

'And panthers, yes . . . But not cows. If we see any armed beeves, you're on your own.'

'Duly noted. But I'm sure we'll be fine in broad daylight. And there's unlikely to be any trouble at the village post office. Apart from some mis-sorted post, obviously.'

'And there's probably a perfectly ordinary explanation for that.'

'I should think so. Do you want that last digestive?'

Pandemonium. That's the only word to describe the scene at the village post office. Actually, that's not quite true. 'Chaos' would describe it adequately, too. As would 'bedlam'. There was a commotion bordering on uproar. All hell, I would venture to say, had broken loose.

Eight villagers wouldn't ordinarily be considered a crowd. But in the tiny space in front of the post office counter, when they were all shouting at the top of their voices and angrily waving fistfuls of letters, eight villagers most definitely were a crowd. Or perhaps an angry mob.

'Gracious me,' said Lady Hardcastle as we opened the door. 'This is pandemonium.'

*Well done, me.*

Lady Hardcastle looked around. She was a head taller than anyone else there and had an excellent view of the situation, whereas all I could see were backs and boots.

Having taken stock of the situation, she ahem'd, but the furious villagers were far too wrapped up in their epistolary rage to notice.

She leaned down to speak in my ear. 'Do you think you could get their attention, dear?'

I nodded, then put my fingers in my mouth and let out my famously ear-piercing whistle.

The throng turned and looked at Lady Hardcastle. The hubbub subsided.

'Good morning, ladies and gentlemen,' she said. 'I take it from the fact that we're all holding bundles of letters' – she held up our own misdirected post – 'that there's been a little bit of trouble here at the post office.'

The hubbub resumed as the villagers waved their own envelopes and began shouting their complaints once more, though this time directing them at Lady Hardcastle. She held up her hands in an appeal for quiet.

'I understand your frustration, my dear friends, really I do. But you can see the effect you're all having on poor Mrs Talbot.'

There was a renewed outbreak of grumbling, but it was less aggressive this time.

'What I propose,' said Lady Hardcastle when it abated a little, 'is that we all leave our misdirected letters here, and come back in, shall we say, half an hour?'

Mrs Talbot smiled uncertainly.

'Half an hour it is, then,' continued Lady Hardcastle. 'That will give Mrs Talbot time to re-sort them and we can all pick up our important correspondence then. How does that sound?'

From my position by the door I could see little other than Lady Hardcastle's back, but from the resigned mumbles and the sound of paper being slapped on a wooden counter I judged that her proposal had been accepted. The jostling as the disgruntled villagers pushed past us on their way out confirmed it.

Moments later, Lady Hardcastle and I stood alone at the post office counter while a tearful Bessie Talbot picked up the jumble of letters and began looking through them.

She sniffed. 'Thank you for that. You're Lady Hardcastle, aren't you?'

'It's my pleasure. And yes, I am. This is Miss Armstrong.'

'Flo I knows,' said Bessie. 'You've been in a few times since me and Jimmy moved 'ere, a'n't you, dear? Always 'as a nice chat, me and Flo.'

'We do,' I said.

'You two's got quite the reputation round 'ere. They all loves you.'

'How wonderful,' said Lady Hardcastle. 'I had no idea.'

'They's in awe of you, too. I've lost count of how many stories I've heard about how you solved this murder or that. I mean, Jimmy and I's a bit worried about what sort of area we's moved into – we a'n't never been anywhere near no murders – but there's comfort in knowin' there's someone on our doorstep who can solve 'em when they 'appens.'

'It is remarkable quite how many murders we've been called upon to solve. And somewhat alarming, I must say. But we solve other conundrums, too.'

Bessie waved the misdelivered letters. 'I wish you could solve this one.'

Lady Hardcastle smiled. 'Perhaps we can. Or we can try, at least.'

'It's beyond me – I just don't know how it happened. I know I sorted 'em right. You expects one or two to go to the wrong address, but I a'n't never seen nothin' like this.' She waved the stack of envelopes again.

'You've run a post office before?' I asked.

'We ran a sub-post office in Bedminster for three years before we come out 'ere. In all that time we 'ad one postcard go to the wrong street, and one gas bill delivered to a number 23 instead of 32.'

Lady Hardcastle nodded. 'It's most peculiar. An error by the postman?'

'Can't see how. Takes a lot of work to mess things up this badly, and Wilf, bless 'im . . . well, it's not that he's lazy, like – takes his job very serious – but I can't imagine him puttin' in that much effort. He likes to get his round done and then get back to his missus and put his feet up with his pipe and a cuppa.'

I laughed. Wilf Harrison had been our postman ever since we moved to Littleton Cotterell and Bessie's assessment was spot on. 'We'll get to the bottom of it. There's bound to be a simple explanation.'

'I hope so,' said Bessie. 'I can't face too many more mornin's like this one. Do you want to wait while I see if I got anything for you?'

'No, dear,' said Lady Hardcastle. 'I'm sure anything we've been sent can wait till second post. We'll leave you to it.'

We said our goodbyes and set off for The Grange.

It was chilly, but in the aftermath of the storms it was suddenly and unexpectedly sunny, so we decided to walk up the hill to The Grange. Most of the trees were already bare, having given up the unequal struggle to hold on to their goldening leaves against the ferocious winds and rain.

The bare branches made the sky look crisp and clean in the sunlight, while the rotting mulch made the road treacherously slippery beneath our boots.

We took our time.

It was a relief when the architectural chaos of The Grange came into view around the final bend. With its Tudor core, its Palladian façade, and its neo-Gothic wing, the home of our friends the Farley-Strouds should have looked terrible, but it had an eccentric charm – in much the same way as did its owners – that made it oddly appealing.

Until earlier that year, those had been the most interesting things about The Grange: its architectural quirks and its quirky owners. But in May we all learned that, for nearly a hundred years, the hodgepodge old building had been the hiding place of a substantial fortune, in the form of treasure looted by an English cavalry major during the Napoleonic Wars. It was legally determined that the treasure now belonged to the present owners of the house, and the Farley-Strouds had gone from impecunious to oofy with the stroke of a coroner's clerk's pen.

Their first act upon becoming suddenly wealthy had been to throw an extravagant party for the villagers, and only once that was over did they do something for themselves: they packed their bags and went to France to be with their only daughter, Clarissa, who was about to have their second grandchild. Clarissa was married to an English aeroplane engineer by the name of Adam Whitman, who worked for Aéroplanes Vannier in Bordeaux. The expense of travel meant that they seldom saw their beloved daughter and their equally beloved granddaughter, but now they were in the money they had been determined to see grandchild number two as soon as he or she arrived in the world.

Beatrice Gertrude Whitman, sister of Louisa Frances, had been born on the 4th of September 1912, and her doting grandparents had stayed in Bordeaux for almost another month. Edna – principal source of village news – had first alerted me to their return last Friday, the 4th of October. Daisy – back-up source and adder of detail, scandal, and off-colour jokes – had confirmed their arrival the following day. Lady Hardcastle – close friend of the Farley-Strouds and scatterbrained nincompoop – had seemingly been in direct contact with the happy wanderers over the weekend but had entirely failed to mention it.

We scrunched up the gravel drive, glad to be on slightly more certain footing after the slithery leaf litter on the road, and arrived at the navy-blue front door. Lady Hardcastle gave the bell pull a self-assured tug and we waited.

After a short while, Jenkins, the Farley-Strouds' butler, opened the door.

He smiled warmly. 'Lady Hardcastle. Miss Armstrong. Do please come in. Sir Hector and Lady Farley-Stroud are expecting you.'

He ushered us in and took our coats.

'They're in the library,' he said. 'Would you like me to show you through?'

'You're very kind, Jenkins,' said Lady Hardcastle, 'but I think we can find our own way by now.'

'Of course, my lady. Do please ring if there's anything further I can do for you.' And with a bow, he was gone.

Sir Hector was at the novelty globe drinks cabinet in the library.

'Come in, m'dears, come in,' he said. 'A little snifter before lunch? Go on. I'm havin' one. Brought some delicious cognac back from *la belle France*.' He waved a bottle at us.

'I won't today, if you don't mind, Hector dear,' said Lady Hardcastle.

He chuckled. 'Not sickenin' for somethin', I hope.'

Lady Farley-Stroud tutted. 'Not everyone's as much of a dipsomaniac as you, Hector. Leave the poor woman alone.'

'Right you are, my little pear drop. How about you, though, young Florence? Surely you'll join me?'

'Would you be offended if I didn't, Sir Hector?' I said. 'It's a little too early for me.'

'Quite right, too, m'dear. Shouldn't drink early in the day. Bad for the whatnots.' He poured himself a generous glug of cognac and waved us to a pair of seats near a window. 'Don't stand on ceremony, sit yourselves down.'

'Yes, m'dears,' said Lady Farley-Stroud. 'Come and make yourselves comfortable so I can tell you all about baby Beattie.'

'You're in for it now,' said Sir Hector with an indulgent chuckle. 'Are you sure you don't want a little livener?'

Lady Farley-Stroud tutted. 'Oh, do be quiet, Hector.'

'Right you are, my little Pontefract cake.'

'Tell us everything,' said Lady Hardcastle.

Lady Farley-Stroud took a deep breath. 'Well—'

She was interrupted by a clamour of barking and the tick-thud of paws on floors as Sir Hector's three springer spaniels hurtled chaotically through the door, pursued by a small white ball of yapping fluff. They bounced their way noisily through the library and out the door at the other end. Some exciting game was clearly afoot.

A woman's voice called from the corridor. 'Minty! Minty, come back here, you naughty girl. I'll not tell you again.'

The owner of the voice appeared at the door.

'Hector,' she said, angrily. 'You have to do something about your wretched, disobedient dogs. They're leading darling Minty astray.'

'They're just havin' a bit of fun,' said Sir Hector. 'Excited to have a new pal to play with. They'll be fine. Come and join us for a preprandial bracer. You know Emily and Florence.'

The woman seemed to notice us for the first time. 'Oh. Hello. Yes. We met at Christmas a few years ago.'

'We did,' said Lady Hardcastle. 'How are you, Joyce, dear?'

Joyce Adaway was Sir Hector's older sister, whom we had, indeed, met during the festivities of Christmas 1909.

She had been widowed in 1898 and, like our late Queen, had worn nothing but black ever since. It gave her a stern, forbidding appearance rather than the sad, respectful look I felt sure she was aiming for, but most of the fault there lay not with her choice of attire but with her stern, forbidding manner. She would not, I felt, be a ray of joyful sunshine even were she wearing a dress made of candyfloss and carrying a basket of kittens.

'Quite well, thank you,' said Mrs Adaway. 'Though I'd be better if darling Minty were not forced to spend so much time in the company of those ill-disciplined curs.'

Clotho, Lachesis and Atropos – unpronounceably named by Sir Hector for the Greek Fates in a characteristic fit of whimsy – were loyal, friendly, gentle and, in the words of Lady Farley-Stroud's lady's maid – my friend Maude Denton – 'a right bleedin' handful'.

Whereas Hamlet the Great Dane got into trouble simply by being too gormless to realize that his enormous size might render some of his more exuberant games a little disruptive, 'the gels', as Sir Hector collectively referred to them, were disruptive by design. If there were tasty treats to be stolen, shoes to be destroyed, or unsuspecting humans to be knocked off their feet, the gels would be there in a cleverly coordinated attack of stealing, chewing and tripping. They were like clockwork toys, haring about the place, bumping into things and people, and generally causing mayhem, all the while appearing to smile gleefully with their long pink tongues lolling out of the sides of their mouths. Fortunately, just like clockwork toys, their motors soon wound down and they were forced into prolonged periods of happy indolence, snoozing on each other in whatever they determined to be the most inconvenient spot for their human housemates.

The sound of furniture being knocked over came from the corridor, followed by the hollow smash of a vase breaking, and the piteous yelp of a small dog. Fussy canine footsteps came trotting back towards the library, and the ball of fluff returned, head down, tail no longer wagging.

'Oh, Minty darling,' said Mrs Adaway as though she were talking to a tiny child. 'What have they done to you, my little precious?'

She lifted the obviously unharmed dog to her ample chest and kissed it fussily, then stopped and plucked a small shard of smashed pottery from its fur and tutted.

Mrs Adaway held up the fragment of vase and looked daggers at Sir Hector. 'You see what your "gels" have done? She might have been killed.'

'Don't talk rot, Joycey. No harm done.'

'No harm? Your hell beasts have smashed a vase on poor Minty's head. At the very least I should have thought you'd be concerned about the damage, even though you clearly care nothing for my poor Minty.'

'If it's the vase I'm thinkin' of, we're well rid of it. Never liked the blasted thing. And little Minty can't have been anywhere near it when it fell. That vase was a hideous monster of a thing – would have squashed her like an overripe tomato. She just caught a bit of shrapnel, what?'

'A bit of shrapnel! Hector, you terrible man. You were always like this as a child. "Don't worry, Joycey, just a bit of fun. No harm done." Well, let me tell you—'

The sound of a man clearing his throat came from just inside the library door. 'Beggin' your pardon, Sir Hector. I wonder if I might have a word?'

'Certainly, Kiddle – you'd be savin' me from a wigging. Come on in.'

The man looked around nervously. 'It would be easier outside, sir.'

Sir Hector stood. 'Of course, dear boy. Of course. But do say hello to Lady Hardcastle and Miss Armstrong first. Dear friends of ours, what? I'm sure you'd get along. Ladies, this is Felix Kiddle, m'new gamekeeper.'

Kiddle knuckled his forehead. 'Pleased to meet you, ladies, I'm sure,' he said with a cheeky smile.

'Pleased to meet you, too, Mr Kiddle,' said Lady Hardcastle. 'But don't hold the poor man up, Hector. Go and do what you need to do.'

'Certainly, certainly. Come, Kiddle, let's take a stroll.'

As he reached the door, the dinner gong sounded in the hall.

Sir Hector turned back. 'Start lunch without me, do. I'm sure this won't take long.'

Mrs Adaway huffed. 'Talking to a servant like an old friend. A new servant, at that. I don't know what the world's coming to, I'm sure.'

Lady Farley-Stroud looked at Mrs Adaway, then towards Lady Hardcastle. She shook her head and rolled her eyes. Lady Hardcastle started to laugh but managed to turn it into a cough. I smiled.

We all rose and made our way to the dining room.

Mrs Adaway calmed a little as the delicious lunch got underway, and Minty – who we learned was a Bichon Frisé and whose full name was Lady Araminta Fluffikins – proved to be none the worse for her adventure with the spaniels. She sat on a chair beside her doting mistress, eating titbits from her hand.

I could see Lady Farley-Stroud scowling at this, but I surmised this was a battle already fought and lost.

I decided to divert her from the subject of dogs at the dining table. 'How was Clarissa? How's baby Beatrice?'

'Beatrice is an absolute darling, Florence m'dear. The bonniest of bonny babies. Clarissa is in fine fettle, too.'

'That's wonderful,' said Lady Hardcastle. 'What does Lou-Lou think of it all?'

'She's only two, bless her, but I think she understands that she has a baby sister. She doesn't seem at all put out by her, so that's a good sign.'

'About the same gap as between Harry and me. When they asked him how he felt about having a baby sister, I gather he said, "I'd rather have aminals." But we rubbed along pretty well.'

'I'm sure they will, too. We didn't see much of Bordeaux, though, I'm afraid. They actually live in a little village to the west of the city and don't have a motor car. Adam goes to work at the aeroplane factory on a bicycle, if you can believe it.'

Mrs Adaway tutted. 'Bicycle, indeed.'

'He might ride a bicycle but at least he doesn't feed his absurd little dog at the luncheon table,' snapped Lady Farley-Stroud.

A battle fought and lost, perhaps, but still with the possibility of a counteroffensive. I intervened again. 'I'm glad to hear everyone's well.'

'We are, thank you, m'dear. And how's your sister?'

'She writes that she's fit and healthy,' I said. 'The baby is kicking and her doctor is pleased with her progress. She's less pleased with looking like a hippopotamus, mind you.'

Lady Farley-Stroud laughed. 'She'll be back to her old self in no time.'

'I'm sure she will. She's looking forward to being a mother.'

'She'll make a good 'un. Lovely woman. She took such good care of dear Agnes Bingle after that business at the Dog and Duck.'

'She made quite an impression,' I agreed.

'A splendid impression. And you'll make a wonderful aunt, too, dear Florence.'

Mrs Adaway looked up from feeding Minty a slice of beef from her fingers. 'Married, is she?'

I opened my mouth to speak, but Lady Farley-Stroud cut me off.

'Don't dignify that with a response, Florence dear. Joyce, you really are the rudest, most—'

'Sorry about that, ladies,' said Sir Hector as he breezed into the dining room. 'What have I missed?'

'Gertie was telling us about baby Beatrice,' said Lady Hardcastle. 'And Flo was keeping us up to date with Gwen's progress.'

'Progress?'

Lady Farley-Stroud sighed. 'She's expectin' a baby, you old buffer. We've spoken of it before. Do try to keep up.'

'Quite right, quite right. Should have remembered. Congratulations, Aunt Florence. Lovely woman, your sister. Very kind. Make a wonderful mother.'

'Thank you,' I said.

'I speak as I find, m'dear. Sorry to be absent, though. Kiddle just wanted to reassure me the lower fields are safe from incursion. Heard about poor Hyde. Nasty business.'

'What was that?' asked Mrs Adaway. 'What nasty business?'

'Mauled to death by a wild dog.'

Mrs Adaway clutched Minty protectively. 'Probably one of *your* wild dogs. We won't let them get you, will we, Minty poppet?'

'You said he was your new gamekeeper,' said Lady Hardcastle, seemingly as keen as I to divert Mrs Adaway from her endless attacks.

'He is indeed. Or he would be if we raised any game. Don't have time for that no more. He just keeps an eye on the woodland and the wildlife so Mogg can concentrate on runnin' the rest of the estate. Splendid fella, Kiddle. Bit of a rogue, but he knows his hollyhocks. He and his wife are livin' in the cottage down by the stream. Got a young son. Good to have the place occupied again.'

Without the funds to manage everything properly, the Farley-Strouds' estate had slowly been falling into neglect and disrepair. It seemed their new-found financial security meant they could hire more staff and begin to take care of things properly. It was good to see.

'You allow him to be far too familiar, Hector,' said Mrs Adaway.

'Nonsense, m'dear,' said Sir Hector. 'Treat a man with respect and dignity and he'll reward you with loyalty and hard work. Chap needs to know he's taken seriously.'

Mrs Adaway tutted. 'It will all end in tears. I blame that Ramsay MacDonald and his Labour Party. Nothing good will come of letting the working classes think they can rise above their appointed station in life, you mark my words.'

'Consider them marked, Joycey. Consider them marked.' Sir Hector leaned across the table towards his wife. 'Pass me a pork pie, would you, my little jelly baby? I do love a pork pie.' As he took the proffered pastry he seemed to notice Minty for the first time. 'Get that ridiculous dog away from the table, Joycey. Dashed unhygienic havin' a dog at the table. Put her out in the garden with the gels.'

Mrs Adaway ignored him and carried on feeding scraps to the pampered pooch.

◆　◆　◆

At home that evening we had little appetite for supper, and we found ourselves, slightly earlier than usual, in front of the fire with glasses of wine and some cheese. I'd found a tin of water biscuits at the back of the larder where Miss Jones had hidden them. Not, this time, to keep them for herself, but because she insisted that her homemade crackers were much better. She was right, they were, but she wasn't there, so the factory-made ones would have to do.

Lady Hardcastle sprawled in her armchair and sipped her wine. 'Joyce is a hoot, isn't she?' she said.

I made a face. 'She's certainly something. And not something warm.'

'Oh, I don't know. She certainly has a lot of love to spare if her treatment of Lady Araminta Fluffikins is any indication.'

'I'm not sure I trust that dog. All that yelping and fussing over the broken vase seemed manipulative. I bet she's a nasty piece of work on the quiet.'

Lady Hardcastle laughed. 'You think she's the ringleader?'

'I wouldn't put it past her. She's probably the wild dog responsible for all the attacks.'

'Hardly. But I hope they find out exactly what's behind them. I can't explain why, but I find poor Sid Hyde being mauled to death a good deal more upsetting than most of the murders we've had to deal with over the years.'

'I know what you mean. For me, I think it's the motivelessness of it. When a person kills another person, no matter how viciously, there's a reason for it. It might not be a completely sane reason, but it's a reason nonetheless – something we can predict, something we can defend against. These attacks seem indiscriminate. As difficult to defend against as a disease.'

'Indeed. I wonder if any of the other farmers over there have seen anything. Perhaps we can give the man from the ministry a head start when he arrives by talking to a few of them.'

I took a bite of my Stilton. 'Perhaps. Who?'

'Someone who won't think we're accusing them of anything. Someone who can understand the bigger picture. Oh, oh – we haven't seen Noah and Audrey Lock for a while, and they were Hyde's next-door neighbours at Chapel Farm. What about them?'

Audrey Lock had been Audrey Caradine when we first met her. She was the widow of Spencer Caradine, local curmudgeon and bully who had died in suspicious circumstances, face down in a beef pie. She'd been having a not-so-secret love affair with her neighbour, Noah Lock, and the two were now happily married and living on Lock's farm. They certainly fit Lady Hardcastle's requirements as sensible people who wouldn't be suspicious of our motives.

'It can do no harm,' I said. 'And Lock's a practical man – he might have an idea of how to deal with the animal before the bloke from the Board of Agriculture gets here.'

'I don't think it's an especially complex problem, dear. One would simply shoot it.'

'If one can see it.'

'One would definitely see it if it were charging towards one, all claws and fangs. I'll be sure to pack a gun.'

'But what about me?' I asked. 'I hate guns.'

'You could wound it with withering sarcasm. And your look of disapproval if it dared to make a mess anywhere would send it skulking away with its tail between its legs.'

'Most amusing. I need a long-range weapon of some sort. I can throw a knife but I doubt it would stop a wild dog. And, once I've thrown it, I find myself without a knife.'

'Bow and arrow? You're a demon with a bow.'

'Not bad, not bad. But not as portable as I'd like.' I thought for a moment. 'Oh, do you remember that Hungarian assassin in Paris?'

She grinned. 'Now we're talking. The chap with the blowpipe.'

'Exactly. Blowpipe, dart with some sort of tranquillizing drug on it, unconscious beast. Bob's your uncle. I still have it somewhere.'

'That's settled, then. We shall visit the Locks. I shall have a gun in my bag, and you shall have your blowpipe. And perhaps we should have a cake.'

'To lure the beast into the open?'

She tutted. 'To give to the Locks. Or a bottle of wine. Some flowers, at least. We'll be dropping in unannounced – we have to take some sort of gift.'

I nodded. 'We'll find something. And now that's agreed, what shall we do for the rest of the evening?'

'I'd quite like to work on that Debussy piece I've been trying to learn, if you can amuse yourself.'

'I'll get my book. Cocoa?'

'With brandy, yes please.'

# Chapter Three

We'd met Noah and Audrey Lock in our first year in Littleton Cotterell, but we'd seen little of them since. Once the trial of Audrey's husband's murderer was concluded, Audrey had sold Top Farm to Sid Hyde and married Noah. She'd moved into Chapel Farm with him and the two of them had set about living happily ever after. They seldom came into the village so they were strangers at the Dog and Duck, but we'd bumped into them a few times at the more important village festivities.

It was fair to say they weren't expecting us when we drove out to Chapel Farm the next morning.

Audrey answered the door. 'Hello, m'lady, Miss Armstrong. Fancy seein' you two here. If anyone had said to me this mornin', "Who do you think will come callin' today, Aud?" I'd never have expected it to be you. What a lovely surprise.'

'Good morning, Mrs Lock,' said Lady Hardcastle. 'It's lovely to see you, too. May we impose upon you for a moment or two of your time? I know you're busy, but we'll be quick, and it might be to your benefit in the long run.'

'You're always welcome here, benefits or not. Come in. No's back for his mornin' break so the kettle's just boiled.'

'Excellent timing, then. And we brought you a cake by way of apology for intruding.'

'No need for apologies, but I never says no to cake. Come on in.'

We walked through the farmhouse to the kitchen. When last we'd seen it three years earlier, it had been neat and clean but a little spartan and impersonal. Audrey had brought her taste for all things warm and cosy and it looked much more like a home now.

Noah Lock, tall and handsome, was standing with a cup of tea in his hand, looking out of the kitchen window at the neat garden beyond.

'That bed would look nice with some daffodils in the spring. I might plant some bulbs later this week— Oh, hello, ladies. I didn't know we had guests.' He put down his tea and turned to shake our hands. 'How splendid to see you.'

'You too,' said Lady Hardcastle. 'I feel rather guilty that we've not seen much of either of you since your wedding.'

'Oh, that's mostly our fault,' he said. 'We tend to keep ourselves to ourselves up here, and when we do go out we prefer to go over to the Hayrick at Chipping rather than to come down to the Dog and Duck.'

Lady Hardcastle smiled. 'Nevertheless, we should have called on you.'

Lock smiled back. 'All right, then: you should. Would you like some tea?'

We both said yes and made ourselves comfortable at the kitchen table while the Locks fussed about together with cups, saucers and teapots. Audrey cut four slices of the cake.

'So, what is it you wants?' said Audrey when she finally sat down. 'We'll do whatever we can for you, won't we, No?'

'Of course. We owe our happiness to you.'

Lady Hardcastle's teacup paused on its journey to her lips. 'Oh, I think that might be overstating things a little – we simply made sure the right people were blamed for the right things. But I'm glad you're happy.'

'We are,' said Audrey. 'But I means it. Whatever you wants, you can 'ave it.'

'You're very kind. We don't need much, though, just a little of your local knowledge.'

'Does it have anything to do with Sid Hyde, by any chance?' asked Lock.

'It does,' I said. 'He bought your farm, didn't he, Mrs Lock?'

Mrs Lock nodded. 'He did. But call me Audrey, love. Are you investigatin' for the police again?'

'Nothing like that,' said Lady Hardcastle. 'We're aware, obviously, that people in the village are upset – Sid Hyde was well liked. They're more than a little worried too, though, so we thought we might be able to put some minds at rest by finding out a little more about what happened.'

'We don't really know much ourselves, love, do we?'

'No, not really,' said Lock. 'We knew nothing about it until Louis Finch – he's Hyde's lead farmhand – came over to ask us for help when he found the body. He was in a terrible state.'

'I can well imagine,' said Lady Hardcastle. 'What did you do?'

'There's not much we *could* do. I just drove him down to the police station in Littleton Cotterell and he reported Hyde's death there.'

Lady Hardcastle nodded. 'Hyde told us about his mutilated sheep the night before he died. Have you had any trouble like that?'

Lock shook his head. 'None. But we keep dairy cattle now. I used to farm sheep, but they're more trouble than they're worth. Disease is a problem with all livestock, but when you add the fragility and breathtaking stupidity of sheep, you spend an extraordinary amount of your working day trying to keep them from just falling down dead.'

Audrey rolled her eyes.

'Audrey was used to cattle,' continued Lock, 'so we changed everything round. With the weather we've had lately we've been keeping them in the byre overnight so they're mostly safe from whatever it is that's doing all this.'

'Have you any idea what it might be?' I asked.

'I've seen my share of animal attacks, but they were all abroad. I've never seen anything like it in England.'

'What was attacking when you were overseas?' asked Lady Hardcastle.

'Hyena in South Africa. Big cats in India – tigers and panthers. I'll grant you I've not been farming in England for very long, but I know our wildlife. We've no predators larger than a badger.'

'And badgers are adorable,' I said. 'Is it something a dog could do?'

'I've heard of dogs attackin' sheep,' said Audrey. 'They can lose control when they smells blood. Don't have to be big, neither. Even a terrier can tear an animal to pieces if it wants. 'S what they's bred for, some of 'em.'

'But they'd not be able to take on a man,' I said.

'An armed man,' added Lady Hardcastle. 'Hyde had his shotgun with him.'

'Finch mentioned the gun,' said Lock, 'so it seems like it was a planned inspection of the perimeter.'

I nodded. 'That's what he told us he was planning when we spoke to him in the pub on Sunday.'

'But according to Finch the gun hadn't been fired,' said Lock. 'So whatever attacked him attacked quickly.'

'This Finch chap,' I said. 'Might he know more than he's said so far?'

Lock shrugged. 'He might. As I said, he was in a bit of a state when we saw him yesterday. But he's a decent chap, and there's nothing about that farm he doesn't know.'

'Did he and Hyde get on?' asked Lady Hardcastle.

'They had their ups and downs, the same as anyone, but they rubbed along well enough.'

Audrey shook her head. 'They 'ad a right fallin' out last week.'

'Over what?' I said.

'They wouldn't say, neither of 'em. But they wasn't 'appy with each other.'

'It'll be something trivial, I'm sure,' said Lock. 'But if you want to know exactly what's going on at Top Farm, Finch is the man to ask. He lives in Woodworthy but he's likely to be at the farm – he's a conscientious chap and he'll want to make sure everything is being properly looked after.'

◆ ◆ ◆

It was a short drive to the Locks' neighbours at Top Farm. The whitewashed farmhouse looked unchanged since we had last seen it more than three years earlier. The flowerpots that used to grace the windowsills had gone, but the sturdy house was still gleamingly well maintained.

We knew it was possible that Louis Finch would be out in the fields – trying, as Lock had put it, to stop the sheep from falling down dead. But we had to start somewhere and there was at least a chance he might be at the farmhouse.

The front door was ajar.

Lady Hardcastle nudged it open a little further. 'Hello? Is there anyone there? Mr Finch?'

There was movement within and I gently pushed Lady Hardcastle behind me as we stepped in to investigate.

'Hello?' called Lady Hardcastle again. 'Mr Finch? Is that you?'

A small man with wispy blond hair peered out nervously from the half-open kitchen door.

'I gots permission to be here,' he said.

'We never doubted it for a moment,' said Lady Hardcastle. 'But we don't have permission at all. May we come in?'

The kitchen door opened wider and the man retreated. With a shrug, I led the way and we followed him.

Little had changed in Audrey's old kitchen – she'd clearly decided to leave the furniture behind when she remarried – and it looked almost as warm and homely as it had when we last saw it.

The man was next to the back door, ready to flee, and had positioned himself so that the large oak table stood between us.

I stepped to one side to allow Lady Hardcastle properly into the room.

'It is Mr Finch, isn't it?' she said.

He glanced nervously between us. 'It is.'

'We're—'

'I knows who you are. There i'n't many round here what doesn't.'

'I'm never sure whether that's a good thing or bad.' She gestured towards the table and chairs. 'Shall we sit down?'

He looked between us again, but then a chair scraped on the flagstone floor as he pulled it out for himself. Lady Hardcastle sat, too, but I remained standing.

'Is the range lit?' I asked.

Finch nodded. 'I put some more wood in it this mornin'. I come up to see Sid, but then I remembered I'd never be seein' 'im again. I 'ad to 'ave a cup of tea.'

'Would you like another while we talk? I'll put the kettle on.'

He didn't object, so I took that as assent. He didn't have to drink it but I wanted to bring a bit of domestic normality to the awkward scene, and there's nothing more normal in an English farmhouse than making a pot of tea.

'I gather you found Sid yesterday morning,' said Lady Hardcastle. 'That must have been terrible.'

'I did. And it was. I a'n't never seen nothin' like it. I won't never forget it, neither, I can tell you that.'

'I can only imagine.'

The truth was that neither Lady Hardcastle nor I had to imagine anything – we'd both seen more than our fair share of horrific, violent death over the years.

'I don't reckon you could, m'lady,' said Finch. 'It'll haunt my nightmares.'

'It must be all the worse because he was your friend.'

Finch cocked his head slightly, as though in thought. 'You're right. We was friends. I'd never 'ave said so before – I was his farmhand and he was my boss. But we was friends. We had our ups and downs – everyone does, don't they? But I knew I could count on him. I hope he felt the same. I just wish . . .'

Lady Hardcastle said nothing, and I tried to keep my clattering to a minimum as I hunted for cups and saucers.

Eventually Finch spoke again. 'I just wish he'd listened to me when I said he should stick with cattle. He insisted sheep would suit the land better, but I knew they's more trouble than they's worth. Noah Lock got rid of his first chance he got. But that were the first time we fell out. If he never had sheep, that . . . that beast what killed 'im would never even have been on his land.'

'You can't think like that, Mr Finch,' said Lady Hardcastle. 'No one is to blame.'

'That's what the doctor said. Just one o' them things, he said. He said the coroner's inquest would just be a formality on account of how it was so obviously an animal attack and that there weren't nothin' no one could-a done.'

'He's right. Who was it?'

'The doctor? I don't know. Wally— sorry, *Sergeant* Dobson brought him over.'

'It wasn't Dr Fitzsimmons from Littleton Cotterell?'

'No, he was out visitin' a patient,' Wal said. 'He did introduce him. Williams, was it? Or Tremayne. Maybe Bramble. From Chippin', he was.'

I tried not to laugh. 'I think I know who you mean. An older fellow? We've never met him, but . . . well, we've heard him described as a bit of a dodderer.'

Finch smiled. 'That sounds like him. I a'n't never been to no doctor so I don't know. I knows Dr Fitzsimmons from seein' 'im about the village, but I've been fit as a fiddle all me life.'

I smiled. 'Good for you. Not many are so lucky.'

'No, they's not. But this fella, this Dr Whatsisname, he said it was tragic what happened to Sid, but there weren't nothin' no one could do about attacks by wild animals like that. They's too quick, see? Poor Sid had his shotgun with him, but he didn't even have time to cock it.'

'He didn't?' said Lady Hardcastle.

'No, m'lady. It was still broken and loaded when I found it, like he hadn't even had time to raise it, let alone shoot it.'

'That's interesting. And what do you think was responsible?'

Finch pondered. 'Only thing I can think of is a big dog. Sheep are slow and gormless, but it would still take sommat pretty powerful to bring one down. And Sid weren't no weaklin', neither.' His voice gave out on him. 'What am I supposed to do now? Who'll take over the farm?'

'Did Mr Hyde leave a will?'

'I think so. I remember him talkin' about it. I think everythin' goes to his brother – that's his only livin' relative. But he works in the quarry over Tytherington – he don't have no interest in farmin'. But even if he decides he wants it, it'll be months afore it's all settled – I can't leave the animals that long. But I can't afford to work for nothin', neither. I just don't know what to do.'

Lady Hardcastle smiled. 'Don't worry on that score. His executors will take over the financial responsibilities of his business until probate is settled. The farm is a going concern so it's in their interest to keep the business running until Mr Hyde's brother decides what he's going to do with it.'

Finch sighed with relief. 'Really? Well, that's a load off my mind.'

The kettle finally boiled and I was able to make the tea and sit down.

'Where did the attacks take place?' I asked.

'Both was down by the spinney.'

'And is that on Mr Hyde's land?'

'It is. Then there's a patch of scrub he never used for nothin', then the woods. Don't know who owns the woods.'

'That would be Littleton Woods, so it's the Farley-Strouds, I think,' said Lady Hardcastle.

Finch nodded. 'Sounds about right.'

'And how far do the woods stretch?' I asked.

'Quite a way. They borders Sid's land in the middle, the Locks up that way, and Bottom Farm down t'other.'

Lady Hardcastle pulled out her notebook. 'Remind me who owns Bottom Farm these days. It's . . . it's . . .'

'Rood,' I said.

She looked hurt. 'Not on purpose. I just can't remember his name.'

'His name is Rood. Jonathan Rood.'

'Ah, yes, that's it. Thank you, dear.'

Finch smiled. 'Nice fella. His wife's an absolute cracker, too.'

'She is,' I agreed. 'You remember? We saw her at the harvest festival. Rood wasn't there, but we spoke to her.'

'Oh, I do remember,' said Lady Hardcastle. 'She *is* very beautiful. And charming with it.'

'That's her,' said Finch.

'And have they had any trouble?' I asked.

'Not that they've said. But they wouldn't have told me – I'm just the help.'

Lady Hardcastle looked up from her note-taking. 'It's possible they haven't – the Locks haven't been bothered.'

Finch nodded. 'Rood don't keep no livestock, and Lock keeps cattle. I reckons it was the sheep that attracted the beast.'

'Quite probably,' I said. I noticed that Finch had already drained his tea. 'Another cup, Mr Finch?'

He peered into his cup. 'I hadn't realized I'd finished it. But no, thank you, Miss Armstrong. I doesn't really have time for another. I gots to see to they stupid sheep.'

'That's quite all right, Mr Finch,' I said. 'I understand. You get on – I'll tidy up here.'

'You're very kind. Thank you. Oh.'

'Oh?'

'What about Doreen? No one would have told her.'

'Doreen?' said Lady Hardcastle.

'Doreen Robinson. She and Sid have been seein' each other this past year. She lives over Woodworthy near me. He said he was goin' to propose. She's goin' to be heartbroken, the poor woman. But I'd best tell her. I'll get over there once I've seen to the sheep.'

After a round of thank-yous and goodbyes, Finch left by the back door and set off across the fields.

Lady Hardcastle sat at the table making notes in her notebook while I put the cups away. Hyde's breakfast things had been sitting in the sink so I washed everything up and gave the worktops a good wipe down.

'What next?' I asked as I hung a frying pan from one of the hooks above the range.

'Since we're here, a visit to Bottom Farm might be time well spent. Hyde's neighbours on the other side might have seen something.'

'They might, indeed. Do you want to look at anything else here?'

'I'm not sure we'd find anything useful. Let's just pop next door and see what they know.'

◆ ◆ ◆

'Next door' was another short drive away down the hill. Bottom Farm – they were as imaginative in their naming of places as in their naming of people – had been owned by Lancelot Tribley when we had first moved to the area, but was now in the hands of Jonathan Rood and his 'absolute cracker' of a wife, Phillis.

I parked in the lane beside the farm gate and we stepped carefully along the mud-slicked path to the stone-built farmhouse. Lady Hardcastle rapped on the door.

After a short while, Phillis opened the door and dazzled us with her smile. 'Good mornin', ladies. Fancy seein' you out here. What can we do for you?'

'Hello, Mrs Rood,' said Lady Hardcastle. 'We're just trying to find out a little more about the animal attacks. May we come in for a moment?'

'You'd be quite welcome to, but I'm afraid I don't know nothin' meself and Jon's away. I knows about poor Sid and his sheep, of course – terrible business – but Jon's never said nothin' else about it. We doesn't keep much livestock, mind, so we haven't had no attacks. But now this business with Sid . . . well, it's terrifyin' is what it is. A wild animal on the loose in our little village? No one is safe.'

'Quite. Which is why we're asking around. We thought we'd gather as much information as we could before the authorities got involved. You know, to try to speed things along a little.'

Phillis rolled her eyes. 'The "authorities". Fat lot of use the Board of Agriculture'll be. But thank you for whatever you manage to do.'

'Entirely our pleasure. When are you expecting Mr Rood's return?'

'He's had to go up Tewkesbury urgently to see his brother but I'm expectin' him home tonight. I can tell him you called – p'raps you could call back tomorrow to see if he knows sommat more?'

'If you're sure that will be all right, then yes, please.'

'Of course. You're sure you won't come in for a cup of tea now, though? Kettle's just boiled.'

'You're very kind, but we'd best be on our way. We'll call again tomorrow.'

'Right you are, m'lady. Mind the path. I keeps tellin' Jon to sweep it but he won't listen.'

'We'll be fine, Mrs Rood. We'll see you tomorrow.'

We picked our way back to the Rolls and I started the engine.

'Where to now?' I said as it purred to life. The electric starter designed and fitted by Lady Hardcastle's friend Lord 'Fishy' Riddlethorpe was an absolute boon.

'Well, I don't know about you, tiny servant, but I'm starving. Lunch at the Dog and Duck?'

'An excellent idea.'

The lunchtime crowd at the pub was as noisy as ever. There was still plenty of work to be done on the farms as they prepared for winter, and the farmhands were taking a well-earned break over a pint of cider accompanied by a pie or one of Old Joe's celebrated doorstop sandwiches.

We found a table in the snug and I went to the bar to order some food.

Daisy was talking to Miriam Grove, the vicar's housekeeper.

'. . . and so I says, "You bloomin' well put that back, Geoffrey Jackson, or I'll tell your mother." So, of course, 'e pokes his tongue out and runs off with it.'

Mrs Grove tutted. 'He's always been trouble, that one. To hear his mother talk you'd think butter wouldn't melt, but I see him and his pals messing about as they come out of Sunday School. Little terrors, the lot of them.'

'Talkin' of little terrors,' said Daisy with a wink in my direction. 'What can we get you, Flo?'

'Two small Mattick's and two ham sandwiches, please, Dais.'

'We gots no ham. I can do you some beef?'

'Beef will be lovely. With a little mustard, please.'

Daisy poured our two glasses of cider from the barrel behind the bar.

'Good afternoon, Mrs Grove,' I said. 'And how is life treating you?'

'Can't complain, Miss Armstrong, can't complain. The vicarage is worried about the wild beast on the loose, of course. Everyone is, though, aren't they? But as for – what do you call them? – tangible problems . . . there's just the post going wonky. And I always say that if the worst thing to happen is some mixed-up post, then you're not having too bad a week.'

'That was peculiar, wasn't it?' I said. 'We left before the postman had been today – were there any further problems?'

'Not today, no. But yesterday was pandemonium.'

I smiled. *Yes*, I thought, *yes it was*.

Daisy put the drinks on the bar. 'Sandwiches'll be a couple of minutes.'

'Thanks, Dais. Can I get you anything, Mrs Grove?'

She inspected her nearly empty glass of sherry. 'I oughtn't. It doesn't do to be sozzled before teatime when you're the vicar's housekeeper.'

Daisy grinned. 'Oh, go on, Mim. The vicar won't mind. He's a broad-minded bloke, our vicar.'

Mrs Grove held out her glass. 'Just a small one, then. Thank you, Miss Armstrong.'

'Were you caught up in the postal pandemonium, Dais?' I said as she poured another sherry.

'More than most,' she said. 'Everythin' was all mixed up at home, at the shop, and here as well. And, of course, it's left to muggins here to go to the post office and sort it all out.'

Daisy lived in the village with her parents, and her father, Fred, ran the butcher's shop.

I nodded. 'When we went in, there were over half a dozen people shouting the odds at poor Bessie Talbot. Herself had to take charge and calm them all down.'

'Poor Bessie,' said Daisy. 'She's lovely.'

'She is. You know everything, Dais – what do you know about the Talbots?'

She grinned again. 'Not much, just that they's a nice couple.'

I sighed. 'Well, I knew that – I've had many a pleasant chat with Bessie. I was hoping for something a little more substantial.'

'They used to run a post office in Bedminster.'

'I knew that, too.'

'Oh, but did you know that Hilda Pantry applied to be postmistress?'

'I did not. Your title of Princess of Gossip is saved.'

'Princess? Who's queen?'

'Edna Gibson.'

'Fair play – she is the Queen of Gossip, I'll give you that. But Hilda was turned down in favour of the Talbots. And a good thing, too, I reckons. Can you imagine that misery guts tuttin' over your telegrams and shakin' your parcels to see what you've been sent?'

'It doesn't bear thinking about,' said Mrs Grove with a theatrical shudder.

Daisy laughed. 'It don't, do it?' She turned as Joe brought out another tray of sandwiches. She put two on plates and added a little mustard before handing them over. 'Your sandwiches, Miss Armstrong.'

'Thank you, Miss Spratt. I'd better get these to Herself before she faints from hunger. Cheerio, Mrs Grove.'

'Ta-ta, dear,' said Mrs Grove. 'Thank you for the sherry.'

I returned to our table with the drinks and sandwiches on a tray.

'There you are,' said Lady Hardcastle. 'I thought I might faint from hunger.'

'I worried you might.' I handed her a sandwich. 'Get that down your neck. It's beef, though – Joe had no ham.'

'With mustard?'

'Of course.'

'What took you so long?'

'Joe was behind with the sandwiches and I had a chat with Daisy about the post office.'

'What did you learn?'

'Not much at first. I worried that her position as chief filler-in of the colourful details of local gossip might be in jeopardy—'

'And no one wants to have to go there.'

'Go where? Oh, I see. I get told off when I say things like that.'

'And now you know why.'

'I do. I feel suitably chastised. But it turns out she won't have to relocate to jeopardy after all. She doesn't know more than we do about the Talbots, but she did tell me that Hilda Pantry had applied to take over the post office and had been turned down.'

'Thank goodness for that. I'd never have received any post at all.'

Mrs Pantry ran the grocer's shop. She was a curmudgeonly woman who disliked people in general, and the upper classes in particular. Her late husband had once read a Marxist pamphlet and convinced her that the bourgeoisie were the enemy of the proletariat.

I nodded. 'You probably never would.'

'It's an interesting titbit, though. For my part, I'm dismayed to have to report that I've been earwigging for all I'm worth and I haven't learned anything at all. Sid Hyde is still the principal topic of conversation, but no one has any fresh insights. I fear we're very much on our own and going nowhere.'

'Ah, well. It's early days yet. And we'll feel better after our sandwiches.'

She patted her tummy. 'I feel better after just two bites. But don't fill up. Remember we promised to go up to The Grange again this afternoon to give Gertie some company.'

'Ah, yes, I hadn't forgotten. And we definitely must go – I'd want some friendly company if I had to spend any amount of time with Sir Hector's sister.'

◆ ◆ ◆

We found Lady Farley-Stroud alone in the library with a pot of tea and a magazine.

Jenkins announced us and she looked up. 'Emily, Florence – thank goodness you're here. Come and have some tea.'

'It's that bad, is it?' said Lady Hardcastle as we made ourselves comfortable.

Lady Farley-Stroud said nothing but instead just nodded towards the other end of the long library. Sir Hector and his sister were talking to a tall, handsome man I'd never seen before.

Mrs Adaway was standing near the far door, looking up at the man and holding out her bewildered dog. 'Dear Mr Pinkard, would you please, please, do me the kindness of examining poor Minty. She's not at all well and I do worry about her so. She's all I have.'

Pinkard smiled warmly and took Minty from her. 'Certainly, Mrs Adaway. Now, let's have a look at you, young lady.' He cast an expert eye over the dog, flexing her limbs and gently pressing her chest and belly. He crouched down and, keeping a firm hand on her collar, set Minty on the floor. She stood obediently and looked adoringly at the deep-voiced man.

Pinkard let go of Minty's collar and looked up. 'She seems to be in fine fettle, Mrs Adaway. What is it that's troubling you about her?'

'I can't put my finger on it, Mr Pinkard, but she's off her food and a mother knows when there's something wrong.'

He smiled indulgently and looked back at Minty, who had rolled on to her back. He scratched the dog's chest. 'Perhaps she's a little out of sorts. Sometimes being away from home can upset them. But you're fine, really, aren't you, girl?'

'But she needs medicine, surely.'

'I think a lean, meaty treat might do the trick. A small chop, perhaps. Nothing too big, and nothing too fatty, just a little something to get her digestion back to normal.'

Mrs Adaway swooped in and scooped up her dog. 'Thank you, Mr Pinkard. Thank you so very much.'

She bombarded the poor man – whom I very much hoped was a vet – with more questions about her wriggling pet.

Lady Farley-Stroud shook her head.

'You can only begin to imagine, m'dear,' she said quietly. 'I do my best to tolerate Joyce – she's Hector's sister after all, and family's family – but she doesn't make it easy. And that wretched little puffball. Well. I mean. Really.'

Lady Hardcastle and I tried not to laugh too loudly.

Lady Farley-Stroud poured the tea. 'Actually, the puffball is rather endearing, if I'm honest. But the way she fusses over it is enough to drive a gel to drink.'

'As long as it's just tea, dear, you'll be fine,' said Lady Hardcastle.

'That man *is* a vet, isn't he?' I asked.

Lady Farley-Stroud laughed. 'Wouldn't it be altogether too splendid if she were bothering Hector's accountant about her stupid dog? But no, that's Robinson Pinkard, the new vet from Chipping. He's here to give the cattle their autumn check-ups. We could never afford to see too much of his predecessor, but since our recent good fortune we've become his best clients. Our animals have never been better cared for.'

'He seems kind,' I said.

'Kind, dear, yes. Kind and expensive. I think those are the key qualifications for a career in the veterinary sciences. Being devilishly handsome is just a bonus.'

Lady Hardcastle grinned. 'Gertrude Farley-Stroud, you rascal.'

'There's life in the old dog yet. But enough of handsome vets, what of you two? It's so good of you to come to see me. I'm not dragging you away from anything important, am I?'

'Not at all, dear. The country's enemies are up to no good, and its friends are little better, but we are excused boots for the time being as a reward for our recent wonderfulness.'

'The London adventure you refuse to tell me about?'

'The very same. At home all we have to worry about is gathering information in anticipation of the intervention by the Board of Agriculture in the recent animal attacks, and calming the village after a postal mix-up. We are otherwise entirely at your disposal as allies in the face of spousal-sibling invasion.'

Lady Farley-Stroud laughed. 'It's hardly an invasion, m'dear – we invited her. She's not a bad old stick, really. She's just . . .'

'We know what she's just. And it's entirely to your credit that you put yourselves out to give her a little much-needed company.'

'I'm a saint. But what's all this about the post?'

'There were some unexplained mix-ups with the deliveries yesterday morning – everyone seemed to get everyone else's letters.'

'Everyone? Well, that would explain why we had so little post yesterday. Has it been resolved?'

'Resolved but not explained.'

'So it might recur?'

'It's certainly a possibility.'

'I wonder—'

Sir Hector had abandoned the poor vet and come to join us. 'Hello, Emily. Hello, Florence.' He sat down and poured himself some tea. 'And hello to you, too, my little liquorice allsort.'

Lady Hardcastle and I saluted him with our teacups.

'It's a little unkind of you to leave poor Mr Pinkard with your sister,' said Lady Farley-Stroud.

'Nonsense, m'dear, he's used to dealing with awkward dumb animals. He'll be fine.'

Pinkard left Mrs Adaway fussing over Minty and he, too, came to join us.

'Ah,' said Sir Hector, 'here's Pinkard now. Any of you gels need a check-up?'

The vet gave a puzzled smile. 'I'm not sure I—'

Lady Farley-Stroud tutted. 'Take no notice of my husband, Mr Pinkard, he labours under the misapprehension that he's funny.'

'Ah, I see.'

'You'll get used to him. Do you have time for a cup of tea?'

'I should love one, actually. Thank you.'

He accepted Lady Farley-Stroud's gestured invitation to sit and then looked at Lady Hardcastle and me. 'I'm sorry, ladies, I don't think we've met.'

'My fault, my fault,' said Sir Hector. 'Lady Hardcastle and Miss Armstrong, this is Mr Robinson Pinkard, FRCVS. Pinkard, these are our good friends Emily Hardcastle and Florence Armstrong, civil servants and solvers of crimes.'

Pinkard stood to shake our hands. 'How do you do? I had no idea I'd be meeting celebrities. I've read of your crime-solving successes in the press, of course.'

'How do you do?' said Lady Hardcastle. 'Some of the stories are true, but we really just dabble – meddle, some say – and point the police in the right direction once in a while.'

'I'm sure you're just being modest.'

'She is,' said Lady Farley-Stroud. 'They're remarkable women and we're grateful to have them living here in our wonderful village. And speaking of gratitude, thank you for taking a look at Mrs Adaway's stup— at her dog.'

'Entirely my pleasure, my lady. There's nothing at all wrong with Minty, but I've enough experience to know that it's usually the owner who needs a little care rather than the animal.'

'Well, if it keeps her quiet for a while, you've more than earned your fee. Thank you.'

I put my cup and saucer on the small table beside my armchair. 'Lady Farley-Stroud told us you were the new vet at Chipping.'

'Newish, certainly. My wife and I have been there a few months now.'

'And before that?'

'Before that I was a partner in a large practice in London.'

'Quite the change, then. How are you finding life in the countryside?'

'It's not so different, to be honest. The bigger change was returning to England after five years in India.'

I smiled. 'We were in India for two years from 1901. It's a wonderful country.'

'It is. I was working for a variety of companies out there, mostly caring for their horses. It's so good to meet someone else who's spent time there.'

'The memsahib and I were out there for a few years ourselves,' said Sir Hector. 'But we came back while you were still a nipper, what?'

'I had no idea, Sir Hector,' said Pinkard. 'What a small world.'

Mrs Adaway finally joined us, her dog clutched tightly to her.

She sat down. 'Minty says thank you,' she said. 'The poor girl's not been at all well.'

Aside from a small amount of frustrated squirming, Minty seemed to be in rude health. And if I were being clutched that tightly to Mrs Adaway's stiffly corseted torso, I, too, might squirm, so it didn't seem like an unreasonable thing for the dog to be doing.

Lady Farley-Stroud, it seemed, agreed with me. 'Nonsense, m'dear. Dog's in fine fettle. Never seen a healthier beast.'

'And if you were a trained veterinary surgeon I might take your word for it, but I prefer to listen to a properly qualified person. She is not well, and Mr Pinkard agrees with me.'

The vet looked uncomfortable. 'Well . . . I . . . ah . . .'

Lady Hardcastle came to his rescue. 'What do you think of the animal attacks, Mr Pinkard?'

'Terrible business. Terrible. That poor man.'

'Terrible indeed. And the villagers appear terrified. It's not like people around here to be so upset – they're usually rather stoic in the face of danger.'

'It's because it's a wild animal,' said Sir Hector with a nod. 'They're used to human malefactors, d'you see? Animals are a different kettle of monkeys. Humans have a primal fear of animals, what?'

'That's certainly how we've been thinking,' said Lady Hardcastle. 'Have you any thoughts on what might be doing it, Mr Pinkard?'

He gave a polite shrug. 'I'm not at all certain, though I hear it attacked a sheep, too. Now, I didn't see the sheep myself and I can only speculate, but here in England the only animal capable of inflicting that kind of damage would be a large dog. If we were in India I might suspect a rogue tiger.' He gave a little laugh. 'But that's not likely in Gloucestershire.'

'Hardly,' said Mrs Adaway. 'But a dog wouldn't do something like that, surely. Well, Hector's Hell Hounds might, but not my precious little Minty Fluffikins.'

She ruffled the dog's head and it took advantage of the momentary loosening of her grip to escape. Minty settled at Mr Pinkard's feet, looking up adoringly at him.

Mrs Adaway huffed.

She ignored us while we talked more about India, and huffed again when Lady Farley-Stroud invited Mr Pinkard to the village's forthcoming Bonfire Night celebrations (to which he agreed to come on the condition that there would be bonfire toffee and sparklers).

Mrs Adaway had thawed a little by the time he said his farewells and left, though some frostiness returned when Minty followed him to the door and had to be shooed back into the library.

By the time we said our own farewells, she was back to herself and casually insulting everyone and everything. Normality was restored.

# Chapter Four

'Good morning, wrinkled one.'

The sheet flipped down. 'Wrinkled?'

'Just a little. Round the eyes.'

'Laugh lines, tiny servant. The legacy of a life of joy and merriment.'

'That'll be it. I bring coffee and toast.'

She sat up. 'Then I forgive you.'

I put the tray on the bedside table and handed her a coffee cup. 'What are we up to today?'

'I rather think we ought to continue our efforts to gather evidence for the Board of Ag.'

'The Board of Ag?'

'The BoA? Ag Board? There must be an easier way of saying Board of Agriculture. Anyway, we ought to call on Rood at Bottom Farm. The Gorgeous Phillis said he'd be back from Tewkesbury so he should be able to help us with our dossier for the AgBo—'

'That's no better.'

'Worse, I should say. But after that I thought we'd nip up to The Grange. Gertie needs all the friendly faces she can muster while Joyce is there.'

'She's not *that* bad,' I said.

'She's not. But to Gertie she is, and she'll allow Joyce to drive her batty if we don't rally round and try to bring some of our customary jollity to the proceedings.'

'Jollity, eh? Is that what we're known for?'

'Most certainly we are. We are rightly celebrated as the local purveyors of mirth and whimsy.'

'Are we, indeed? And in our capacity as village jesters, are we invited to lunch or will we just be there to jingle our cap bells and wave our pigs' bladders?'

'Lunch, I think.'

'Mrs Brown makes a fine lunch – I look forward to it.'

The brakes squealed slightly as we drew up outside the farmhouse at Bottom Farm, and I made a mental note to check them later. I didn't know much about brakes but I was reasonably certain that a noise like that wasn't one Rolls-Royce would have designed into the system. They made much of the smoothness and quietness of their engines – shrieking brakes would undermine their philosophy of refinement and elegance, I felt.

I had parked behind a large car painted an uninspiring shade of chestnut brown.

'It seems we're not their only visitors,' said Lady Hardcastle as we alighted. 'I wonder who that could be.'

'I've never seen the car before,' I said. 'It's a Rover, isn't it?'

'It is.' She smiled wistfully. 'I sometimes miss our little Rover, you know. It was much littler than that, of course, but it went to a good home. Dinah loves it.'

I nodded. 'Talking of Dinah, would it help to get our favourite journalist out here to cover the animal killings?'

'It very well might. I shall telephone her later and see what she says.'

By now we had reached the farmhouse door and Lady Hardcastle raised her hand to knock.

But before she could execute her customarily cheery rat-a-tat, the door opened.

It was the stunning Phillis Rood. 'Good mornin', m'lady, Miss Armstrong.'

Lady Hardcastle smiled warmly. 'Good morning, Mrs Rood. I hope you don't mind us dropping in unannounced once more.'

'You's not unannounced – you said you'd come today. You wants to speak to Jonny about the animal attacks.'

'Yes, we do. Is he at home?'

Phillis pointed. 'He's out in the yard with the vet. They won't mind if you goes over there. He said he wanted to talk to you.'

'Thank you very much.'

'Come back for a nice cup o' tea when you're done.'

'Thank you – we might.'

So the Rover belonged to the vet. That was one mystery solved, at least.

We set off in the indicated direction for the farmyard and quickly found Rood and Pinkard inspecting a carthorse outside one of the barns.

'Good morning, Mr Rood,' said Lady Hardcastle. 'And Mr Pinkard, too – how nice to see you again.'

Pinkard gave a friendly smile and a nod of greeting. 'Good morning, my lady. Rood, this is Lady Hardcastle and . . . I'm sorry, my dear, I've completely forgotten your name since yesterday.'

'Armstrong,' I said, with a smile of my own.

'Of course. Do forgive me, Miss Armstrong. I've been meeting so many people these past few months that I'm finding it hard to keep up.'

'Think nothing of it.'

Rood tugged at the peak of his flat cap. 'Mornin', m'lady. Miss Armstrong. The wife said you'd be callin'. Sorry I missed you yesterday. I was up Tewkesbury.'

'Visiting your brother, I believe,' said Lady Hardcastle.

He gave a little chuckle. 'That's right. No secrets when our Phillis is about.'

'Your wife said the visit was urgent. Is he unwell?'

'My brother? Oh, he's fine, thank you – there weren't nothin' wrong with him. He put me on to a dealer up there who's gettin' me a new seed drill. I needs it as soon as possible so I can plant me winter wheat, and I wanted him to get things movin' for me.'

'That's good to hear. Did your wife tell you why we called?'

'She said you were askin' about Sid, but she didn't say more.'

'Ah, I see. Well, your neighbours are concerned that there's a wild animal on the loose, but since Mr Hyde's death, the villagers are very frightened, too. We've said we'll try to find out as much as we can before the men from the Board of Agriculture get here so that we can hasten their work in discovering the creature and putting an end to its horrible activities.'

'I understands. We're worried, an' all. We doesn't have no livestock to speak of, not like the neighbours, but we keeps a couple of pigs and a few chickens. And there's the draft horses, of course – couldn't cope with losin' them. But still it's nothin' like Sid or the Locks. I brings 'em all in overnight now just in case. Course, with the weather gettin' colder we'd bring 'em in most nights anyway, but we's takin' no chances now, even if we has a mild night.'

'That sounds very wise,' I said. 'Have you seen anything of the creature?'

'Not a hair. But it's like I said: we doesn't have fields of livestock like t'others so it wouldn't have no reason to come here.'

'Of course. I was just wondering if you'd seen it passing across your fields. Especially over the weekend.'

'No, I reckon it would stay close to Littleton Woods over by Sid's land. Better cover. Hunters don't like open ground, they likes concealment. When I has to go over that way come plantin' time, I'll have a shotgun with me, though, I can tell you.'

Pinkard nodded. 'A sensible precaution. And one that would definitely do the job, I should think. I stand by my assessment that this is the work of a large dog. Lost. Hungry. Possibly hurt. Most strays will just try to find a friendly human to look after them, but every once in a while a lost dog will revert to its instinctive ways. It'll feed and protect itself the only way it knows how, and that's when they become dangerous.'

'That makes a good deal of sense,' said Lady Hardcastle. 'Assuming you're correct, how would one go about tracking and trapping such a dog?'

'From my experience of dealing with wild dogs in India, I'd say leave it to the professionals. A cornered, frightened dog is a very dangerous animal indeed. I'd not recommend that anyone not properly trained in handling such an animal go anywhere near it.'

'But from what you say, you're suitably trained?' I said.

Pinkard smiled. 'I am, yes. I have a lot of experience with dangerous animals.'

'So if we find the dog, we could call upon you to help us deal with it?'

'Absolutely you could, and I'd be happy to.' He gave a wry smile. 'Though unless you manage to trap it – and I most emphatically urge you not to try – it would be long gone by the time I arrived.'

'Point taken,' said Lady Hardcastle. 'So what can you recommend we do to help the men from the Board of Agriculture?'

Another wry smile. 'It's more likely to be the *man* from the Board of Ag, and keeping out of his way would be the best thing.

Not because you're likely to be any hindrance – I'm sure you'd be most helpful – but because he's likely to drive you quite mad. Civil servants have a way of doing things, and it's not always the quickest and most practical way.' He looked suddenly crestfallen as he realized what he'd said. 'Oh, I didn't mean . . .'

Lady Hardcastle laughed. 'Don't worry, Mr Pinkard – no offence taken. We've certainly met our fair share of that sort of civil servant over the years. I'm still trying to find a way to deal with them effectively, but I can't help but think that avoiding them isn't really the answer. We shall have to continue to find out what we can, and hope that we can speed the board's actions so that the matter is resolved as swiftly and safely as possible.'

'Well, good luck to you, my lady. And don't forget: if there's anything I can do to help – anything at all – telephone me. I'll be happy to assist you in any way I can.'

He and Lady Hardcastle exchanged calling cards and we bid the men goodbye.

◆ ◆ ◆

We drove straight from Bottom Farm to The Grange, where I parked with exaggerated neatness close to the front door.

Jenkins greeted us warmly and we were shown, as so often, to the library, where this time we found Lady Farley-Stroud dozing in an armchair.

He cleared his throat. 'Lady Hardcastle and Miss Armstrong to see you, my lady.'

Lady Farley-Stroud snorted, and jerked upright. 'Thank you, Jenkins. How's lunch coming along?'

'Mrs Brown says it will be ready to serve in half an hour, my lady.'

'Splendid.'

'Will there be anything else?'

'No, thank you, Jenkins, that'll be all.'

She discreetly wiped a trickle of drool from her chin with a handkerchief and waved us to the other comfy chairs arranged around the low table. 'Welcome, m'dears. Lovely to see you both, as always.'

'I hope we didn't interrupt your nap,' said Lady Hardcastle.

'Nonsense. I shouldn't be nappin' anyway. Makes me look like one of those old duffers you see in the comedy plays. "The batty old gel's asleep in her armchair again." On the other hand, at least while I'm asleep I'm free of the irritation brought by Joyce and her ridiculous dog.'

'I'm a firm believer in the importance of napping,' I said. 'Herself doesn't agree, but I swear by the half-hour snooze.'

'I shall quote you the next time Hector teases me for fallin' asleep in the afternoon. Though he's a fine one to talk.' She tutted and rolled her eyes. 'But enough of my inability to stay awake. How are you, m'dears? What news do you bring to distract me from the frustration of my sister-in-law?'

'Precious little, I'm afraid,' said Lady Hardcastle. 'Where is the lovely Joyce, by the way?'

'Lovely, my eye. She's out walking the cur in the grounds. If we're lucky they'll fall down the ha-ha and break their necks. Gone but not missed.'

Lady Hardcastle laughed. 'You don't mean that.'

'I'd push 'em over m'self if I thought I could get away with it.'

'Then you do need a distraction. Let me see . . . Actually, I have no real news at all. To tell you the truth, I was hoping you might have something jolly to distract *us*.'

'Aside from Joyce . . . I mean, honestly, how can someone who actually has the word "joy" in her name bring so much misery? Aside from her, everything is going swimmingly. The arrangements for Bonfire Night are all very much in hand and there's very little still to be put in place in the final few weeks. Young Daisy will be in charge of the catering team. The village fireworks committee is collecting scrap wood for the bonfire and building our Guy. And dear Noah Lock has volunteered to take charge of the fireworks themselves. He was a military man, you know – knows a lot about explosives.'

'I knew he'd been an army officer but I wasn't aware he had any explosives expertise,' said Lady Hardcastle. 'Good for him. And good for you, Gertie. Well done.'

'Thank you, m'dear. In fact, it's all going so well that I've been able to begin planning the Christmas party. We'll be able to afford a proper feast this year so I want to make sure that everything is as splendid as it can be.'

'How wonderful. And if you need anything from us, you have only to say.'

'Absolutely,' I said. 'Always happy to help.'

'Well, I'm sure we shall need your piano accompaniment as usual, Emily dear. And Florence, I seem to remember you being rather adept at organization. People still talk about the stage you built for the village show last year.'

'I didn't build it,' I protested. 'That was Charley Hill and his men.'

'Ah, but you were the one who came up with the plan and marshalled our limited resources to get it all built in time for the show. The village still thinks of it as the Florence Armstrong Stage.'

'I'm flattered. And in that case, yes, I'm happy to try to organize something. That was fun.'

'I don't think we'll need anything on that scale, but your entertainment background might come in very useful backstage as we try to marshal the traditional villagers' show.'

The chaos of the Christmas concert at The Grange was a cherished part of the celebrations, and I wasn't sure I'd be doing anyone any favours by bringing too much order to the proceedings, but I'd certainly be pleased to be involved in some way.

'As I said, happy to help.'

'Splendid. We should arrange a series of meetings where—'

I was spared having to think of excuses for not attending a series of meetings by the noisy arrival of Sir Hector and the new gamekeeper.

'. . . and that's why Cook always keeps the ham on the top shelf of the larder.'

Kiddle chuckled politely.

'Hello, ladies,' continued Sir Hector, almost without taking a breath. 'Just tellin' Kiddle here about the day the dogs worked together to steal that ham. Dashed clever, my gels.'

'I remember it well,' said Lady Hardcastle. 'Mrs Brown was not best pleased.'

Sir Hector gave his familiar bark of a laugh. 'Never pleased about anything, that woman. But that's not the reason I've dragged Kiddle up here. Poor chap don't need to be listenin' to my wheezy old stories. I've brought him up to speak to you, Emily.'

'To me?'

'Well, to you and Florence, of course. You were talkin' about the animal attacks with Pinkard yesterday so I thought you'd want to know what Kiddle has seen. Tell 'em, m'boy.'

Kiddle looked momentarily uncomfortable to have to be addressing the three of us. We must have looked like some sort of tribunal sitting there in our armchairs, staring up at him expectantly.

'Well,' he began, 'what's happened, see, is there's been a few hares and rabbits taken. I wouldn't have thought nothin' of it – foxes'll take the occasional rabbit if they gets a chance, I've even seen a weasel have a go – but this weren't like foxes. Or weasels. This were violent. Messy – beggin' your pardon. Sommat big and angry took they rabbits. I was thinkin' it could be that dog as everyone's talkin' about, so I reckoned I ought to tell someone.'

'Thank you, Kiddle,' said Lady Hardcastle. 'I'm glad you did. Where did you find the remains?'

'Down near the woods. They—'

There was a screeching wail from the direction of the ballroom at the back of the house.

'Help! Help! Minty's gone! Minty's gone!'

Mrs Adaway had obviously come in through the French doors on the terrace and now bustled her way into the library, red-faced and dishevelled. Her hair was loose from its pins and she was panting from the effort of hurrying back from her dog walk.

Lady Hardcastle stood. 'Joyce dear, whatever is the matter? Here, take my seat. Can we get you anything?'

'No time for sitting, you stupid girl. There's a panther loose in the grounds.'

Lady Hardcastle suppressed a smile. She'd been called stupid more than once – I'd pointed out her stupidity several times that week already – but she was seldom referred to as a girl. It seemed to please her. 'A panther, dear? Are you quite sure?'

'Of course I'm sure. I know a panther when I see one, thank you very much. M'late husband and I lived in Argentina in the '80s – I've seen more than my fair share of big cats.'

'And it was in the grounds?'

'Large as life. It frightened poor Minty and she ran off into Littleton Woods to get away from it. We must save her before it eats her.'

Kiddle was already on his way towards the door. 'Don't you worry, Mrs Adaway, I'll find your dog. Lovely little thing, she is. But she'll be right as rain, just you see.'

He was gone.

Mrs Adaway gave a little sob. 'Do be careful.'

She fainted.

◆ ◆ ◆

Mrs Adaway came round quickly and we managed to heave her into one of the armchairs, where she fussed and fidgeted like an anxious child.

'Will he be all right, your man? Will he be able to save darling Minty? What if it eats her? I couldn't bear it. I couldn't bear it.'

'Hush now, Joycey,' said Sir Hector with unexpected warmth. 'He's a good man, Kiddle. Knows what he's about. He'll find the pup. Bring her back safe.'

'But he's up against a panther, Hector. Is he armed? I've seen a panther gut a man. It gutted him.'

I was still unconvinced she'd actually just seen a panther – it was much more likely simply to be a large dog – but I didn't feel it was quite the right time to argue with her about it. Instead I said, 'What exactly happened? Where were you?'

She seemed slightly taken aback by my directness. Perhaps she was still struggling with the idea of having a servant in the library if they weren't serving tea. 'Oh. Well. Yes. We were walking about the grounds, d'you see? We passed Clarissa's elm tree. Minty loves that tree for some reason – runs round and round it, barking joyously up at its branches. I do like to think it's because she knows it's her cousin's tree.'

Sir Hector had planted the elm tree in 1880, on the day his only daughter was born, and it was known in the family as Clarissa's tree.

'That might be why, yes,' I said. 'And then what?'

'We reached the edge of the grassland, near the coppice – do you call it the coppice, Gertrude?'

Lady Farley-Stroud shook her head. 'If it's where I'm thinking of, we call it the grove. A little stand of trees before the woodland proper?'

'That's the place. So we arrived at the grove and I saw a flash of movement in the trees beyond. Off in the middle distance. Just a suggestion of it. Out of the corner of my eye, d'you know?'

'I know exactly what you mean,' I said.

'Frightened me, I can tell you. I don't frighten easily, but that gave me the willies. Minty must have seen it, too, but it didn't frighten my brave little girl – it intrigued her. She ran off towards the trees where we'd both seen the movement, and disappeared. Gone. I called her back, but she ignored me. And that's when I saw the panther.'

Lady Farley-Stroud clearly had no qualms about starting – continuing, more like – an argument with her sister-in-law. 'Are you absolutely certain it was a panther? You know what you're like. You thought that crow in the herb garden was a golden eagle the other day.'

Mrs Adaway harrumphed. 'It was the way the light caught its plumage.'

'And do you not think it possible that it was the way the light caught the dog's . . . plumage that made you believe you'd seen a panther?'

'It was a panther,' said Mrs Adaway emphatically.

It was Lady Farley-Stroud's turn to harrumph.

Further sniping was forestalled by the arrival of Jenkins, who announced that lunch was served in the dining room.

'I can't possibly eat anything,' said Mrs Adaway once he had gone.

Sir Hector took her by the hand and tried to heave her from the chair. 'Nonsense, Joycey – got to keep your strength up, what? Got to be ready for when little Minty comes bouncing in. You'll be no good to her if you're weak with hunger while she wants to play. Kiddle will be back with her any minute.'

'Leave me be, Hector,' said Mrs Adaway, but she didn't physically resist and he led her to the door.

Ladies Hardcastle and Farley-Stroud followed, with me at the rear.

In the dining room we found that Mrs Brown, the Farley-Strouds' curmudgeonly cook, had laid on a formidable spread.

There was an awkward moment as we sat and wondered if Mrs Adaway had been correct after all. Should we behave as though nothing had happened, as though she hadn't just seen a large animal heading off in pursuit of her curious dog? Or should we, as she seemed to be suggesting, put such indulgences as lunch to one side as we waited anxiously for news from Kiddle?

We were saved from our discomfort by the lady herself, who fell upon the food as though she'd been on starvation rations for a fortnight. Apparently, eating would be fine.

Conversation, though, was stilted, despite Sir Hector's best endeavours. I made one or two efforts at cheery, distracting chatter, too, and Lady Hardcastle did her best to bubble, but mostly we just ate.

Despite the dearth of clocks in the Farley-Stroud household, we were all aware of the passage of time, and there was a growing sense of unease at Kiddle's prolonged absence.

Eventually, Lady Hardcastle put her napkin on the table and stood. 'I think we ought to go down to the woods to make sure Kiddle is all right. What do you say, Flo?'

I rose. 'I was hoping you might suggest it. I don't suppose you brought a—'

'In here,' she said, holding up her artist's satchel.

'Then let's not hang about.'

'I ought to come with you,' said Sir Hector.

Lady Hardcastle shook her head. 'No, Hector, it's best you stay here. We know what we're doing.'

'I'd be in the way, what?'

'I didn't say that. You'll be more use back at the house in case we miss Kiddle and he needs help when he gets back.'

'Say no more.'

We made our way to the dining room door.

'What did she bring?' muttered Mrs Adaway.

Lady Farley-Stroud was sufficiently well acquainted with our ways to know that I had been about to say 'gun', but she chose to keep that titbit from her sister-in-law. 'Sketchbook, m'dear. Likes to record everything.'

'I hardly think—'

But we had already closed the door, so I never found out what she hardly thought.

We retraced Mrs Adaway's steps to the ballroom, and out through the French doors on to the terrace.

Lady Hardcastle looked out across the grounds.

She pointed. 'Well, there's the grove.'

'And beyond that, the woods,' I said. 'It's a fair way. No wonder the old girl was puffed.'

'Best foot forward and all that.'

The sun was out, but the air was crisply autumnal as we strode across the lawn towards the steps leading down into the ha-ha. We were through the gate at the bottom and up the other side in no time and we resumed our hurried pace towards the grove, following Mrs Adaway's trampled footprints in the longer grass.

'Whom are we believing?' I asked.

'About the nature of the creature?' said Lady Hardcastle. 'All my instincts, not to mention my dimly remembered scientific training, want me to resist the idea of "believing" anything at all. Evidence is what counts.'

'Well, yes, but what evidence do we have?'

'Precious little, as far as I'm aware.'

'I suppose we have a couple of sightings.'

'We do. But is Joyce a credible witness, do we think? Is young Billy, from the Dog and Duck? Both insist they've seen a big cat. Both even go so far as to say it's a panther. But our available experts are less convinced. Pinkard – an experienced vet – suggests that it's more likely to be a dog. Noah Lock has similar experience of animal attacks abroad, but he was non-committal. He mentioned hyenas and big cats, but he, too, seemed to be leaning broadly dogwards, simply based on probability. We don't get many big cats in Gloucestershire, after all.'

'Mrs Stitch's moggy is a little on the hefty side.'

'I doubt he could be bothered to stroll to the end of her garden, much less heave himself over the wall and off to the woods to eviscerate a sheep.'

We had, by now, reached the grove. The grass showed signs of more trampling where Mrs Adaway and Minty had stopped when something in the woods had caught their attention. Tracks continued towards the trees.

I pointed them out. 'That'll be Kiddle. I doubt Minty weighs more than half a stone wet through – she'd barely have moved the grass as she passed, so those aren't her tracks.'

'Agreed,' said Lady Hardcastle.

She reached into her satchel and drew out a Broomhandle Mauser to which she deftly attached a wooden shoulder stock.

'That's quite a weapon you've been hauling about there,' I said.

'One likes to come prepared. I'd prefer something with a little more stopping power, but this does at least have the advantage of being quite portable.'

'Just make sure you don't miss. I don't want to have to try to defend you from a ravening wild beast.'

'You'd defend me? How touching.'

'Of course I would. I like that dress and I'd hate to see it torn open and covered in blood. The cleaning and repairs would take forever.'

She tutted and we walked cautiously on.

Kiddle's tracks led us very clearly to the edge of the wood, but no further. Once the grass had thinned among the trees, there was much less to guide us and we had to rely on our rudimentary tracking skills to point us in the right direction.

Some scuffed leaf litter here, a crushed fern there – someone or something had definitely passed this way.

As the trees closed in around us I began to feel an irrational unease. It might be more dangerous to walk along a city street at night – along *some* city streets in the daytime – but woods and forests provoke some primeval fear. Our ancestors must have *really* hated forests.

We pressed on in silence, eyes sweeping for signs of danger.

I stepped on a small pile of rotting leaves, and the dried stick they were covering broke under my weight with a loud snap.

Our heads turned in unison towards the sound of the growl.

Lady Hardcastle's gun came up.

We edged forwards, towards the sound.

The growl came again.

This time, though, I heard it more clearly. It wasn't a big cat. It wasn't even a big dog. It was a tiny dog.

'Minty?' I called. Why would I say it as a question? What was I expecting? 'Why yes, Miss Armstrong, it is I, Lady Araminta Fluffikins. How delightful to see you again.'

Still, we didn't know what else might be there, so we continued our cautious approach.

As we drew nearer, Minty began barking, and as we passed the last tree concealing her from view, we saw why.

She was covered in blood, and standing guard over the body of Felix Kiddle.

◆　◆　◆

Kiddle groaned, and I rushed towards him while Lady Hardcastle scanned around with her gun raised.

Minty snarled and tried to see me off, but she wasn't a stupid dog and seemed to quickly work out that even against a human as small as me, it was a fight she couldn't possibly win. I managed to get her to let me examine her, and found that she was unhurt. The blood wasn't hers, but that of the man she was guarding. I tried to encourage her to go to Lady Hardcastle, but she refused to abandon Kiddle and sat loyally by his side. A small growl warned me I was only there under sufferance and that any false move would be met with the full force of her tiny wrath.

Kiddle groaned again.

He had been badly mauled. Something's teeth – or, more likely, claws – had ripped raggedly through his heavy outdoor clothes as though they were made of chiffon. I was distracted briefly by the thought of a gamekeeper in a chiffon evening gown, but the blood oozing slowly from the wounds to his arms, belly and legs brought me back to reality.

The animal hadn't caught any arteries, and he had only lost a small amount of blood. Enough to make a mess, but not enough to endanger his life. His grogginess, I quickly ascertained, came from the head wound, probably sustained when he had fallen and hit it on an exposed tree root.

'Kiddle,' I said. 'Felix. Can you hear me? You're badly cut, but you're going to be all right.'

'Minty,' he moaned.

'She's here. She's safe. She's been looking after you.'

'Big cat. Huge. Black. A panther. It tried to get her. Poacher. Dick Durbin. Tried to save her. Tried to fight it off. It turned on us both.'

'Where?'

He pointed.

'I'll go,' said Lady Hardcastle. 'You stay here with Kiddle.' She rummaged in her satchel and produced a silk scarf and a hip flask. 'You'd best clean those wounds.'

I opened the flask. Brandy. Of course it was.

I had no idea if there was enough alcohol in Herself's best cognac to sterilize open wounds, but it was better than nothing.

'This is going to sting a bit,' I said as I poured a tiny splash of brandy on to the first of the gashes.

His agonized gasp confirmed I'd been correct.

I cleaned him as best I could while trying not to add too badly to his pain. On closer inspection, the wounds were quite shallow and his clothes had withstood more of the attack than I'd given them credit for. Still, he was a mess, and one or two would certainly need stitches.

I worked as quickly and delicately as I could, while keeping one eye and both ears open for the return of the cat. There was no sign, though, and the next thing I saw was the return of Lady Hardcastle.

Kiddle saw her, too. 'Durbin?'

She shook her head. 'He didn't make it, I'm afraid. Very badly mauled.'

The gamekeeper tried to sit up.

I put my hand on his chest and pushed him gently down. 'No, you'd better stay where you are. We'll get help to you.'

'But I need—'

'You need to wait here. There's nothing you can do for Durbin, and if you get up and start trying to dash about you could do yourself some damage.'

'I didn't plan on doin' no dashin', I just wanted to—'

'Nevertheless. You rest here and we'll take care of everything.'

Lady Hardcastle crouched beside me. 'You're fleeter of foot than I, so you get back to The Grange and summon help. I have the gun, so I'll keep watch.'

'Right you are,' I said. 'If we can get Sir Hector's car down here to the edge of the woods, we can have Kiddle safely back at the house by the time Dr Fitzsimmons gets here in his cart.'

'I think he refers to it as a carriage, dear, but yes, that sounds sensible.'

'Carriage, my eye – it's a cart.'

'It is, but allow the man his vanity. And it's a sudden death so we should get Sergeant Dobson up here as well.'

I nodded. 'Of course. Are you sure you'll be all right?'

She patted the Mauser. 'We'll be fine. And Minty will look after us, won't you, dear?'

She ruffled the dog's bloodstained head and I set off back to The Grange.

# Chapter Five

I ran back to the house and was hurrying past the library when I heard Sir Hector calling to me.

'We're in here, m'dear.'

I entered and found him looking out of the window while Mrs Adaway and Lady Farley-Stroud sat uncomfortably upright in two armchairs near the fire.

'Have you found him?' said Sir Hector.

I opened my mouth to speak.

'Never mind his stupid gamekeeper,' interrupted Mrs Adaway. 'What about my poor, dear Minty?'

I frowned. 'Kiddle is badly hurt, but he should be fine with the right care. He's been mauled by a big cat and he needs a doctor at once.'

'I'll telephone Fitzsimmons,' said Sir Hector.

'Thank you. And would you tell Sergeant Dobson as well, please? The animal killed a man – Dick Durbin.'

'The poacher? Bit of a rogue, that one, but he didn't deserve that. Poor fella. That'll be my second call.'

'I don't care about the blessed poacher, either,' said Mrs Adaway, angrily. 'What about Minty?'

'Minty is unharmed,' I said. 'She's covered in blood and will need a bath, but none of it is hers.'

'Oh, the poor thing. The poor, dear thing.'

I shook my head.

Lady Farley-Stroud saw me and rolled her eyes. 'Your concern for your fellow man is touching, Joyce.'

'My *fellow* man? One is a servant and the other a criminal. I hardly think those are my fellows.'

'Well, that just about sums you up. I have never—'

Sir Hector held up his hands. 'Ladies! I will not have this unseemly bickering. A man is dead. Another is badly hurt.'

'But—' began Mrs Adaway.

'And your absurd dog is fine, Joyce,' said Lady Farley-Stroud.

'Well. Really. I've never been spoken to like—'

'And that, I feel, is at least half your problem. Someone should have pointed out long ago what a dreadful old bat you are. Perhaps then we'd—'

'Ladies!' said Sir Hector, even more forcefully. 'Stop this at once.' He turned to me. 'My apologies, Florence. You shouldn't have to witness this terrible behaviour when you're a guest in our home. I do apologize.'

He meant well, of course, but this actually put me in a rather awkward position. How was I expected to respond to that? I smiled and nodded my acknowledgement but said nothing.

He seemed to realize his blunder. 'Would you mind awfully comin' with me, Florence, m'dear? If Fitzsimmons starts askin' complicated questions I shan't know what to say, what?'

'Of course, Sir Hector. Lead the way.'

I followed him out of the library towards the hall, where the telephone was mounted discreetly on the wood panelling beside the door.

He picked up the earpiece and rat-a-tatted on the handle to attract the attention of the operator.

'Hello, m'dear,' he said, as though he knew her personally. 'Be a sport and connect me to Dr Fitzsimmons in Littleton Cotterell, would you?' He turned to me. 'Connectin' me now.' He grinned. 'What ho, Fitzsimmons. Hector Farley-Stroud. Got a bit of an emergency, what? . . . No, the memsahib's right as ninepence . . . Joyce, too. In rude health. Or should that be rude and healthy?' He gave a little chuckle. 'No, it's young Felix Kiddle, m'new gamekeeper. Had a bit of a mishap with a cat . . . No, we don't have a cat. Wild cat in Littleton Woods. Big one by all accounts. Mauled the poor fella . . . Not sure, old chap. Hold on.' He looked to me. 'Wounds?'

'Slashes to his arms, legs and abdomen,' I said. 'It didn't look as though there was any damage to the muscles, nor to any major blood vessels. He's lost some blood but it's under control. We cleaned the wounds with alcohol as best we could but he took a blow to the head as he fell and wasn't fit to make his own way back to the house.'

'Hear that, Fitzsimmons? . . . Good show. Hold on . . .' He looked at me again. 'Can the quack get his carriage to the wounded man?'

'I shouldn't have thought so,' I said. 'But your motor car should be able to make it. Perhaps we could bring him back to the house?'

'Cracking idea.' Back to the telephone. 'Hear that, old chap? . . . That's it, meet us up at the house . . . Cheerio for now.'

He hung up. 'Ring for Jenkins, would you, m'dear? I'll telephone the rozzers.'

I pressed the servants' bell while Sir Hector made the call to the station. By the time he had arranged for Constable Hancock to ride up with the doctor, Jenkins had arrived and was waiting politely for instructions.

'Jenkins. Good man. Want you to get Bert to drive Dewi down to the woods in the motor car. Need them to bring a wounded man back to the house. Kiddle's been attacked by the wild beast that's been causin' all the trouble.'

'Of course, sir.'

'Might be tricky, mind you. Got anything we could fashion into a stretcher?'

'There are some sturdy poles in the gardener's shed, sir. If we fold a blanket—'

'Splendid. Leave the details to you, what?'

'Yes, sir. I'll see to it at once.'

'Thank you. Once you've done that, would you serve coffee in the library, please.'

'Of course, sir.'

Jenkins hurried off and I followed Sir Hector back to the waiting, bickering, sisters-in-law.

'Alcohol, eh?'

'Hip flask,' I said.

'Ha!' he barked. 'That's our Emily.'

It took quite a while for all the comings and goings to come and go but, eventually, Kiddle was taken back to Dr Fitzsimmons's home for treatment, Durbin's body was brought to the house to await the mortuary van, Minty was taken for a bath by her anxious owner, and Lady Hardcastle was given coffee in the library.

She had asked Constable Hancock to join us and he perched, straight-backed, on the very edge of an armchair, his police helmet on the arm beside him.

'Bad business, that,' said Sir Hector. 'Sure I can't offer you a snifter? Calm the nerves?'

'Thank you, Sir Hector,' said Hancock, 'but not while I's on duty. I'll need a pint or two down the Dog and Duck later, mind. I a'n't never seen nothin' like that.'

Lady Hardcastle looked puzzled. 'I thought you were the one who went to see Sid Hyde's body.'

'I was, m'lady, but 'tweren't nothin' like that. His wounds were clean slashes, rest 'is soul. But Durbin . . . they was more like rips. Like he was torn open.'

'When you say "slashes", what do you mean? Like a knife?'

'Like a knife, yes, but . . . but not like a knife. Four cuts all lined up like they was made by an animal's claws.'

'Parallel?'

'That's the word. Parallel.'

'But in your view they could have had a different cause?'

'Two different animals, you mean?'

'Very much like that, yes.'

'I suppose so. But I don't like the thought of there bein' two ferocious animals out there. It's bad enough there bein' just one.'

Lady Hardcastle nodded. 'I see. Hector, would you mind if I used your telephone to make a call to Bristol? And would you mind awfully if we stayed a while longer? I'd like to get Inspector Sunderland out here. And the police surgeon. We'll need to hang on to Durbin's body, too, I'm afraid.'

'A detective?' said Lady Farley-Stroud before her husband could answer.

'Yes, Gertie. I rather think there's been a murder.'

There was another long wait before our friends from the Bristol Police arrived. We spent it in conversation with Lady Farley-Stroud, who brought out her planning files for the Bonfire Night celebrations and the Christmas party. There were lists, schedules and sketches. There were copies of orders, invoices and correspondence. I'd known for years that Lady Farley-Stroud was a keen committee chairwoman and an enthusiastic organizer of village life, but I'd had no idea she took it all to such extremes. It was a pity she'd never had the opportunity to run a business – she and Sir Hector wouldn't have had to wait until they found hidden treasure at The Grange to make their fortune.

I was rather relieved when Jenkins appeared at the library door to announce two more visitors. I'd just agreed to take on even more responsibility for the entertainment at the Christmas party, and I was worried what else I might find myself drawn into if Lady Farley-Stroud were allowed to continue.

'Inspector Sunderland and Dr Gosling are here, m'lady,' he said as he ushered them into the room.

'Cave,' said Sir Hector with a chuckle, 'it's the rozzers.'

Lady Farley-Stroud sighed. 'Good afternoon, gentlemen. Take no notice of my husband.'

Inspector Sunderland smiled. 'Good afternoon to you both.'

Dr Gosling, meanwhile, was grinning. 'I always love coming here. And it certainly is the rozzers.' He winked at Sir Hector.

'Would you care for some tea?' asked Lady Farley-Stroud. 'Or coffee?'

The inspector smiled. 'Perhaps later, my lady. For now I'm keen to find out what prompted Lady Hardcastle's urgent summons.' He turned to Lady Hardcastle. 'You were a little cagey on the telephone.'

She smiled. 'Walls have ears, Inspector dear. And telephone operators certainly do. Recent events have caused something of a stir in the area and I didn't want the gossip to get a head start on us.'

'I am intrigued.'

Lady Hardcastle stood. 'Well, I hope you'll think it was worth the trip after all that.'

'We'll always answer your call, old girl,' said Dr Gosling.

'We will,' agreed the inspector. 'So, what's going on?'

'I think it would be easier if we showed you,' said Lady Hardcastle. 'Excuse us, Gertie dear – I just need to show them the . . . well, you know.'

Lady Hardcastle led the way, with Sunderland and Gosling following. I hurried off to the servants' hall to collect Constable Hancock and we caught up with the others just as they were approaching the old stables, which now functioned as the garage for the Farley-Strouds' car.

Dr Gosling was talking to Lady Hardcastle. 'Am I just here to keep the old boy company?'

Lady Hardcastle patted his arm. 'You're here because of your invaluable expertise in the field of forensic pathology.'

'I think you might just be buttering me up.'

'I might, indeed. You never know with me.'

She pulled open the stable door and went over to a man-sized shape on the ground that was covered by a canvas tarpaulin. She drew back the sheet to reveal Dick Durbin's body.

Dr Gosling approached and knelt beside her. 'Chap's definitely deceased. You see these slippery, pink bits and bobs on the outside? They should all be on the inside.'

Inspector Sunderland sighed. 'Show a bit of respect, Gosling. This was a human being.'

'Sorry, old chap. Doctors, you know? Gallows humour and all that. What did this to him?'

'A large cat,' said Lady Hardcastle. 'Probably a panther.'

Dr Gosling frowned. 'I see. The wounds are certainly consistent with something like that. So if you know how he died, where do I come in?'

'For the matter of that,' said the inspector, 'where do *I* come in? You're sure it was an animal?'

Lady Hardcastle nodded. 'We have a witness.'

'I see. But animal attacks aren't really a matter for the CID, not even if the animal is a rare and exotic one.'

'Indeed no,' said Lady Hardcastle. 'But murder most definitely is a matter for the CID. Constable Hancock, would you be good enough to tell the inspector what you told us when you first saw Mr Durbin's wounds.'

'What I said, sir, was that them's not the same as the wounds I saw on Sid Hyde when I saw his body on Monday mornin'.'

Inspector Sunderland took out his notebook and began writing. 'And who was Sid Hyde? Should I know him?'

'He was a farmer, sir. From Top Farm. Good as gold. Not known to the police, sir.'

'Yes, but why—'

Lady Hardcastle stood. 'Sid Hyde was the victim of a supposed animal attack. He'd lost one of his sheep, and was patrolling his land to protect the rest when the same animal which slaughtered his sheep took his life, too. Or so everyone thought.'

'And you no longer think so?'

'Not now the constable has seen the victim of a real attack, no. Constable?'

'Hyde's wounds were cleaner, sir,' said Hancock. 'Like they was made with a blade, not an animal's claw.'

Sunderland carried on writing. 'So you think Hyde was murdered, and the killer made it look like an animal attack?'

'That's exactly what I think,' said Lady Hardcastle.

'Did he have any enemies, this Hyde?'

'Everybody loved old Sid,' said Hancock. 'Good as gold, he was, like I said. Always put his hand in his pocket down the Dog and Duck. Do anythin' for anyone, he would.'

'And he hadn't upset anyone recently?'

'Not so far as I knows, sir, no.'

'Do you have any suspects in mind, my lady?'

Lady Hardcastle shook her head. 'I've only just realized the poor fellow was probably murdered. We've been trying to find out more about the wild animal so we could help the man from the Board of Agriculture when he gets here.'

'And what did you find out?'

'Precious little. One young farmhand said he saw a large black cat, but everyone else was convinced it must have been a dog.'

'It would make more sense,' said the inspector. 'Not a lot of panthers in the West Country.'

'Well, quite. We were prepared to go along with the dog theory on the balance of probabilities alone. But now we have a reliable eyewitness who is adamant that he saw a panther.'

'And who's that?'

'Hector's gamekeeper: Felix Kiddle.'

'Where can I find him?'

'He'll be at Dr Fitzsimmons's house this evening – he was attacked by the creature, too. He's hurt, but not life-threateningly. If the doctor can somehow keep infection at bay, he should pull through. I imagine the doctor will send him home in due course, but I'm afraid I don't know where that is. Sorry. Hector never said where he lived.'

Dr Gosling was standing with us now. 'If we want to take this further, I ought to have a look at Mr Hyde's body for myself. Where is it, Constable?'

'Mortuary at Stroud, sir. Coroner's inquest set for next Tuesday.'

'I think we'd better get up there and have a look. Sunderland?'

'I agree. I'd rather know more about both deaths before I make a report and start asking questions.'

'Thank you,' said Lady Hardcastle.

'We haven't done anything yet, my lady.'

'No, but you've taken us seriously, and that's always appreciated.'

'I'd never question your opinion on matters of murder.'

'You're very kind. We'll leave Gertie and Hector to get some peace and quiet now, so if you have any news and don't mind delaying your journey home by dropping in on us, we'll be at the house.'

'If it's not too late I'm sure we can manage that. Come on, then, Gosling, we'd better get cracking.'

'We better had, but I'll need to make a couple of telephone calls first, if the Farley-Strouds don't mind. I presume you told the mortuary at Stroud to take Mr Durbin's body, Constable?'

'I did, sir. That's our regular procedure.'

'Of course. I'd prefer he came to my mortuary, though, so I need to make the arrangements. It's too late to stop the Stroud men, so would you mind waiting here to fend them off and then hand him over to my chaps when they get here?'

'Not at all, sir.'

'Good man. It might take a while.'

'Don't you worry about that, sir – they always looks after me downstairs at The Grange.'

Dr Gosling laughed. 'I'm sure they do. Well, goodbye for now, ladies, but I hope to see you later with news. Sunderland – will you accompany me inside to listen to my charming telephone manner?'

'I think I'll wait in the car, thank you.'

'As you wish.'

We all left Hancock to guard the body, and walked towards the house. Dr Gosling scuttled off to ask to use the telephone while Inspector Sunderland gave us a cheery farewell and went to sit in his car.

Lady Hardcastle and I went inside to say our goodbyes to the Farley-Strouds and then set off for home.

◆ ◆ ◆

My first task upon our return to the house was to trudge upstairs to the attic to fetch the blackboard and easel that had become known as the crime board. Since her days as a student of natural sciences at Girton College, Lady Hardcastle had preferred to do her thinking on a blackboard where others could see what she was up to and collaborate as necessary. Or something like that. She had explained it to me often, but the thing I most associated with the crime board was not its usefulness in making sense of complicated situations, but the tedium of lugging it downstairs every time it was needed.

And it was needed often. We had moved to Gloucestershire in 1908 for a quiet life in the country, away from the frantic pace and ever-present death and danger of London – but, unbeknown to us, we had chosen England's murder capital as our new home. When we had first met Inspector Sunderland of A Division of the Bristol Police, he had gleefully informed us that there were more murders per head of population in our chosen part of Gloucestershire than in any other region in the country. A person was more than twice as likely to be murdered here, he told us, than anywhere else.

It didn't take us long to discover that not only was he absolutely correct but, as we'd already noted, the people of the area were now so accustomed to their neighbours being done in that it barely caused a flicker. Unless an animal was suspected, of course, and then there would be flickering aplenty.

I made sure to make a proper amount of fuss and noise as I installed the crime board in the dining room, where Lady Hardcastle was sitting at the table preparing the sketches that we would pin up to aid our contemplation of the case.

Edna and Miss Jones had gone home for the day, so I made a pot of coffee and joined Lady Hardcastle at the dining table.

She was an excellent artist and more than capable of talking and drawing at the same time, but I tried not to interrupt too much anyway. Instead I sipped my coffee and attempted to marshal my thoughts. I still had no idea what was going on, and if Inspector Sunderland and Dr Gosling returned with the anticipated confirmation that Sid Hyde had been murdered, I was almost certainly going to be expected to offer insights and opinions as well as coffee and biscuits.

Frustratingly, I'd come up with exactly nothing by the time the doorbell rang.

I led the inspector and the police surgeon to the dining room and left them with Lady Hardcastle while I made another pot of coffee and put some of Miss Jones's freshly made madeleines on a plate.

I returned to the dining room to find them making dinner arrangements.

'Ah, Flo,' said Lady Hardcastle, 'welcome back. How do you feel about Humphrey's in Bristol for dinner on the twenty-second?'

'Of October?'

'Yes.'

'I have no idea when that is, nor what else I might have planned, but in principle it sounds splendid.'

'It's a Tuesday and we have nothing on. There's a skittles tournament at the Dog and Duck on the Wednesday, but the rest of the week is free.'

'Then count me in. Humphrey's has a splendid menu.'

'Over to you, then, gentlemen. If wives and fiancées are also free, we have a plan.'

'Dolly's usually free on Tuesdays,' said Inspector Sunderland.

'Splendid,' said Lady Hardcastle. 'What about Dinah?'

Dr Gosling shrugged. 'Not a clue. She's always jaunting off hither, thither and yon. I can't keep up with her.'

'Well, do remember to ask, won't you? It would be lovely for us all to get together again. It's been an absolute age.'

The two men nodded and murmured in agreement.

'So,' she continued, 'what did you find at Stroud?'

'Man-made injuries,' said Dr Gosling. 'As Hancock suggested, the gashes on the deceased's torso were caused by sharp, smooth-edged blades, probably iron or steel.'

'Blades?' I asked. 'Plural?'

'I'd say, so, yes. The wounds have the characteristics of slashes – quick strokes, not slow, deliberate cuts. To get them so evenly spaced and perfectly parallel would take great skill. I'm sure you could do it, or perhaps your butcher Mr Spratt, but it would be beyond most people. And there are slight differences between the cuts which *could* just be caused by differences in speed and force between slashes, but are more likely to be slight differences in sharpness between the connected blades.'

'So you're imagining something like an artificial claw?' said Lady Hardcastle.

Dr Gosling shrugged. 'Not my job to imagine, old thing. I present the medical facts and then you and Sunderland do the imagining. All I'm qualified to do is make a statement to the coroner. Which I shall do.'

'And what do you think, Inspector?'

The inspector swallowed a mouthful of madeleine. 'From what Gosling says, some sort of arrangement of blades does seem to have been used. I can imagine four knives lashed together and used as a single weapon, certainly.'

'So we think someone wanted Hyde dead,' I said, 'and tried to cover their tracks by making it look as though it was the same animal that had killed his sheep?'

'It's as good a starting point as any,' said the inspector. 'I know we spoke about it earlier but I can't quickly find it in my notes. Do you mind going through it again?'

Lady Hardcastle and I nodded our assent.

He took out his notebook. 'Thank you. Who would want him dead?'

Lady Hardcastle replaced her coffee cup carefully on its saucer. 'As far as we're able to tell at the moment, no one.' She began holding up her sketches. 'His neighbours on one side are the Locks – you remember Noah Lock and Audrey from the Caradine case?'

'I do. Nice people.'

'Very nice indeed. They spoke well of Hyde and seemed to have no disputes with him.'

'Am I right in thinking Lock is a military man?'

'He was an officer, yes. Served overseas. India and South Africa.'

'So he could handle a knife, too.'

'I should think so,' said Lady Hardcastle. 'He certainly looks like the sort of man you'd want by your side in a fight. But I'm struggling to see a motive.'

'It's usually land if farmers are involved.'

'Perhaps.' She riffled through her drawings. 'To the other side, at Bottom Farm, are the Roods: Jonathan and Phillis. Again very pleasant, and again, no obvious disputes with Hyde.'

'I say,' said Dr Gosling. 'Is that sketch of Mrs Rood accurate?'

Lady Hardcastle flipped it towards her and checked. 'As accurate as my limited skills allow, dear, yes.'

'She's a bit of all right, isn't she?'

'A handsome woman,' agreed Inspector Sunderland. 'Could Hyde have been making unwanted advances? Is Rood the jealous type?'

'It's possible,' conceded Lady Hardcastle, 'but Hyde was walking out with a woman from Woodworthy . . . umm—'

'Doreen Robinson,' I said.

'That's it. Thank you. Hyde's farmhand said he was devoted to her and planned to propose.'

'And what about this farmhand?'

Lady Hardcastle held up the relevant sketch. 'Louis Finch. Another one who didn't have a bad word to say about Hyde. He was devastated by Hyde's death and extremely worried about the potential loss of his own job. He clearly didn't understand how the legal side of things worked and seemed surprised and relieved when I explained probate and inheritance.'

The inspector was making notes as usual. 'And who inherits?'

'Hyde's brother, we think. He works at the quarry at Tytherington.'

'Did you get a name?'

'Sorry, no.'

'If he has financial troubles, that might give him a motive.'

'It might, indeed, but we've no idea, I'm afraid. We know nothing about him other than what Finch said, and that was just that he has no interest in farming.'

Inspector Sunderland nodded. 'Have you spoken to anyone else?'

'There's Hector's gamekeeper, Felix Kiddle – the other victim in today's attack.'

'Ah, yes. I'll call at Fitzsimmons's tomorrow and get an address for him. Did he know Hyde?'

'Everyone knew Sid Hyde, dear, but we've heard nothing to indicate that there might have been bad blood between them.'

'This Hyde chap is coming across as some sort of saint.'

'Hardly. He was just an easy-going, well-liked man, that's all.'

'Whom somebody wanted to kill.'

'Well, yes, there is that. But so far I'm struggling to find a reason for it.' Lady Hardcastle held up yet another sketch. 'Then there's a young local lad whom we know only as Billy. He seems to be the first to have identified the wild animal as a panther – although, obviously, no one believed him. But when the creature attacked Kiddle and Durbin it became clear that he'd been right all along.'

'No one believed him? Did they rib him?'

'His pals did, of course.'

'Did Hyde?'

Lady Hardcastle smiled. 'No, Hyde didn't believe him – he was still insistent that a dog had killed his sheep – but he wasn't dismissive or rude. But young men of Billy's age deal with things a little more directly – they're more likely just to punch a chap in the mouth if they feel slighted. I can't picture him painstakingly strapping four knives together and lying in wait in the early hours of the morning to take his revenge on Hyde, even if he *had* said anything.'

The inspector shrugged. 'It would back up his story about the big cat.'

'Even so . . .'

'I'd still like to speak to the lad.'

'Oh, I wouldn't dream of presuming to suggest otherwise – at the very least he might have more information about the panther – but my impression is that he's not the sort of young man to commit premeditated murder.'

Sunderland smiled. 'In my experience, very few murderers give that impression, right up to the moment when they slash someone open with a fake claw.'

'That's very true, dear. But that's all I have, I'm afraid.' She held up a beautiful drawing of a fierce black cat. 'Oh, but I do have a panther.'

'So you do. You're really rather talented, my lady.'

'Thank you, dear.'

He finished making his notes. 'Well, I think this is enough for me to be getting on with for now. Thank you.'

'Our pleasure. Will you stay for dinner?'

'I'm afraid I have to get back to Bristol.'

Dr Gosling nodded. 'And I'm having dinner with Dinah. I expect she'll want to write a story on all this, too.'

'Ah, yes,' said Lady Hardcastle. 'Dinah. I'd been meaning to call her with a tip when it was just the wild animal killings, but now it's an actual murder I expect she'll want it even more.'

'I expect so. Always on the lookout for a good story, our Dinah.'

'She knows where to find us if she needs introductions to the main players.'

Inspector Sunderland frowned. '*After* I've spoken to them, please. I'm all for helping the press, especially when it's Miss Caudle, but I'd like to take the first run at the witnesses.'

There was a little more small talk while we polished off the madeleines, then we said our goodbyes and waved our friends off to Bristol.

# Chapter Six

Thursday dawned, bright and sunny, but there was a chill in the air so I decided to do my exercises in the drawing room. It wasn't the first time since the spring – the September storms had driven me indoors – but it definitely felt as though the summer was over now that it was the cold rather than the rain that was stopping me from exercising in the garden.

I got started and lost myself in the calming motions. I thought time must have run away from me but the clock said otherwise and I had already washed and changed by the time Edna and Miss Jones arrived together. It suddenly struck me that I'd never asked how they managed to do that.

'How do you manage to do that?' I asked as they took off their hats and coats in the boot room.

'Manage what, my lover?' asked Edna.

'Arriving together. You live miles apart.'

'Hardly miles,' she said with a smile. 'A few hundred yards, maybe. I calls on 'er on my way through. I says hello to her ma, has a quick gossip – she likes a gossip, does Annie Jones – and then we walks over together.'

I smiled. 'It's obvious when you think about it. What was today's gossip?'

Her eyes opened wide as she put her hand on my arm. 'You i'n't never goin' to believe it. You know how Sid Hyde was killed by a lion?'

'I'm not sure anyone ever mentioned a lion.'

'Did they not? Well, it don't matter anyway. Sid Hyde was' – her eyes widened further and her grip on my arm grew tighter – '*murdered.*'

I tried not to laugh. And failed. 'By a lion?'

She frowned. 'No, silly, by a human man. What do you think of that?'

'Well, it certainly makes more sense than a lion. How did you find out?'

'Wally Dobson was in the Dog and Duck last night. Singin' young Sam Hancock's praises, he was. It was Sam who worked it all out, see?'

'Good old Sam. Did Sergeant Dobson mention Dick Durbin and Felix Kiddle?'

'There was sommat, but I didn't catch it. What do you know?'

I briefly recounted the events of the previous afternoon, including the confirmation from Sunderland and Gosling that Hyde had been killed with iron or steel blades.

She seemed disappointed. 'So you already knew?'

'Sorry.'

'But there *was* a lion.'

'A panther.'

'Same thing, i'n't it?'

'Sort of. A panther is certainly a big, scary cat and you'd definitely not want it curled up in front of your fire.'

'It'd keep the mice under control, mind.'

'Mice, rabbits, sheep, annoying neighbours . . . you'd have no more problems with any of them. As long as it didn't eat *you*, you'd be fine.'

Edna laughed. 'Bit of a gamble, certainly. Still, it's a relief to know Sid weren't killed by a wild animal.'

'But Dick Durbin was.'

'Yes, but he was probably up to no good.'

I didn't fancy trying to get her to explain the concept of a police panther, keeping the region safe from n'er-do-wells by eating them whenever it thought they were 'up to no good'. Instead I offered her a cup of tea. 'Or coffee if you prefer – I'm making Herself's starter breakfast.'

'I wouldn't say no.' She turned to Miss Jones. 'You'll 'ave one, too, won't you?'

'I wouldn't say no, neither. What did you think of them madeleines?'

I smiled. 'They were wonderful – thank you. Inspector Sunderland was particularly impressed.'

'That's good to hear. I wants to improve my pastry skills, see?'

'There's not much improvement needed. Can we have breakfast for half past eight today, please? We've nothing on as far as I know.'

'Course you can.'

I took the coffee and toast upstairs.

The lump underneath the covers snuffled a little as I entered and put down the tray, but didn't stir. I opened the curtains a chink but it was still misty so I left them closed.

I contemplated the sleeping mound for a moment, then decided to leave her be. If the coffee and toast were cold by the time she woke I could always make more.

I stepped quietly towards the door. I had my hand on the handle when I heard the sheet flick down.

'Is that you, Flossie?'

'None other,' I said as I turned round.

'Where are you going?'

'I brought up your starter breakfast, but you seemed comfy so I thought I'd let you snooze on for a bit.'

'You're kind. What time is it?'

'Half past seven.'

She sat up. 'Half past seven? This will never do. Why did you let me lie in?'

I frowned. 'Why would I not? We have no plans today.'

'We're going to Bath.'

'We are?'

'I'm sure I told you.'

'I'm sure you didn't. Why are we going to Bath?'

'An old Girton chum of mine, Sarah Laycock-Bartles, lives there. We're going to see her.'

'How lovely. We've lived in the West Country all these years and we've never been to Bath.'

'Well, quite. We can do a little sightseeing and then meet Sarah. She's just the sort of expert we need.'

'And what sort of expert is that?'

'She's a zoologist specializing in unusual animals and the sightings thereof. She's often quoted in the newspapers. Whenever there's a strange beast abroad in the countryside and "an expert says . . .", odds-on she's the expert. They refuse to mention her name – their readers would explode at the breakfast table if a woman were being quoted as an expert.'

'It would take up an awful lot of space, too.'

'It *is* quite a handle, to be sure, but I started life as a Featherstonhaugh so I'm no one to talk.'

'It would take at least three lines in a newspaper column to name you both.'

'Another reason for their maintaining her anonymity. But I'd like her opinion on the Beast of Littleton Woods and she has agreed to meet us at a quiet tearoom near the abbey.'

'Right you are. When do we leave?'

'I have consulted *Bradshaw's* and there's a train from Chipping Bevington at eleven minutes past ten.'

'I'd better get breakfast on, then. See you at eight?'

'I'll be ready, dear.'

I left her to her coffee and toast and went downstairs.

'Sorry to drop this on you, Miss Jones,' I said, 'but can we have breakfast for eight instead, please? Herself wants to go out.'

Edna looked up from her tea. 'Anywhere nice?'

'A trip to Bath,' I said. 'We've lived here all this time and we've never been to Bath.'

'I went there once with our Dan and my sister. It wasn't a patch on Weston. No sea, for a start.'

'There's hardly ever any sea at Weston.'

'True, true. But there's no donkey rides at Bath, neither.'

'But there are the Roman baths, and the Pump Room. And Jane Austen lived there for a while.'

'I don't know her. One of Lady H's friends, is she?'

'She was a writer. In Regency times.'

'Oh, *that* Jane Austen.'

'You've read her?'

'No, but I've heard of her, of course. So that's an attraction, is it? That some woman who wrote books an 'undred years ago lived there for a bit?'

'Well, when you put it like that, I'm sure I'll be as disappointed as you were. But I'd like to see her house.'

Miss Jones was tending to the sausages. 'I thought you'd be workin' on solvin' the mystery of the killer beast.'

'And that's the real reason we're going. Apparently, Herself has a friend there who knows all about strange animals. We want as much information as we can get hold of before the chap from the Board of Agriculture turns up.'

'Well, he'd better get on with it as soon as he can – everyone's terrified. Our ma won't even let the cat out.'

I smiled. 'We've a real-life human murderer loose in the village – Sid Hyde wasn't killed by the Beast. Is no one saying anything about that?'

'There's always a murderer loose in the village. Part of livin' in Littleton Cotterell, that is. A wild animal's different. Our ma's pal Mrs Stitch says she saw a pair of glowin' eyes lookin' over her garden fence when she went out to check on her chickens afore bed. In a shockin' state, she was.'

'Oh dear. Did it get them?'

'The chickens? No, they's fine. And layin' a treat. I got some of their eggs for your breakfast.'

'I reckon,' said Edna, sagely, 'it's precisely *because* it's a wild animal that everyone's in a tizzy. We all thinks we can reason with a human murderer, don't we? But you can't reason with no wild animal. And we thinks we can outsmart a murderer, or outfight him. Can't beat a wild animal in a straight fight.'

I nodded. 'I'm sorry, I hadn't thought of it like that. We'll definitely do everything we can.'

'Thank you,' said Miss Jones. 'I know you'll solve it – you solves everything.'

'I wish I had your confidence in us, Blodders. Do we have any mushrooms?'

'Will that help find the Beast?'

'No, but they'll go nicely with breakfast.' There was a clatter in the hall. I looked at the kitchen clock. 'Is that the post? Already?'

Edna picked up her teacup and sat back in her chair. 'Only one way to find out, my lover.'

◆　◆　◆

There was absolutely nothing wrong with the post. This was undoubtedly a good thing – I very much wanted the Talbots to succeed. But I freely confess I was also a tiny bit disappointed – I thought the chaos brought about by the misdelivered letters had been rather funny.

Everything in our house went to plan, too, and breakfast was eaten, coats and hats donned, and the car boarded in plenty of time for the drive to Chipping Bevington railway station.

I parked in our usual spot away from the station building, and we walked across the gravelled yard towards the door. We were only halfway there when we were intercepted by Old Roberts, the stationmaster (and porter – it was a small station).

'Good mornin', m'lady. Good mornin', Miss Armstrong. I didn't know you was travellin' today. London again, is it? Are your bags on your motor car?'

'Just a day trip to Bath today, Roberts,' said Lady Hardcastle. 'A tiny bit of business and a little sightseeing.'

'Sounds like a nice day out, m'lady. Mrs Roberts and I went to Bath once. It wasn't a patch on Weston.'

I smiled. 'I've heard that. No donkeys, apparently.'

'Not a one. A few pigeons was all we saw.'

'I do love a pigeon,' said Lady Hardcastle. 'And how is Winnie? Her ankle has recovered, I hope.'

Roberts's wife had taken a tumble in the summer and sprained her ankle, and Lady Hardcastle had further endeared herself to the station manager by sending flowers.

'She's right as rain, m'lady, thank you for askin'. Back to her old self, you might say.'

By now I would have expected to be in the ticket office buying our tickets from Young Roberts, Old Roberts's son, but we were dawdling. Something was up.

Lady Hardcastle thought so, too. 'You seem to have something on your mind, Roberts, dear. Is all well?'

He stopped dead and looked about, as though checking he couldn't be overheard. 'Can I ask you for some advice, in confidence?'

'Of course. What troubles you?'

'I shouldn't really be botherin' you, but I doesn't know who else to ask.'

'Whatever it is, you can tell us.'

'Thank you, m'lady. What it is, y'see . . . I was in the station office a few weeks back, mindin' my business, and the telephone rings. It was the regional controller, Mr Billen. He says, "Hello, Bob." He never calls me Bob. Only ever calls me Roberts. "Hello, Bob, old pal," he says, "how do you fancy a drink at the Railway Arms?" Now, in all the years I've worked here, no regional controller has ever invited me for a drink. Not once. So I says, "Is sommat the matter, Mr Billen?" And he laughs, all bonhomie and jolly-good-fellow, and he says, "My dear Bob, nothing's the matter. I just want to get to know you a little better. I think we might have a lot in common, you and I." And he says it like we's best pals even though, until then, the most he'd ever said to me was "Do you have the passenger numbers for August?" I didn't know what to make of it.'

'And did you meet him?'

'I did, m'lady. Couple of weeks ago, afore the storms. And he comes in the Railway Arms, expensive suit and pocket watch. And all the railwaymen, they's lookin' down at their pints, tryin' not to be noticed. And he buys a whisky for hisself and a pint for me and says we should go and sit in the snug. So I goes in there with him and he starts talkin' about this and that, about people we both knows on the railways, about the new timetables – all normal stuff. But all the time he's sort of hintin' at sommat. Like he's tryin' to get me to admit to sommat.'

'Admit to what?'

'He kept on about bendin' the rules, and knowin' some people would take a sweetener. But I a'n't never done nothin' like that and I told 'im so. But he winked and said, "You never know what you might do if the price is right." So, o' course, then I thinks he's not accusin' me of nothin', he's tryin' to sound me out. See if I'm open to bribes, like.'

'I must say, it certainly sounds like that to me,' said Lady Hardcastle. 'And you wish to know what to do about it?'

'In a nutshell, m'lady. See, I'd normally go to the regional controller with sommat like that . . . but . . . well . . . he *is* the regional controller, i'n't he? And I doesn't want to take it higher, 'cos what if I's wrong? I doesn't want to slander the bloke.'

'I see your difficulty, I really do. So here's what I propose: Miss Armstrong and I shall look into your Mr Billen—'

'Bernard Billen, m'lady.'

'Indeed. We shall make discreet enquiries about Mr Bernard Billen and try to find out if he's a wrong'un. And if he's up to no good, we'll attempt to ascertain your best course of action. How's that?'

'I knew you'd have the answer, m'lady. Thank you. I's glad I ran into you. But I don't want to hold you up any longer – the Bath train's due in four minutes.'

We left Old Roberts and hurried to the ticket office.

Bath, it turned out, was a great deal less disappointing than Edna and Old Roberts had led us to believe it might be. We took a meandering route from the station to the Royal Crescent, making sure to pass some sights of interest that Lady Hardcastle had noted in her guidebook.

First there was Sydney Place, where Jane Austen had stayed while complaining about the noise from the people enjoying themselves in the nearby pleasure gardens. I had always been fond of Austen's writing but I'd never had much of an opinion of her as a woman. Somehow this act of deliberate curmudgeonliness – moving next to somewhere noisy and then complaining about the noise – endeared her to me greatly.

Still following the guidebook, we found astronomer William Herschel's house on New King Street, where he discovered Uranus, to the amusement of generations of schoolboys. Lady Hardcastle treated me to a lecture on all his other achievements, as well as those of his sister Caroline.

From there we made our way to a house near the New Theatre Royal, where Beau Nash had lived for a time. Sadly, it wouldn't have been convenient for the theatre because the old Theatre Royal was somewhere else.

We admired the Royal Crescent from Victoria Park and then made our way back towards the abbey, the Roman Baths and the Pump Room, all of which we explored.

Our excursion nearly at an end, we made our way to a quiet tearoom in a back street where we found a toothy, bespectacled woman of about Lady Hardcastle's age sitting at a table in the corner, apparently waiting for us.

She stood. 'Emily. Darling. It's been altogether too long.'

They kissed cheeks.

'You didn't live so close before,' said Lady Hardcastle.

'True, true. But Cumbria is beautiful – you should have come up.'

'I do regret not making the effort.' She gestured towards me. 'This is my friend, Florence Armstrong. Flo, this is Sarah Laycock-Bartles. We were at Girton together but we haven't actually seen each other since . . . when?'

Miss Laycock-Bartles smiled as we all sat. 'Some time in the early nineties, I think. You'd not long married Roddy. There was a party at your brother's place. Twenty years ago? No, it can't be. Good heavens.'

'Good heavens, indeed. Several lifetimes ago.'

Miss Laycock-Bartles touched my hand. 'We've kept in touch, dear, of course, so I know all about you.'

'Not *all* about me, I hope,' I said.

'Only the scandalous bits,' said Lady Hardcastle.

A uniformed waitress arrived with a pot of tea and some large toasted buns.

'I hope you don't mind,' said Miss Laycock-Bartles, 'but I took the liberty of ordering some Sally Lunn buns.'

We tucked in while the two old friends reminisced a little.

Miss Laycock-Bartles seemed to become suddenly aware that I was being excluded. I didn't mind, of course, but she wasn't to know that.

She gestured towards my plate. 'What do you think?'

I looked down. 'Of the bun? Delicious. A bit like brioche.'

She smiled. 'They are rather yummy, aren't they? And how about the city? Have you been before?'

'No, never. I'm dismayed by the absence of donkeys – though I can't say I wasn't warned – but it's otherwise splendid.'

This seemed to delight her. 'It is rather light on donkeys, now you come to mention it. But listen to us chattering on. Your telegram said you wanted to pick my brains, Emily. I must say I was a little taken aback. What vital insights, I wondered, could a zoologist offer an amateur sleuth? I know nothing of murder and intrigue.'

'Ah, my dear Sarah,' said Lady Hardcastle, 'but you're Britain's foremost expert on unusual wildlife.'

Miss Laycock-Bartles struck a musical-comedy actress's 'who, me?' pose. 'Well . . . I couldn't possibly say.'

'Have you heard about the Beast of Littleton Woods?'

Miss Laycock-Bartles looked suddenly serious. 'I have not. Please tell.'

Between us, Lady Hardcastle and I related the story of the mauled sheep, the killed poacher and the injured gamekeeper.

'Good heavens. This is exactly the sort of thing I study. Usually the sightings come to nothing and my job is to disappoint people and say it was a large dog. But there are witnesses this time?'

'Three,' I said. 'A farmhand who wasn't entirely sure, a wounded man who was sure but was also concussed, and an old lady who's absolutely adamant—'

'—but who might have been a little hysterical,' interrupted Lady Hardcastle. 'She'd lost her dog.'

'They all say panther,' I concluded.

Miss Laycock-Bartles nodded. 'It's remarkable if it's true. There have been no sightings in the West Country for years. The last big cat I heard of was in Norfolk.'

'That's a shame,' said Lady Hardcastle. 'When I remembered what a wiz you were I'd rather fixed on the idea that you'd be able to tell us all about it.'

'No can do, I'm afraid. If it really is a big cat – and the odds are very much stacked against it – it's not been seen in the area before. I'd certainly know about it if it had.'

I took a sip of tea. 'You say the sightings are usually false?'

'Usually, yes. People let their imaginations run away with them. They see something big moving in the distance, usually on a misty morning. Or a pair of eyes reflects the lamplight as they walk along a quiet lane at night. So far there have been no confirmed sightings of actual big cats anywhere between Inverness and Penzance. The most promising was the Beast of Buxton – they're always the Beast of Somewhere. A monstrous, shaggy creature, so the accounts said. There were sightings all through the Peak District and it was blamed for a number of animal mutilations. It turned out to be a sheep that had become separated from its flock and hadn't been shorn for a few seasons.'

'How very disappointing,' said Lady Hardcastle. 'I presume it wasn't responsible for the animal mutilations.'

'No, that was a local innkeeper trying to drum up trade. Beast tourism is big business. From what you've said, I'd not get your hopes up that yours is any more real. You've reasons to doubt all three of your witnesses.'

'It's not likely to be a sheep, though,' I said. 'It most definitely attacked two people. A cow, perhaps, but not a sheep.'

Miss Laycock-Bartles looked puzzled. 'A cow?'

'Private joke, I'm afraid, dear,' said Lady Hardcastle.

'Ah, yes. Sorry.' She winked at me. 'Or possibly a donkey, what? But in reality, I'd put my money on a dog. In almost all cases of actual physical attack, it's a dog.'

'Hmm,' said Lady Hardcastle. 'Thank you, dear. That's disappointing but helpful.'

'Sorry. But I'll keep an eye open for reports of other sightings. One never knows.'

Conversation returned to news of mutual acquaintances while I savoured my bun and watched the good people of Bath as they went about their business, oblivious to the threat of monstrous dogs. And sheep. And cows.

◆  ◆  ◆

Despite having been out all day – or perhaps because of it – we decided to go out again in the evening, and took a stroll across the village green to the Dog and Duck.

The pub was lively, even for a Thursday night, and we found ourselves, as we so often did, standing at the bar trying to attract Daisy's attention. It was oddly pleasing to see once again that we were so much a part of the village that it didn't cross the minds of any of the regulars even for a moment to offer us a seat. Anywhere else, and it would have irked me considerably – on Lady Hardcastle's behalf, if not my own – but here I took it as a sign of acceptance.

Daisy was busy at the other end of the bar so we chatted while we waited for her.

'What did you think of Sarah's reaction to our news?' Lady Hardcastle asked me.

'I'm a little disappointed, if I'm honest. With three witnesses saying it's a panther, I rather thought it might actually be . . . you know . . . a panther. But your cryptozoologist pal—'

'I say, that's a splendid word. One of your own?'

'It suddenly came to me. But, splendidly named or not, she's poured cold water on the panther idea.'

'She has, rather, hasn't she? I'm always inclined to accept the pronouncements of an expert in these matters, but how do we explain away the testimony of three witnesses?'

'I didn't help there, did I?' I said. 'I was trying to be all scientific and open-minded but, thinking back, I seemed determined to discredit them.'

'It was the right approach, I think, but it does feel like we've taken a backwards step. Heigh-ho.'

'Heigh, as you say, ho.' I turned to look down the bar. 'Whom do you have to set a panther on to get a drink round here?'

Lady Hardcastle laughed. 'Leave her be, tiny one. She's . . .' She trailed off and looked at the tobacco-smoke-stained ceiling.

'She's what?'

'Hmm? Oh, I'm so sorry. I've spent much of the day racking my brains trying to think whence I might know Bernard Billen. And, now I've remembered, I'm wondering what on earth I might do about it.'

'And whence *do* you know this Billen chap?'

'He was on a charity committee I served on a couple of years ago in Bristol. A thoroughly unremarkable man, as I recall. As puffed up and full of himself as all men in his position tend to be – the regional controller of a railway, dontcha know – but otherwise entirely without anything to mark him out from the herd.'

'And did you think him capable of corruption and malfeasance?'

'Everyone I meet on that sort of committee is capable of sleaziness and wrongdoing, dear. I think it's one of the selection criteria.'

'It would certainly explain why you're invited to serve on so many.'

'Well, quite. I'm the worst of the lot. Other than those vague impressions, though, I can't really recall anything about the fellow. But I've promised Old Roberts I'd look into it for him so I suppose I ought to find out more. At least I have a head start now I've remembered I've actually met him.'

'We'll figure it out,' I said. I remembered something of my own. With a smile, I said, 'Did you know Old Roberts's Christian name was Robert?'

'I actually did, yes. I think Gertie told me. And if that news has delighted you, you'll be beside yourself when you find out what he and Winnie named Young Roberts.'

'Oh, I do so hope it's what I think it is. Go on.'

'He's called Robert, after his father.'

'Utterly wonderful.'

'Oh, but there's more. He's also named Robert after his grandfather.'

'So he's Robert Robert Roberts? I could never have hoped for more. My faith in humanity is restored. Oh, here's Daisy. At last.'

'Sorry about that, ladies, it's busy in here tonight. What can I get you?'

'Two brandies, please,' I said.

She began pouring Old Joe's 'best' brandy into two mostly clean glasses. 'Where've you two been, then? Blod said you'd gone out for the day.'

'A trip to Bath.'

'Nice. I much prefers Bath to Weston for a day out – not so many donkeys.'

'I honestly didn't expect you to say that.'

"S'true. I loves it there. See anything nice?'

'Houses.'

Lady Hardcastle tutted. 'Houses where very famous people once lived.'

I shrugged. 'Houses. And the baths and the abbey. We ate buns with a friend.'

Daisy laughed. 'Lovely. It certainly sounds like you had a better day than I did.'

'Why?' I said. 'What happened to you?'

'I saw a rat, didn't I?'

'You live in the countryside, Dais, there are rats everywhere.'

She frowned and shook her head. 'Not like this one. Huge it was. Blimmin' enormous. Like three or four rats standin' on each other's shoulders wearin' a rat costume for the pantomime.'

'Big, then?'

'You a'n't seen nothin' like it.'

'I wouldn't be so sure,' said Lady Hardcastle. 'We've seen some pretty big rats. Remember the sewers in Salzburg, Flo?'

I nodded. 'They were very big rats.'

'I guarantees you they Austrian rats weren't nothin' compared with the one I seen out in the yard.'

Billy the farmhand had arrived at the bar with his empty glass. 'You still on about that rat, Dais?'

'Yes, Billy, I am. And you'd be goin' on about it, too, if you'd seen it. Big as a cat, it was.'

The farmhand laughed. 'And you're sure it wasn't a cat?'

'After the ribbin' you took t'other night when you said you'd seen a big cat down by the stream, I'd-a thought you'd be a bit more sympathetic to someone who's seen a big rat.'

'Sorry, Dais, you's right. You seen what you seen.'

'Thank you. Another pint in there, is it?'

Billy the farmhand took his cider back to his friends and sat down.

'The thing is, Dais,' I said, 'a rat's a rat. I mean, you can get some pretty big ones, but there's a limit, isn't there? Your average rat comes in a range of sizes from about here' – I held my hands a few inches apart – 'to here.' I opened them a little wider. 'What you're describing is something like this.' I held them absurdly wide.

Daisy shook her head. 'Bigger'n that.'

'Really? Like this?' Wider still.

'More like that, yes.'

'Gracious,' said Lady Hardcastle. 'If it really is a rat, I shall give serious consideration to moving house.'

'It could help carry your bags, I reckon. And if there's any more of 'em, then I'm comin' with you. We should evacuate the whole village and get Flo's brother-in-law to bomb it flat.'

My twin sister, Gwen, was married to a battery sergeant major in the Royal Artillery, and I smiled at the thought of him and his comrades bombarding our little village to rid it of giant rats.

'Or,' I said, 'we could keep our eyes open and find out what it really is.'

'It's a rat.'

I smiled again. 'And find out what sort of rat it is.'

'I can't ask for more.' This talk of oversized rodents had delayed the pouring process, but our drinks were finally ready. 'Here you goes.'

'It wasn't a badger?' suggested Lady Hardcastle.

Daisy sighed as she took my money. 'Badgers got stripy heads and they only comes out at night. This was broad daylight and there weren't no stripes.'

'An albino badger, then?'

'It were brown, not white, and it weren't nowhere near as big as a badger.'

Lady Hardcastle smiled. 'Then, as Flo says, we shall keep our eyes open and try to fathom out exactly what it is.'

'It's a rat.'

'Changing the subject to less contentious matters,' I said, 'Gwen's well.'

'I'm pleased to hear it. She's due end of December, i'n't she? Give her my love, won't you? She's a lovely girl, your sister. She wouldn't tease me about the rat.'

'You don't know Gwen at all if you think that, but thank you, I'll pass it on.'

'I thought she was the nice one. It's Aunt Flo you has to watch out for.'

'Aunt Flossie, if you don't mind – my family only ever call me Flossie.'

'That's very sweet. You'll make a wonderful aunt and she'll make a lovely mother.'

'Thank you very much. In the meantime, though, I think I'm just the local dog and rat catcher.'

'And railway investigator,' said Lady Hardcastle. 'Don't forget that.'

We left Daisy to her work and found a space at a table with Edna and her husband, Dan. It was a fun evening.

# Chapter Seven

After all the recent shenanigans, we had no plans for Friday, so breakfast was a reasonably relaxed affair. For a while.

Lady Hardcastle suddenly threw down her slice of toast.

'Dancing plague,' she exclaimed.

We'd previously been discussing whether we needed to order some more petrol for the Rolls, so this outburst came as something of a surprise.

I gave her my best puzzled look. 'A sea lion painting Impressionist landscapes with blancmange.'

'I beg your pardon?'

I shrugged. 'I thought we were playing Whimsical Non-Sequiturs again.'

'Oh, I see. Understandable. No, there was an unexplained outbreak of uncontrollable dancing in . . . now, where was it? Karlsruhe? Stuttgart? No, no, it was France. Strasbourg. Sixteenth century. Hundreds of people dancing themselves to complete exhaustion for no reason.'

'Fascinating. And . . . ?'

'It just popped into my head. A peaceful town, everyone minding their own business, and then suddenly they're collectively seized by this unexplained, uncontrollable obsession. I was thinking about Billy's giant cat, and then Daisy's giant rat, and wondering if we're going to see a rash of similar sightings over the coming days. Something strange happened in the minds of those Strasbourgeois four hundred years ago. Perhaps the same is happening here.'

'Some sort of collective derangement, you mean?'

'It's as good an explanation as any. We've already observed that people seem more affected by the animal attacks than by the human murders they've all seen and heard about. Perhaps it's triggering some primal psychological response.'

'Perhaps. It would explain the apparent corroboration from Kiddle and Mrs Adaway, too. How do we stop it?'

'I don't think we can. We could find out what's really going on, I suppose, but I'm not sure there's any urgency – these things tend to burn out on their own. We just need to make sure no one does anything reckless or dangerous.'

'Torches and pitchforks?'

'I was half joking before, but I'm genuinely concerned about that now, yes.'

'They're a sensible lot. Reason will prevail.'

'I hope so.'

'Oh, but what if it's not collective derangement at all? What if Daisy's right?'

Lady Hardcastle's fork paused midway to her mouth. 'And she really did see an improbably huge rat?'

'Exactly that. A giant rat could take on a sheep. I've seen normal-sized rats attacking a dog.'

'And the giant cat?'

'Bred by the same scientist who made the giant rat. He was experimenting with a special growth serum, intended to alleviate hunger by producing larger crops and animals for food, but some spilled in his laboratory and he accidentally made a giant rat. And then, obviously—'

'He made a giant cat to get rid of the giant rat?'

'It would explain all the observed phenomena. But he has to be stopped.'

'He does?'

'His ultimate aim is clearly to make giant cows. And we all know that cannot possibly end well.'

Lady Hardcastle laughed and her bacon-laden fork resumed its journey to her mouth.

'Oh,' I said. 'And it would explain Old Roberts's problem, too. The scientist would need large quantities of dangerous chemicals, and he's trying to avoid suspicion by having them delivered in secret . . . so he's bribing the regional controller to falsify the shipping dockets . . . but he still needs to make sure the staff at the final destination are looking the other way.'

'Have you ever considered writing any of these flights of fancy down?'

'Who'd want to read the ramblings of a downtrodden lady's maid?'

'You make an excellent point, tiny one.'

'Do we have plans for today?'

'None whatsoever. I was hoping to get some work done in the orangery.'

'It feels almost like a day off.'

'It does a bit. I think I'll need a break by eleven – I usually do. We can have another think about plans then. Do you have things to keep you amused until thirst forces me back into the house?'

'Amused? I suppose so. I'd like to write a couple of letters, and I need to find a way to get that mysterious stain out of your green dress. I think that'll keep me busy.'

'It's mustard.'

'On the back of your skirt?'

'I was using some mustard powder to portray snow in a photography project – it shows as white in black-and-white photographs.'

'Why not use talc, or bicarb, or—?'

'Because I used mustard. And I spilled some. A lot, actually. And it sort of got on my dress. Sorry, dear.'

'At least I know what it is now.'

We finished our breakfast and went our separate ways. She to her studio, me to the kitchen to try to soak the mustard out of her dress.

By the time I'd finished my letters to Gwen and Ellie, it was getting on for eleven o'clock, so I put away my pen and went through to the kitchen.

Miss Jones helped me put a tray together and I stopped in the hall to pick up the post. Fresh letters and news from the outside world would go well with our elevenses, I thought.

It was a good plan, let down only by the complete absence of the post.

I was just setting the tray down in the drawing room when Lady Hardcastle came in.

'Have you picked up the post?' I asked.

She laughed. 'No, dear, I have servants to do that for me. I thought you knew.'

'I forget sometimes. But if you've not picked it up, then we've had no post.'

'That's irksome. I'm expecting a couple of things. I wonder if there's still trouble at the post office.'

'There could be. I could pop up there and check if you like – I'd enjoy the walk.'

'We could both go – I worry about Bessie after the near riot we saw the other morning.'

'That's not a bad idea, actually. Things did get a little fractious.'

She nodded. 'Very well, then. But not right away. Didn't you say something about cake?'

'I haven't mentioned cake.'

'Oh. Is there no cake?'

'There's tea here, but no cake. We've only just had breakfast.'

'Hmm. If we walk up to the post office to check on Bessie, would that justify cake, in your puritanical opinion?'

'Not entirely, but it would make it less gluttonous.'

'Splendidly splendid. Cake, please, then we can go up to the post office together.'

The scene inside the post office was . . . quiet desperation.

The counter area was deserted, and the only sign of life was a weary Bessie Talbot sniffing back tears as she sorted letters into pigeonholes.

'Bessie?' I said. 'Is everything all right? We were worried about you.'

Despite the ringing of the bell on the door and our loud footsteps on the polished floorboards, she had been oblivious to our presence and the sound of my voice seemed to take her by surprise.

She turned with a start. 'What? Oh, hello, Flo. Hello, Lady Hardcastle. I didn't notice you comin' in. How can I help you?'

She put down the bundle of unsorted letters and came to the counter.

'We were actually wondering if we could help *you*, dear,' said Lady Hardcastle. 'After all the trouble earlier in the week, and then no post today . . . well, as Flo said, we were worried.'

Bessie smiled weakly. 'You's very kind. But it's nothin'. I'm just a bit behind with me sortin'.' She sniffed.

'Was it muddled again?' I asked.

She fiddled distractedly with a bowl of walnuts that sat on the counter. She picked one up and opened it with a pair of nutcrackers. We had to wait until she'd eaten the nut before she replied.

'Completely,' she said. 'I checked it twice, then nipped out the back to have a cup of tea with Jimmy before Wilf arrived to start his round. When I come back to help him load his satchel, it was all messed up. I been tryin' to sort it ever since.'

Lady Hardcastle frowned. 'Tell me again how you work, dear. What's the procedure?'

'Much as I just said. We gets a big sack of post from the main office at Chipping Bevington. I sorts it into they pigeonholes behind the counter. Then I goes back to see Jimmy, we has a cuppa, and I helps him with the books and ledgers. Then Wilf turns up and I ties each address's letters with a ribbon and hands them to him in the right order so he doesn't have to rummage about in his bag as he goes on his round – the next address is always on the top. I doesn't bundle 'em till the last minute in case we gets another delivery from Chipping. It doesn't happen often, but it's a right nuisance when it does.'

'And you're sure everything was correct before you went back to see your husband?'

'Absolutely sure. I checked twice. Everythin' was just as it should be.'

'It sounds as though someone is coming in and deliberately messing things up,' I said.

Bessie nodded and cracked another walnut. 'I thought that. But who? And how? We'd hear the bell ring when they come in the door. And why? Why would anyone put me to this much extra work every day? I's exhausted.'

I looked at the door. It might be possible for someone taller than I to reach up and muffle the bell as they opened it, but it would still be very awkward. Then again, Bessie had been so

120

distracted when we arrived that she hadn't registered our presence, even with the ringing of the bell. If she had been out in the back room with Jimmy, engrossed in bookkeeping, tea drinking and gossip, would either of them have noticed even an unmuffled bell?

'Is it just today?' asked Lady Hardcastle. 'The mixed-up post, I mean.'

'No, it's been every day since that first time on Monday. Tuesday and Wednesday weren't so bad but today has been terrible. It's as though someone has come in and moved absolutely everythin'. Who would do such a thing? What have we ever done to deserve it? I's at the end of me tether, I can tell you.'

We commiserated with poor Bessie for a few minutes more, then took our post to save poor Wilf from walking up the lane later on.

Just as we were leaving, I spotted a flyer pinned to the noticeboard by the door. The board usually hosted the meeting schedules of the many village groups and their calls for new members. There were occasional For Sale notices, and the odd plea for people to be on the lookout for missing cats. On top of all the usual miscellanea today was a sheet of plain foolscap paper. Neatly written in a bold confident hand, it said: *Meeting Regarding the Wild Animal on the Loose. Village Hall. Friday Evening. 7 o'clock.*

I nodded towards the notice and Lady Hardcastle nodded back. We left.

At home, I made a fresh pot of tea and cut two more slices of the Madeira cake Miss Jones had baked earlier. I carried the tray through to the drawing room, where Lady Hardcastle was reading her post.

She waved a letter at me. 'Helen Titmus is going ahead with her "Man, the Destroyer of Worlds" photographic exhibition in Brighton. She couldn't find a gallery to host it but she's managed to rent the shop next door to her studio and is going to launch a gallery of her own.'

'Good for her,' I said. 'We should go down and see her – show our support.'

'We should, we should. Brighton's such a pig to get to from here, though. But let's not let that put us off. She's our friend, after all.'

We knew Helen Titmus through Lady Hardcastle's sister-in-law, and we'd met her again in London a few months earlier. She'd spoken of her intention to mount the exhibition and had spent some time on that London trip taking photographs that she hoped to be able to include. It was actually quite exciting to see it all coming together.

'Are there donkeys?' I asked.

'In the exhibition? I doubt it. It was landscapes, wasn't it?'

'At Brighton, you ninny.'

'I don't know, but I doubt that, too. Pebbly beach, you see. Not good for donkeys. It has two piers, though. At least I think it does.'

'I love a pier. Let's go. When's the exhibition?'

'She doesn't say, but one imagines it might take a while to organize everything. I shall write back and ask for more details.'

'Excellent. Or it will be if we ever get her reply.'

'Well, quite. I saw you looking at the door at the post office. Do you think someone could be sneaking in?'

'It's certainly possible,' I said. 'Though extremely improbable. They'd have to be at least as tall as you to reach the bell and muffle it before it rang. Probably taller, actually. And it would be an awkward move. They'd have to hold the bell as they sneaked in round the partially open door and then muffle it again as it closed. Getting out would be just as bad.'

'I'd wondered if it might be a prank by some of the naughtier village boys, but that makes it seem much less likely.'

'They can be quite ingenious, though. Or industrious, at least. Tying everyone's door knockers together on Balaclava Road took some doing. I'd bet they could fasten a scarf to a stick to muffle the bell.'

She laughed. 'Or sitting on each other's shoulders, wearing a long mac. Either way, it's a lot of trouble to go to for a prank. There's no other way in, is there?'

'The back door opens into that narrow road that serves all the shops. Someone could get in, but they'd have to get past the Talbots as they worked in the back room. There's a storeroom with an outside door, I think, but I don't think you can get to it from the main office – the door must be out the back somewhere.'

'What about Hilda Pantry?'

I shrugged. 'She'd have the same problem – they'd definitely notice her sneaking through their parlour. But if we're allowing the possibility that ingenious schoolboys could muffle a bell with a scarf on a pole, there's no reason a grumpy grocer couldn't do the same. I'm not sure any of her pals are strong enough to carry her on their shoulders, though.'

'It would certainly make sense if it were her, though. You said she wanted the post office. Ruining things for the Talbots and driving them out would give her another shot at the job, don't you think?'

'I certainly wouldn't put it past her. She's a nasty piece of work, that Hilda. But I still can't see how she'd get away with it, day after day. Surely someone would see her.'

'One would have thought. Could Jimmy be doing it? What do we know of him?'

I sipped my tea as I thought. 'It's possible, I suppose, but what would he gain from it?'

'The same as our putative village boys: it's a jolly wheeze.'

'Except it's not really all that jolly, is it? She's in a terrible state.'

'He might be trying to drive her mad.'

'To what end?' I asked.

'Perhaps all is not sunshine and roses chez Talbot. Perhaps he loves another and wants rid of her.'

I chuckled. 'Finally rid of his charming, delightful wife, he and the Widow Pantry would be free to build a retail empire to conquer Littleton Cotterell and surrounding districts.'

'Now you're just being silly, dear. Honestly. Oh, but what if Bessie already *is* mad? What if she's slipping into some manner of fugue state and rearranging the letters herself, completely unaware of what she's doing?'

'You're drifting far outside my area of expertise. I specialize in mending dresses and biffing baddies on the beak – I leave psychiatric disorders to my elders and betters.'

'As well you should. Your imagined educational shortcomings notwithstanding, I think we've proved something conclusively: we haven't the foggiest idea what's going on.'

'Not a clue.'

She thought for a moment. 'We ought to go to the village meeting this evening.'

'Even if only to make sure there are no torches and pitchforks,' I agreed.

She nodded and took a bite of cake.

◆ ◆ ◆

We arrived at the hall at about five to seven to find it already filled with cheerfully chatting villagers. The ceiling lamps cast an uneven, flickering light and gave the room an ominous air in contrast to the almost festive feel of the gathering below.

We found seats in the back row and settled to watch the proceedings.

Jagruti Bland came in, accompanied by Hamlet, who seemed thrilled to see so many potential human playmates. Lady Hardcastle and I moved one space along the row of chairs to allow them to sit next to the aisle.

Jagruti smiled. 'Thank you, ladies. If Hammy starts playing up I might have to make a quick getaway.'

'It's lovely to see you both,' said Lady Hardcastle.

'It's lovely to see you, too. But seeing us both isn't entirely my choice. James is trying to write his sermon so I thought I'd get Hammy out of the house to give him some peace. I hope he doesn't misbehave.'

'Oh, I'm sure he will, dear. Husbands are wont to misbehave when they're left alone in the house.'

Jagruti looked alarmed. 'No, no, I meant the dog.'

'She knows what you meant,' I said. 'Take no notice.'

Lady Hardcastle grinned.

A few moments later, Angelina Goodacre, the bicycle maker from the Dower House, squeezed along the row to sit next to me.

'Hello, Flo,' she said.

I smiled. 'Angelina. Come to see the fun?'

'Wouldn't miss it. One of my favourite things about country life, the village meeting. People in towns and cities don't get involved in quite the same way.'

'It's not always a good thing,' I said.

'But it's always fun. If they don't take to the streets with pitchforks and flaming torches by the end of the evening I shall be very disappointed.'

I raised an eyebrow.

She laughed.

It was a few minutes past seven by the big clock on the wall when Mrs Gardner, secretary of the embroidery club, stood up and took her place at the lectern to address the packed hall.

Hush descended.

Mrs Gardner cleared her throat. 'Good evening, ladies and gentlemen. It's gratifying to see so many of you here. We've called this meeting to air everyone's concerns about the dangerous wild animal terrorizing our village.'

'We don't need to air our concerns,' said a male voice from the audience. 'We all know what our concerns are: there's a wild beast attackin' people and livestock. The question is: what are you goin' to do about it?'

'We'll get to possible solutions in a moment,' said Mrs Gardner. 'First I'd like to—'

'We don't much care what you'd like to do,' said another voice from the other side of the hall. 'We wants a plan of action. We could sit about here discussin' it all night, but it won't save my animals. It won't bring Sid Hyde or Dick Durbin back to life, neither. We needs to *do* sommat.'

A chorus of *yeah*'s and *that's right*'s spread round the hall. Then people started standing up one by one, shouting their own suggestions.

Angelina leaned towards me with a grin. 'Two bob says they're out there with torches and pitchforks before the pub closes.'

'You joke, dear,' said Lady Hardcastle, 'but that's actually my greatest worry.'

'I'm not joking,' said Angelina. 'I've seen this sort of thing before.'

Mrs Gardner, meanwhile, was attempting to restore order. 'Please, ladies and gentlemen, please.' She held up her hands in an appeal for calm. 'I understand your concerns, but we must approach this in a rational and civilized manner. We—'

'We can't go out alone at night,' said a woman near the front.

'I's afraid to go out at all,' agreed a woman from the other side.

'We's keepin' our cat indoors,' said another.

Mrs Gardner still had her hands up, trying to calm things down. 'Again, I understand. But we need—'

'We needs to round up all the dogs,' shouted a voice. 'That's what we needs. It's a dog what's doin' it.'

'Like that'n there,' shouted another.

Heads swivelled to regard Hamlet, who was sitting placidly by Jagruti's side. If dogs could smile, I imagined he'd be grinning from ear to ear – he liked people and always seemed pleased to be among them.

The people, though, had begun to feel differently.

A woman two rows ahead of us stood and brandished her umbrella at him. She shouted something about a 'monstrous beast' and took a step towards him.

Hamlet, sensing a fun game in the offing, jumped to his feet and bowed in that way dogs do when they're playing. He barked joyously, but the problem with Hamlet's barks, even the most joyful ones, was that they really did sound as though they issued from the throat of exactly the sort of monstrous beast the woman feared.

The woman flinched away. 'It's him. He's the one that's doin' it. He wants puttin' down.'

A chorus of agreement followed.

Lady Hardcastle stood and gently took Jagruti's arm, lifting her up and propelling her towards the door.

'Come along, dear,' she said. 'I think it's time we were all elsewhere.'

Hamlet was disappointed at the sudden curtailment of the game with his new friend, but responded to the gentle tug on his lead and dutifully followed. He offered a resonant bark of farewell as he went out the door.

I backed out, facing the room and prepared to fend off anyone who might follow but, for all their bravado when confronting a harmless dog, no one seemed keen to take me on.

Outside, Lady Hardcastle was talking to Jagruti. '. . . him home, dear. Make sure he stays indoors for the next couple of days if you can. I know he needs his exercise, but if they don't see him, they'll probably forget about him.'

Jagruti nodded. 'But—'

'Don't worry,' I said, 'we'll walk you back to the vicarage.'

'No, Flo dear, it's all right. Hamlet will look after me.'

'We really must insist,' said Lady Hardcastle. 'I honestly don't think there's any danger from the beast, but I'm worried that some hothead might come out and try to take Hamlet from you.'

'They'd have their work cut out,' said Jagruti. 'He's a loveable old softy most of the time, but he won't let any harm come to me. He's very protective.'

'Nevertheless,' said Lady Hardcastle, taking her arm.

It was only a short walk from the village hall to the vicarage, and we were there almost as soon as we had left.

Mrs Grove answered the door and Jagruti handed her Hamlet's lead. The dog followed her inside, but Jagruti remained on the doorstep.

'It's so very kind of you to look after us like this,' she said. 'Will you come in for some tea?'

'Thank you, dear, but no,' said Lady Hardcastle. 'I think we'd better get back to the meeting.'

'Another time, then, perhaps?'

'Most definitely. Have a safe evening.'

We waited until Jagruti was inside and then made our way back in the direction of the hall.

I looked up at Lady Hardcastle as we walked. 'Do you really think it's a good idea to go back in there? They'll just turn on us. At the very least they'll ask us a lot of questions we simply can't answer. I'm sure Angelina will let us know if things get properly ugly.'

She thought for a moment. 'I agree up to a point. But I'm concerned that we're really not very far from torches and pitchforks. Mrs Gardner was no match for the louder ones in there. I rather feel the need to—'

'Read the riot act?'

She laughed. 'I was going to say something about being the voice of calm rationality, but perhaps a bit of schoolmarmly sternness might be in order instead.'

I took the lead and opened both doors at once in what I hoped might be a dramatic and attention-grabbing manner.

No one noticed.

I quickly realized that by describing the scene in the post office as pandemonium I had left myself nowhere to go to describe the chaos that greeted us inside the hall. Almost everyone was on their feet, and absolutely everyone was yelling at the top of their voice.

I turned to Lady Hardcastle and had to shout to make myself heard. 'Are you still sure this is a good idea?'

'It's a terrible idea, but we can't leave them like this. Please do your uncouth whistling thing.'

Somewhat uncertainly, I did as I was asked and was astonished when it had the desired effect. The room fell silent and all eyes turned to us.

Lady Hardcastle strode past me down the aisle that had been left between the rows of chairs and made her way up on to the stage. I followed.

No one said a word.

She gestured for Mrs Gardner to move aside and turned to address the crowd.

'Ladies and gentlemen,' she said – as promised, in her best schoolmarm voice. 'This is *not* the way we behave in Littleton Cotterell. Sit down.'

There were mutterings of dissent.

'Sit. Down,' she said, somewhat more forcefully.

There was a shuffling of feet and a scraping of chairs as they meekly did as they were told.

'I know you're frightened – I'm rather frightened myself. And I know you all want to be able to do something – anything – to protect yourselves and your loved ones from this animal. But threatening the vicar's wife's dog and shouting at one another is *not* the way to go about it.'

'We needs—'

'Did I give you permission to speak, Mr Dimmock? I did not. You *need*, Mr Dimmock, to take sensible precautions against attack. If it's at all possible, you should travel in pairs, especially at night. The animal has been seen in the daytime, but it seems to be sticking to the woods, so avoid the woods unless you absolutely have to go there. Most of all, though, it is absolutely essential that we all remain calm and that we take no rash actions. No one should take it upon themselves to attempt to hunt the creature, no matter how skilled you imagine yourselves to be. Someone could get hurt.'

There were renewed mutterings, but more subdued this time.

'Despite the misgivings I've heard, the authorities – in the form of the local police and the Bristol Constabulary – *are* looking into this, and they will have answers and solutions in short order. Until their enquiries are complete, no one has any fresh information to give you, and nothing good will come from angry speculation. I suggest we all return to our homes and do what the villagers of Littleton Cotterell do best: look after each other.'

I was expecting at least a little dissent but, as was so often the case, authority emanated from her in mystical waves and the assembled villagers began to button up their coats and make their way out of the hall. As instructed, they left in pairs.

Lady Hardcastle turned to Mrs Gardner. 'I think that went rather well, dear. Well done.'

We followed the stragglers out, leaving Mr and Mrs Gardner to lock up as we set off to return to the house.

As we entered the lane, Lady Hardcastle put a hand on my arm to stop me.

'What?' I said.

'Shh. Up ahead. A black shape just crossed the road.'

I peered into the gloom, but my eyes were no match for hers. 'Another badger?'

'No, it was taller. And so much more graceful. Beautifully so.'

'A cat?' I asked.

'If it was, it was a blimmin' big one.'

I crouched into a fighting stance. I was unarmed and had no idea how to fight a wild animal, but it was all I could think of in the moment. 'Is it still there? What's it doing?'

I could hear the rustling of her coat and dress as she moved about, trying to get a better view of whatever it was.

'No,' she said. 'It went into the field. I think we're safe to go home.'

We proceeded cautiously up the lane to the house, then locked ourselves inside.

# Chapter Eight

Saturday dawned, misty and chill, and I briefly contemplated exercising in the garden. There's something magical about fog. I think it's the way it muffles sound as well as visibility, and makes the world feel smaller and more intimate. But I took one step outside the back door and changed my mind. Romanticized notions of a world made miniature by mist were no match for prosaic notions of Flo frozen to death by the autumnal chill.

When we arrived home after the events of the previous evening, I had suggested that perhaps we ought to make our presence felt in the village in the morning.

'I'm not so sure,' said Lady Hardcastle as she sipped her cocoa. 'I think we stunned them all into obedience for now, but in the proverbial cold light of day they might be less susceptible to my charms. We'll have no new information to give them, after all. I think we should just leave things be for a while.'

The plan for today, then, extended only as far as popping up to The Grange, and we didn't intend to go there until eleven. We wanted to make sure everyone there was all right after the attacks, and provide a jolly diversion to stop them dwelling too much on the death of Durbin and the injuries to Felix Kiddle.

With a relaxed day in the offing, I prepared Lady Hardcastle's starter breakfast for eight and took it up to her, expecting that she'd be taking advantage of the late start to indulge herself with a lie-in.

She was already sitting up and reading. 'Good morning, Flo dear. Is that my coffee and toast? You're a tiny marvel.'

'I very much am. You're awake early.'

'Your tone conveys surprise with an undertone of disapproval and admonition. You think me a slugabed, I perceive. You have a very expressive voice, you know.'

'I think you might be overstating your own powers of perception there. You *are* a slugabed, and you know full well I think so. I've never hidden it. On more than one occasion I've had cause to say, "Get up, you lazy mare," when we have things to be getting on with.'

'Ah, yes. But today I'm wide awake and raring to go. Join me?'

'Thank you, but I think I'll wait till breakfast proper. Curtains? It's misty out, but it might make the place feel a little less . . . fuggy.'

She laughed. 'Yes, please. And could you lift this piece of toast to my mouth? It's too heavy for me.'

'Get stuffed, there's a dear.'

'I'm *trying*, but the toast is too heavy.'

'Breakfast is at nine. I'll be up to sort your hair out at a quarter to.'

'Right you are.'

I left her chuckling to herself and went back down to Edna and Miss Jones in the kitchen.

◆ ◆ ◆

The library at The Grange was clearly everyone's favourite room, and we found Sir Hector, Lady Farley-Stroud, Joyce Adaway and Lady Araminta Fluffikins sitting together-apart near the fire.

Sir Hector was at a reading table surrounded by tools and feathers. It took me a short while to work out that the strange device in front of him held a fishhook, and that he was tying flies.

He turned and looked over his spectacles at us. 'What ho, ladies. Excuse me not gettin' up – bit tied up, what?' He lifted his left hand to show that it was tangled in fishing line, with a hook stuck through the side of his index finger.

'I didn't know you fished, Hector,' said Lady Hardcastle as she leaned in to look at what he was up to.

'Used to go with Jimmy Amersham all the time. You remember Jimmy?'

'I do. I'm told you and he were terrors in your day.'

'Ha! Still are, according to some.' He nodded towards Lady Farley-Stroud. 'Poor old fella's not been well lately – dicky ticker, dicky knees, you know how we old chaps get. He's improvin' slowly and I suggested we plan a trip for the spring. Give us both something to look forward to when he's better, what? And that reminded me how much I enjoyed this side of it, too.' He indicated the fly-making gear. 'So I thought I'd tie a few new flies. Get my eye in.'

'It looks fascinating.'

He disentangled himself from hook and line. 'Fascinatin' and a little bit uncomfortable.' He dabbed at the spot of blood on his finger with a handkerchief. 'Talkin' of wounds . . . telephoned Fitzsimmons this mornin' – he told me your man Sunderland called round yesterday to ask after Kiddle.'

'Yes – he wants to talk to everyone involved now it's a murder inquiry. Did he say how Kiddle was?'

'Fitzsimmons stitched him up and saw him home. His wife's takin' care of him now. Weak from the loss of blood, he said, and very fragile, but the next few days will see if he escapes infection. We've all got our fingers crossed for him.'

'Indeed. He's a fit man – he should pull through.'

'Thanks in no small part to brave little Minty,' said Mrs Adaway from the other side of the room.

Lady Farley-Stroud let out an aggressive *pfft*. 'If it wasn't for *brave* little Minty, he wouldn't have been out there in the first place. It was only because the stupid little cur took fright and ran off that poor Kiddle had to go out looking for it.'

'Her,' said Mrs Adaway.

'It,' repeated Lady Farley-Stroud. 'If *it* were as brave as you say, *it* would have come back to the house with you when you took fright yourself.'

'*She* stayed with your gamekeeper after the panther attacked him, even though she knew it had already killed that poacher fella.'

'*It* has less sense of what's going on around it than an aspidistra. It had no idea who had been killed or injured – it was just too stupid to find its own way home.'

'Well, I never. I—'

Lady Hardcastle had been expecting to have to distract Lady Farley-Stroud from worrying about Kiddle and Durbin. But if either of us had thought about it for even a few seconds longer, we'd have realized it would be more likely that we'd have to break up a fight between Lady Farley-Stroud and Mrs Adaway.

Lady Hardcastle raised her eyebrows at me and beckoned. We made our way over to join the combatants.

She indicated the teapot on the low table. 'Is there any left in that pot? I'm spitting feathers, as our housekeeper says.'

'It's not very fresh, dear,' said Lady Farley-Stroud. 'I'll ring for more.'

She got up and went to the servants' bell while we made ourselves comfortable on the sofa that separated the two warring women's armchairs.

'Obviously we came to make sure that everyone was all right after Wednesday's horrifying events,' said Lady Hardcastle, 'but I must confess to an ulterior motive.'

Lady Farley-Stroud resumed her seat. 'Oh?'

'You're not after money, I hope,' said Mrs Adaway.

'Oh, do shut up for a few moments, Joyce,' snapped Lady Farley-Stroud. 'Go and walk Brave Minty or something. Watch out, though. I've seen rabbits on the grounds. Wouldn't want the bunnies to scare her off into the woods again.'

'Well!' said Mrs Adaway as she snatched up Minty and stalked towards the door. 'We shall see you at lunchtime when you've calmed down a bit.'

The door slammed.

'I'm sorry about that,' said Lady Farley-Stroud with a smile. 'Now, what was it you wanted?'

'Just a bit of background on a mutual acquaintance, that's all. Do you remember Bernard Billen from that charity committee we served on a couple of years ago?'

So this was her diversion? The railway business? It was better than nothing, I supposed.

Lady Farley-Stroud nodded. 'I do indeed. Pompous fella, looks a bit like David Lloyd George.'

Jenkins arrived and Lady Farley-Stroud asked for more tea. To my delight, she also asked if Mrs Brown would send up some cakes.

Lady Hardcastle waited until he'd gone.

'That was him. And you're right, he *does* look like the chancellor. I'd quite forgotten that. Anyway, Flo and I were at Chipping Bevington station the other day, on our way to Bath—'

Lady Farley-Stroud beamed. 'I do so love Bath. Did you see the house where Jane Austen stayed?'

'It was part of our little tour, yes.'

'You're a great reader, Florence – you must have loved it.'

I smiled. 'I did. Shame about the donkeys, though.'

A frown from Lady Farley-Stroud. 'What donkeys?'

'Exactly.'

'Anyway,' said Lady Hardcastle, emphatically, 'while we were at the station, Old Roberts sidled up to us and told us a story about Billen inviting him unexpectedly for a drink. He's come to believe that Billen was sounding him out – trying to get him involved in something fishy.'

Lady Farley-Stroud gave a throaty laugh. 'I shouldn't be at all surprised. He's definitely a wrong'un, that Billen.'

'Do you think so? We said we'd look into it on Roberts's behalf, but I wasn't convinced we'd find anything amiss.'

'Oh, I could tell you stories about Bernard Billen. It's a wonder he hasn't been up on charges. Corruption, embezzlement, you name it. I can only assume he has *connections* who insulate him from that sort of thing.'

'Gracious,' said Lady Hardcastle. 'So you think it's likely he really was trying to recruit Roberts for something not entirely legal?'

'I've known Roberts for years. Salt of the earth and an excellent judge of character. If he thinks Billen was up to no good, he's probably right.'

'Then we need to look further.'

'It does sound like it, m'dear. But I thought you were investigatin' the Beast. It's still on the loose.'

'There's really not a lot we can do. To be honest, there never was – it's a matter for the authorities. All we were doing was trying to gather information to help them. And now Inspector Sunderland is investigating Sid Hyde's murder, we'd be getting under his feet if we carried on roaming the district asking questions about panthers.'

'That's certain, is it? You mentioned murder when you were talking to Hector just now but I wasn't sure I'd understood correctly.

I know you thought so on Wednesday, but your friend Dr Gosling was going to confirm.'

'And confirm he did. Hyde was definitely murdered and Sunderland has taken the case. Which leaves us free to investigate Billen.'

'And try to fathom what on earth's going on at the post office,' I added.

'Indeed, yes,' said Lady Hardcastle. 'So we'll not be sitting idle.'

Lady Farley-Stroud gave another chuckle. 'I'd never allow you to sit idle, m'dears. Always plenty to be done around the village.'

Sir Hector joined us. 'Make sure you're always busy, ladies. You'll get roped in. Roped in, I tell you.'

'Don't talk such rot, Hector.'

'Shutting up now, my little jelly bean.'

The tea and cake arrived and we tucked in. The earlier acrimony seemed to have been forgotten and I judged our mission a successful one.

◆　◆　◆

We left the Farley-Strouds in reasonable spirits and went out to the Rolls. As we were getting in, little Minty scampered over to us and I crouched to make a fuss of her. She wasn't an unpleasant little dog and she seemed genuinely pleased to see us.

Her owner was close by. 'Hello, m'dears. Is she bothering you?'

'Not at all,' I said. 'She's a very friendly young lady.'

'I never managed to thank you for saving her on Wednesday.'

'Think nothing of it,' said Lady Hardcastle.

'Honestly, there was no saving to be done,' I added. 'She was standing guard over Kiddle by the time we got there.'

'Nevertheless, I'm grateful to you. If there's ever anything I can do for you in return, please just let me know.'

'Thank you,' said Lady Hardcastle and I together.

Mrs Adaway gave us a smile and a curt nod. 'Minty, come. Leave the nice ladies to their business.'

The little dog trotted off and we clambered into the car.

'Well, she's a different woman when she's not with Lady Farley-Stroud,' I said once I was sure Mrs Adaway was out of earshot.

'Almost likeable,' agreed Lady Hardcastle.

I started the engine. 'We had a situation like it below stairs at my first job in Cardiff. Two of the parlour maids absolutely despised each other. On their own they were the loveliest girls you could ever hope to meet, but whenever they were together the atmosphere was poisonous.'

'How dreadful. How was it resolved?'

'The butler had words. No improvement. The housekeeper had words. Still no improvement. But then one day they came to blows over whose job it was to sweep the sitting room. The lady of the house heard the commotion and they were both sacked on the spot.'

Lady Hardcastle smiled. 'That would definitely resolve things, but it's not much help to us. I fear we can't sack Joyce, and it would be extremely difficult to dismiss Gertie – I gather she's involved in some sort of dalliance with the owner of the house. But I do wish they'd reach some sort of accommodation. It's quite uncomfortable in there at the moment.'

'It is indeed. But now that we've escaped, what are we going to do? Go home?'

'That was my intention, certainly. At least, it was until I hit upon the idea of diverting Gertie with talk of Bernard Billen. Now I'm considering a trip back to Chipping Bevington station. I think I'd like to know more about Old Roberts's disquieting encounter with the regional controller.'

◆ ◆ ◆

By the time the engine had purred to a stop and we stepped out of the Rolls at Chipping Bevington station, Old Roberts was upon us with his porter's truck.

'Good afternoon, ladies,' he said with a smile. 'No luggage again? And where might you be off to today?'

Lady Hardcastle gave him a warm smile. 'Good afternoon, Roberts. We're not travelling today. As a matter of fact we came to speak to you.'

'Me, m'lady?'

'You, Mr Roberts. Is there somewhere we might talk in private? I don't wish to keep you from your work but I'd rather we weren't overheard.'

He drew a battered watch from his waistcoat pocket. 'It's about time for my lunch, m'lady. Our Robert will cover for me.'

He turned and set off to the station building. We followed. Once inside, he had a quick word with his son at the ticket office, then led the way through a door marked *Station Manager*.

He invited us to sit.

'So, ladies, what can I do for you?'

'When we saw you on Thursday on our way to Bath, you asked for some advice about your encounter with Mr Billen.'

'That I did. I do hope you didn't mind. I was at my wits' end, I can tell you.'

'We don't mind at all. I said we'd make some discreet enquiries about your man Billen, to see what sort of fellow people think he is.'

'I remembers. Have you found anythin'?'

'We have, and it didn't take long. It seems Mr Billen does, indeed, have something of a reputation for . . . how can I put this without potentially slandering the man? Slight lapses of moral rectitude?'

'You mean he's a crook?'

'Some might think so, certainly, but his crookedness remains so far untested by the courts. Let's be generous to the man and call him a rogue.'

'I knew he wasn't quite square, that one. There was sommat about him.'

'Have you had time to think more about what he might have been after?'

Roberts shrugged. 'That's just it, see? There's not much I has control over. Trains and timetables is all dealt with by . . . well, by him. Or his office, anyway. Passenger fares is, too. I suppose we oversees the loadin' and unloadin' of goods bein' sent on regular trains. And the mail, o' course. But I can't see what he'd want with any of that.'

'It probably won't be his scheme,' said Lady Hardcastle. 'Not directly, anyway. If there *is* anything going on – and we can't be certain of it – he'll be acting as a paid agent. His part in it will simply be to grease the wheels for someone else's illicit enterprise. For a handsome reward, naturally.'

'Then I doesn't have a clue. There's all sorts who might want free access to a railway. Thieves, especially, but anyone who wanted to move people or goods about the country. White slavers, even.'

'Why would the railway be particularly useful, though?' I asked.

'Because we moves so many things in a day, and most of 'em's anonymous. Just a wooden crate with a label. Let's say you nicks a priceless paintin' from a gallery in London. One o' they darin' night-time burglaries they talks about in the papers. Come the mornin' the coppers'll be looking for it everywhere, so you can't hang about. If you wants to sell it – and you would – you needs to get it as far away as possible, as quick as you can. You could put it on a wagon, but it's easy to stop wagons on the road and search 'em. But if you's got it on a train, with all the proper paperwork, i'n't no one goin' t'look twice at it, especially if you've bribed a few key men along the route. I don't usually inspect the crates that pass through here anyway, but if I'd taken a few bob to look t'other way, I'd make sure no one else inspected it neither.'

'This is an interesting possibility,' said Lady Hardcastle. 'So we have "moving stolen goods", but what else is there? It could be something dull but profitable, like share manipulation. He might want to set up small but plausible "problems" that would push the share value down so he could snap up railway shares at a knock-down price.'

'Or property speculation,' I suggested. 'The railway abuts some prime land. Could there be a way of using his influence over the trains to affect land value?'

'I can't see how for the moment, but that's a possibility, too. The problem is that until Billen shows his hand, we shan't know what he's up to. And by then it will be too late.'

At this moment, Young Roberts entered bearing a tea tray. 'Don't mind me. I just thought you might like a cuppa. Our dad's rubbish at offerin'.'

'Oh, thank you,' said Lady Hardcastle. 'And biscuits, too, I see. You spoil us.'

He smiled. 'All part of the service at Chipping Bevington station. Did I hear Mr Billen's name just then? He gets about a bit, don't he? He—'

His father turned towards him. 'You don't want to be payin' no attention to us, m'lad. Nothin' for you to worry about.'

'No,' said Lady Hardcastle. 'Let him speak. What is it?'

'All I was goin' to say is that, after he took our dad for a pint t'other day, I seen him in the Railway Arms one lunchtime talkin' to Wilf Dunmead. Seems he's talkin' to everyone. I's wonderin' when I might get *my* free pint.'

'Who's Wilf Dunmead?' I asked.

Old Roberts turned back to us. 'New signalman out at Littleton Junction. Used to be another bloke ran that box – Jimmy Brown – but he retired down to Brean with his missus.'

'Oh, now that's even more interesting,' said Lady Hardcastle. 'What sort of chap is Dunmead? Is he honest?'

'He's not a bad bloke. Come to us from Dursley. He's always got a few fiddles on the go, but who hasn't?'

'So he might be open to a bribe?'

'He might. You never knows.'

'One never does. But since he's the most recent person to speak to Billen, maybe we should have a word with him ourselves. He might tell us something.'

'I doubts it,' said Old Roberts. 'He's not goin' to tell the famous local sleuth he's doin' somethin' shady, is he?'

'Oh, of course not. But he might let something slip. At the very least he might inadvertently confirm that Billen's up to no good. Where might we find him?'

'He takes his lunch at the Railway Arms. You'll find him there with a pie and a pint,' said Young Roberts.

'What does he look like?' I asked.

Young Roberts held out his hand, palm down. 'Short fella. About this tall. Stocky. Big broad nose. He's prematurely bald, but you won't tell 'cos he never takes his signalman's cap off.'

'Sounds easy enough to find,' I said. 'How long will he be there?'

Old Roberts looked up at the impressive clock on his office wall. 'He's only supposed to be there till two, but his signalman's mate's just a young lad who don't make a fuss if he takes a bit longer. He always reckons the lad can deal with the local traffic so he says he don't need to be back at the box until the 3.06 to Penzance goes through.'

Lady Hardcastle stood. 'Thank you. I hope you don't think us too rude, but I'd quite like to catch him at his lunch if I can. He'll be less on his guard with a beer in his hand.'

'It'll be cider,' said Young Roberts. 'He likes a glass of cider, does Wilf.'

Lady Hardcastle smiled. 'Duly noted. We'll get to the bottom of this for you, Mr Roberts.'

We hurried out and returned to the car.

The Railway Arms was close to the marshalling yard between Chipping Bevington station and the signal box at Littleton Junction. It was an easy journey, especially by car, but only if you already knew the way. Or had a decent navigator. Lady Hardcastle was an excellent navigator and had led us out of a number of sticky situations over the years, but today she was distracted by her notebook.

I reached a T-junction. 'Is it left or right here?'

'Hmm? Yes, I should think so.'

If she was that distracted, there would be no profit in asking again, so I simply plumped for the right turn. I had set off, it turned out, in the opposite direction from the pub.

A few minutes later, Lady Hardcastle looked up from her notebook. 'What are we doing out here?'

'We're going to the Railway Arms.'

'This isn't the way to the Railway Arms, dear. This is the way to . . . actually, I've no idea where it's the way to, but I do know it's not the way to the Railway Arms.'

I sighed, but once again decided there would be no real benefit in arguing and instead found a suitable spot to turn round so we could head back the other way.

The pub, when we finally arrived, was busy. Off-duty drivers, porters, and other staff from the nearby marshalling yard sat about chatting noisily. We looked around the smoke-filled room but there was no one resembling the description we'd been given by Young Roberts. We couldn't be certain, though. It was clear that – unlike in the friendlier village pubs – women were seldom, if ever, seen in the Railway Arms, and we didn't want to draw too much attention to ourselves lest we provoke any kind of hostility.

Our cursory inspection over, we headed towards the bar, where a young barmaid greeted us.

'Good afternoon, ladies. You lost?'

Lady Hardcastle smiled. 'Actually, we did get a little lost on our way here, but no, this is where we intended to be. The stationmaster at Chipping Bevington suggested we might find Wilf Dunmead here.'

'Bobby Roberts? He's a lovely bloke, i'n't he? What do you want Wilf for?'

It seemed strange to hear Old Roberts referred to as anything other than Old Roberts.

Lady Hardcastle nodded. 'Mr Roberts – Bobby – wanted us to have a quick word with him about something.'

'You just missed him, I'm afraid. Always comes in 'ere for his lunch, he does. We didn't used to see so much of 'im, but now he's transferred to Littleton Junction he's in 'ere every day. He's another lovely one.'

'Is he?'

'Oh ar. Kind and friendly, like.' The barmaid looked around furtively. 'Not like some of 'em,' she whispered.

'Oh, then I'm sorry we weren't able to buy him a cider.'

'He'd have loved that, an' all. He's not been 'avin' a good time at home lately.'

'That's a shame. It's always worse when it happens to the nice ones.'

'It is,' agreed the barmaid. 'He's had more than his fair share of it, has Wilf. Started in the spring, see? His poor wife fell terrible ill when their youngest was born. It was touch and go whether she'd pull through. Then the baby was poorly – lovely little thing, she is, but born too soon. Weak lungs, they reckons. So they had to deal with all that. And now his mother-in-law's fallen sick, too.'

'That's terrible,' I said. 'The poor man.'

'It is. Doctor's bills would have done for 'em, but that's the beauty of workin' for the railway, i'n't it?'

I frowned in puzzlement 'It is?'

'Oh ar. They takes care of you, see? One day he's in here tellin' his mates all his troubles, next in comes some bloke called Billen lookin' for him. Like you were just now. Only this time Wilf's here so I points him out, and the fella takes Wilf a pint of cider – he does love his cider – and they has a chat.'

'Could you hear them?' asked Lady Hardcastle.

The barmaid laughed. 'No, and it weren't for lack of tryin', I can tell you. But it didn't matter in the end because, when the fella'd gone, Wilf came over to the bar and gets hisself another drink. "Well, that was a stroke of luck," he said. "That was a fella from the Railwaymen's Benevolent Society. They's goin' to take care of all the doctor's bills and set us on our feet again." He was the happiest I'd seen him for months, bless him.'

'Thank goodness for the Railwaymen's Benevolent Society,' said Lady Hardcastle.

The barmaid smiled. 'That's exactly what Wilf said. "Thank goodness for the Railwaymen's Benevolent Society," he said. He's been like a new man ever since. A proper spring in his step, like.

It's amazin' what a difference it can make when someone lifts your burden, i'n't it?'

'It is indeed,' agreed Lady Hardcastle. 'And this Mr . . . Biffen, did you say?'

'Billen.'

'That's it, sorry. This Mr Billen sounds like some manner of guardian angel.'

'I reckon that's what he must be. Although for a time I thought he was Mr Lloyd George. I seen his picture in the *Daily Mirror* – Lloyd George, that is, not Billen – and they's the dead spit of each other.'

'How funny,' said Lady Hardcastle. She paused for a moment and then said, 'But we mustn't hold you up. We'll have to pop back another time.'

'Right you are. Shall I tell Wilf you was lookin' for him?'

'No, it's all right. It wasn't important and I shouldn't want to add to his troubles by making him think it was. We were just doing a favour for Mr Roberts. Since we were passing this way, you understand.'

'I shall keep mum, then. Like you says, no point in worryin' him.'

We ran the gauntlet of curious stares back to the door and left.

Now I knew where we were, the drive home was much more straightforward and we were back at the house in no time.

After dinner that evening we sat in the dining room with our wine and reviewed the crime board. As far as we were aware, there had been no progress on the one actual crime we were tracking, and we'd heard nothing from the post office, so we were left discussing the only thing that had happened on that chilly Saturday: the Case of the Corrupt Railwayman.

Lady Hardcastle refilled our glasses. 'I wonder if we should be a little more circumspect in our conversations with Daisy.'

'How do you mean?'

'That charming young lady in the Railway Arms was not entirely unlike our own dear Daisy Spratt, did you not think? She didn't know us from Adam—'

'We're very differently built and much better dressed, for a start.'

'Nevertheless, we didn't even ask her about Dunmead's meeting with Billen, but there she was, giving it all up to complete strangers.'

'Daisy's a gasbag,' I said, 'but she's not indiscreet. She knows when to keep mum.'

'You're right, of course. I shouldn't doubt her. But it's remarkable how many revealing details can spill out while a friendly person is simply trying to sing someone's praises. That girl only wanted us to know what a lovely chap Dunmead is, and what a terrible time he's had. But in doing that she told us he'd taken a bribe from the regional controller.'

'Only because we know he's the regional controller and not a representative of the Railwaymen's Benevolent Fund. Is there even such a thing as the Railwaymen's Benevolent Fund?'

'I confess I have no idea. It has a plausible ring to it.'

'It does. And if it does exist, it's possible that Billen might be the regional administrator.'

'It's possible, certainly, but I remain unconvinced that someone as high up in the company – and as obviously self-important, let's not forget . . . Honestly, dear, you have no idea what a pompous little man he is. Quite dreadful . . . I'm sorry, what was I saying? Oh, yes, someone like Bernard Billen surely wouldn't be travelling the region dispensing charitable largesse himself. And if he did drag himself away from being important at his important desk in his important office, he'd definitely travel with flunkies and at least one newspaper reporter. There's no value in playing Lord Bountiful if there's no one there to see it.'

I couldn't disagree. 'So Billen has bribed a signalman at Littleton Junction, then. Does that help us work out what he's up to?'

'I'm not certain it does, no. He has control of the routing of trains in the immediate area. Perhaps he can divert traffic to a quiet part of the marshalling yard where things can be secretly loaded or unloaded. That would fit Roberts's speculation about moving stolen goods. He jumped on the idea of artwork rather quickly – has there been anything like that in the press lately?'

'Nothing I can recall. But I didn't get the impression he was referring to anything specific – it was just an idea that popped into his head because we were pressing him for possible explanations of Billen's activities.'

Lady Hardcastle tapped her wine glass against her teeth. 'It's a stumper. I'm going to go out on a limb and suggest that he didn't murder Sid Hyde, though.'

'While riding on a panther.'

She laughed. 'And mis-sorting the mail at the local post office as he galloped by.'

'Do panthers gallop?'

'I think technically they do. Isn't a gallop when all four feet of a four-legged animal are off the ground? When a cat's running at full pelt, they do that coiling and stretching thing, don't they? Like a big spring. They definitely have all four feet off the ground then. But I think you're right. It's horses. Horses gallop. Panthers . . . lope?'

'Too lackadaisical.'

'Charge?'

'Too rhino-y.'

'Scamper?'

'Too whimsical.'

'Run like the clappers?'

'That'll have to do. Coffee in the drawing room?'

'With cake. And cards.'

I cleared away the dinner things and we retired to sit by the fire.

# Chapter Nine

Sunday was . . . well, it was Sunday. Nothing happens on Sundays. I think even the Beast would have been taking its ease and preparing itself for the labours of the week to come.

Sundays were Edna and Miss Jones's day off, so I spent the morning in the kitchen making the Sunday roast. It had never been much of a feature in my young life when the circus was on the road, but once my mother took my sister and me back to Aberdare to look after our grandmother it became a firm favourite.

For years I thought it must be the most complex and challenging of meals to prepare. My mother would install herself in the kitchen from about nine in the morning, and woe betide anyone who dared enter and disturb the intricate preparations for The Roast. Three hours later, a delicious dinner would appear, and I firmly believed that the whole of those three hours had been spent in diligent toil – peeling, slicing, stirring, basting, until each component of the meal was a triumph of rich, savoury perfection.

It was only when I came to cook the meal for myself that I learned there was almost nothing to do. The peeling and slicing took a few minutes. The basting, where it was even required, was a few seconds of spooning fat on to meat. The stirring came at the end when the gravy was made and was another few minutes of barely noticeable effort. It belatedly dawned on me that the closed kitchen door and all the stern injunctions to keep out were my mother's way of making a little bit of time for herself, away from her squabbling twin daughters and her own demanding mother.

I needed no such respite, but I did enjoy the contemplative pottering and the quiet sitting down in a comfortable kitchen chair of making a Sunday roast.

And that was pretty much that for Sunday.

There was a frost when I woke on Monday morning, so there was no internal debate about where to exercise. I was a little later than usual, but there would be plenty of time before Edna and Miss Jones arrived so I made myself comfortable in the drawing room.

As I slowly moved and stretched, I wondered how Herself would feel about turning the morning room into an exercise room. We seldom used it these days, and with the morning sun streaming through the windows it would make a nice place to practise my t'ai chi. Or what about one of the spare bedrooms? We needed one for Harry and Lady Lavinia, of course, and another for little Addie. But under most circumstances that was the most guests we ever had and—

There was a knock at the door.

'Sorry to bother you,' said Miss Jones, 'but have you got a minute?'

I nodded as I finished stepping up to grasp the bird's tail. 'For you, Blod, always.'

She smiled. 'Were you planning to go into the village this morning?'

'I don't have any plans at all for this morning. Or for the rest of the day, come to that. What do you need?'

'Fred's lad came Saturday with the order but there was no beef shin. I wanted to make a nice stew for you, see? If you happened to be passing the butcher's, could you pick some up for me? He should have it there – it was on the order.'

'I always enjoy a stroll round the village. When do you need it?'

'I was going to cook it in the oven to make it easy. I'd like to have it on before we leave at twelve, then you'd just have to take it out at, say, two-ish. I'll make you up some dumplings and you can pop those in when you warm it up. A good stew always benefits from being allowed to stand for a bit. Could I have the beef by eleven? Is that inconvenient?'

'Not in the least. Can you do me a favour in return, though? Can you get Herself's starter breakfast on while I get changed?'

'Of course. I'll give you five minutes and then get it all going for you.'

And so it was that two hours later, washed, dressed and breakfasted, I was putting on my winter coat and preparing to venture out into the chill.

Lady Hardcastle saw me in the hall on her way to her study. 'Where are you off to? Anywhere nice?'

'To the butcher's,' I said. 'We need beef shin.'

'Does Fred not deliver anymore?'

'He does. There's an explanation, but not a fascinating one. Do you need anything from the village?'

'A quarter of humbugs, please.'

'Of course. I do like a humbug.'

'And chocolate limes.'

'Right you are.'

'And some toffee.'

'Uh-huh.'

'And doughnuts.'

'I'll see you in a little while.'

I closed the door before she could order any more sugary treats and set off down the garden path.

The sky was clear but the air was still distinctly chilly. At least the sun had melted off the thin film of frost, and the lane felt reasonably safe underfoot as I walked along it towards the village green.

I should like to be able to report the state of the trees and hedgerows, but my notoriously poor memory for matters horticultural means that I have no idea what I saw apart from that it was all largely leafless.

Hardy little sparrows flitted from the hedgerows at my passing, and I spotted a pair of buzzards hovering over a nearby field, so there was at least some life I could recognize. Obviously, if the buzzards had their way, at least one life would soon be extinguished and converted into dinner – I guessed mouse, but buzzards will often take a young rabbit or hare if there's one carelessly loping about – but that was the way of things in the countryside.

I skirted the frosty green – I was wearing new boots – and greeted a few villagers as I made my way to Spratt's. As I drew near, I saw a familiar creature sitting outside, its lead tied to a lamp post. It was Lady Araminta Fluffikins.

I crouched to greet her and she snuffled my gloved hands, her fluffy little tail fluttering excitedly. 'Hello, Minty. Is someone from The Grange doing some shopping? Did they bring you for a walk as a treat? It must be torture having to sit out here when there's all that tasty meat inside.'

I ruffled her little dandelion head and stood. She pulled against the lead and tried to follow me as I went towards the shop door, but it held fast and she sat resignedly back down on the chilly pavement.

The bell tinkled and the door scraped against the sawdust that coated the floor.

It was not, I immediately discovered, a member of the Farley-Strouds' household who had brought Minty with them for her morning constitutional, but Mrs Adaway herself.

And there she was, deep in conversation with Fred Spratt.

'. . . and the vet says she absolutely must have only the finest meat. It's for her delicate constitution, you see?'

'You're in luck, then, Mrs Adaway – I only sells the very finest meat. Now, what can I get for your lovely dog? Some nice beef skirt? A little tripe, perhaps?'

I could have sworn Mrs Adaway actually batted her eyelids. 'Oh, I think we can do a little better than that, don't you, Mr Spratt?'

Fred's wife, Eunice, sat beside the cash register with her knitting. She saw Mrs Adaway's eyelids batting and rolled her own eyes at me.

'I like a lady who knows her mind,' said Fred with a smile. 'How about a nice bit of steak? I got some lovely rump.'

She gave him a wink, for goodness' sake. 'I bet you have.'

More eye-rolling from Eunice.

Mrs Adaway carried on. 'But I think Minty deserves a fillet. The vet said she needed a treat, and that was before the poor dear's recent shock.'

'We heard about that,' said Fred as he selected a pair of fillet steaks from his display and showed them to her. 'She was there when Dicky Durbin and Felix Kiddle were attacked, they said.'

'She was. She bravely protected Kiddle after the beast had mauled him. If it hadn't been for her, it might have come back and finished him off.'

Eunice must have been getting dizzy by this point.

'A fine dog for a fine lady.' Fred indicated the steaks. 'Which one do you think?'

'Oh, let's go mad – we'll have both.'

He weighed the steaks and wrapped them while Eunice rang up the total on the till.

Mrs Adaway paid barely any attention to her change, and instead continued to stare adoringly at Fred Spratt.

She noticed me only as she prepared to leave. 'Oh, hello, Florence dear. What a lovely day.'

'Bright, if a little bracing,' I said.

'Always a little brighter and more bracing in the right company.' She winked at me and breezed out.

'I think you have an admirer there, Fred,' I said.

'What do you mean? Don't be daft.'

'He's oblivious, bless 'im,' said Eunice. 'Always 'as been, even when 'e was younger. I practically 'ad to throw meself at 'im afore he'd notice me.'

'I don't know what you're both talkin' about,' said Fred. 'She was just bein' friendly.'

'Course, I don't blame 'er,' said Eunice with a wink of her own. 'He's still a bit of all right, i'n't 'e?'

'A handsome and vigorous man,' I said. 'He drives the women of the village wild.'

Fred sighed. 'Can I help you with somethin', Flo? Or are you just here to help my lovely wife torment me?'

'A little of both,' I said with a smile. 'Do you have some beef shin?'

Fred held up a triumphant finger. 'More than that, I gots *your* beef shin.' He disappeared out to the back of the shop and the cold room.

Eunice looked up again from her knitting. 'That Mrs Adaway's a funny one, i'n't she?'

I nodded. 'Most peculiar.'

'Did 'er dog really protect Felix Kiddle?'

'We certainly found her sitting by his side, covered in his blood. But whether she was protecting him or hoping he might protect her, we'll never know.'

'We saw his wife Saturday – popped in for some sausages. He's on the mend, she says.'

'That's good news. He seemed like a nice chap.'

Eunice nodded. 'There's certainly others I'd rather see mauled by a lion.'

'Panther,' I said.

'I thought it was a lion. Everyone's sayin' it's a lion. 'Cept them as thinks it's the vicar's dog.'

'No, definitely a panther. Felix described it quite clearly.'

Fred returned with the beef.

'There you are, m'dear. One pound o' finest beef shin. I put it out for the lad to deliver t'other day but 'e forgot it. Hold on . . .' He disappeared again and returned moments later with another package. 'And a pound of sausages on the 'ouse for your trouble.'

'I don't have any troubles, Fred, but thank you.'

He winked. It was an epidemic. 'You 'as now – they sausages 'as nearly gone off.'

Eunice tutted. 'Take no notice, dear. He made 'em this mornin'.'

'Just my little joke. Anythin' else?'

'No, just this,' I said. 'Well, this and most of the sweet counter at Mrs Pantry's.'

'Your Lady Hardcastle's got a proper sweet tooth, a'n't she?' said Eunice.

'A whole mouthful of them.'

She pushed out her top plate with her tongue. 'I 'ave, an all, but they i'n't me own.' She cackled and slid her false teeth back into place.

I put the beef and sausages in my shopping basket. 'What do I owe you?'

Eunice consulted her book. 'Nothin', m'dear, we's already billed you for it.'

We said our goodbyes and I strolled on to Pantry's Pantry and Holman's the baker for Lady Hardcastle's sweet treats.

♦ ♦ ♦

I might have had no real plans for Monday, but Lady Hardcastle was nowhere near as free of ambition. She emerged from her photographic studio in the orangery shortly before noon, still dressed in her overalls, and found me in the drawing room, boots off, feet up, reading the newspaper.

She seemed puzzled. 'You're not ready.'

I looked up from a story about a priceless painting stolen from a London art dealer. 'Ready for what?'

'Our trip to The Grange.'

'I had no idea we were going to The Grange. I thought we'd been there quite enough already lately.'

'As I keep saying: Gertie needs as many people around her who aren't Joyce as possible. I assumed you knew we'd be going.'

'Did you, indeed?' I looked her up and down. 'You're not ready, either. Unless you're going in your overalls, of course. Is that the plan? Scandalize Mrs Adaway with your outlandish dress?'

'It will take me mere moments to slip out of this and into something altogether more afternoony.'

'It will take me less time than that to put my boots back on. Do we have time for a sandwich before we go?'

'We're invited to lunch.'

'This really does seem like the sort of thing you should have told me.'

'I'm telling you now.'

'I can't argue with that. Will we be back by two?'

'I doubt it, why?'

'I promised Miss Jones I'd take the stew out of the oven at two.'

'Can't she do it?'

I looked up at the clock. 'They both leave at midday and it's nearly that now.'

'Oh, yes. Of course. Well, can't you—'

'I'll have a word. Go and put your frock on.'

I followed her out in my stockinged feet and, while she galumphed upstairs to change, I went through to the kitchen. Miss Jones assured me that if she added a little extra water and put the casserole at the bottom of the oven, it would be fine until at least four, and might even benefit from the extra time.

With dinner rescued, I buttoned my boots, put on my hat, and sat with my overcoat beside me on the arm of the chair.

I waited for Lady Hardcastle to return.

I waited a little longer.

Half past twelve came and went, and I was considering an uncouth yell up the stairs to ask what on earth was going on when she arrived at the drawing room door.

'Come along, Flossie, quicksticks. No time for dawdling in armchairs.'

I stood and picked up my coat. I was composing a pithy rejoinder, with possible reference to her own unhurried approach to appropriately clothing herself, but she was already out the door before I could decide on the most devastating form of words. By the time I had locked the front door – I still couldn't break the habit of locking our front door, even though no one else in the village seemed to bother – she was already behind the wheel of the Rolls, engine running.

Much has been written on the subject of Lady Hardcastle's devil-may-care attitude to driving, and many were the local cyclists, pedestrians, horses, dogs and chickens whose lives had been made just that little bit more terrifying by their encounters with her as she sped along the roads of Gloucestershire. Even a trip to The Grange could be as exciting as a motor race with her at the wheel, but that day we arrived without having had to apologize to anyone along the way.

By unlucky chance, Sir Hector had been seeing to something just outside the front door, and found himself perfectly placed to be gently peppered by a spray of damp gravel as Lady Hardcastle slewed to a halt.

'What ho, old gel,' he said with a wave. 'Always know how to make an entrance, what?'

We alighted.

'Hello, Hector dear,' said Lady Hardcastle, warmly. 'Have you been out with the dogs?'

'No, why?'

'You look like you were standing next to a dog when it splashed through a muddy puddle, dear – your trousers are peppered with little damp dots.'

'Ah, well,' he said with a smile. 'Can't be helped. We seem to be seein' a lot of you lately. Not complainin', mind you – always a pleasure to see you.'

'We felt Gertie might need allies.'

He nodded sagely. 'Say no more, old sport, say no more. The old sibling can be a trial sometimes. I get round it by bein' elsewhere as often as I can. Used to deal with her the same way when we were children. Joycey's always easier to bear when she's in a different room, what?'

'Well, poor Gertie doesn't always have that option, so we've come over to keep her company for a while.'

'You'll stay for lunch?'

'Wouldn't miss it. Where *is* your lovely wife?'

'Library, I think. Leave you to it. Places to be, things to do.'

Sir Hector beetled off to hide from his sister, and we let ourselves in and found our own way to the library.

Lady Farley-Stroud was sitting in her favourite chair, reading a magazine.

Of Joyce there was no sign.

She peered at us over the top of her reading glasses. 'Hello, ladies. What a lovely surprise. I didn't know you were comin'.'

So it wasn't just me, then.

'Of course we were,' said Lady Hardcastle. 'We arranged it the other day over tea and cakes.'

'I'm sorry, m'dear – completely slipped my mind. Must be goin' doolally in me old age. Come in and sit yourselves down. Have some tea.'

I was still uncertain whether Lady Hardcastle was at fault there, but I said nothing and just made myself comfortable beside her on the sofa. I poured the tea while Lady Hardcastle addressed Lady Farley-Stroud's concerns about her own mental acuity.

'Nonsense. You've a lot on your mind. Speaking of which, where's your houseguest?'

'I don't know and I don't much care. She breezed in after takin' the dog for a walk, gigglin' like a schoolgirl. I asked what on earth had put her in such a good mood, and she said she was in love. She claimed Fred Spratt had made advances to her at the butcher's and that his feelings were entirely reciprocated.'

I had to work hard not to spit out my tea.

'She said what?' I asked when I had swallowed my mouthful.

'She said she was buyin' fillet steak for that pampered little powder puff and that Fred had been flirtin' with her.'

'I was at the butcher's myself and that's not what I saw. She was the one who was flirty and suggestive. There was eyelid-batting and some winking. Fred was just Fred – polite and friendly. And Eunice was there as usual, too. He can be a bit mischievous sometimes, and he does sometimes flirt with customers, but he means nothing by it.'

'Ha!' Lady Farley-Stroud's bark of a laugh was very much like her husband's sometimes. 'I knew Fred wouldn't be makin' passes. Especially not at that silly old bat.'

Unbeknown to us all, Mrs Adaway and Minty had arrived at the library door.

'Who's a silly old bat?' she said.

Lady Farley-Stroud barked again. 'Ha! You are, you silly old bat. Young Florence here was at the butcher's this mornin' and she's told a completely different story. You were the one who was flirtin', not Fred.'

'Ah, but she didn't witness the whole conversation. She came in when we were almost done. I know what happened.'

'And Florence knows what she saw. Tell her, Florence.'

I smiled nervously. This was a fight I didn't really want to be part of. 'Mrs Adaway is right – I did arrive towards the end of the conversation. I didn't see Fred flirting but, obviously, I didn't see what happened before I got there.'

'Ha!' barked Mrs Adaway – they were all at it. 'Y'see, Gertrude, you dried-up old crone? You're just jealous because I can still attract a man and you're lumbered with my idiot brother. Fred wants me. He's far too good for that dreadful Eunice woman. She's not a fit consort for such a magnificent man.'

Lady Farley-Stroud shook her head. 'You're deludin' yourself, you silly old bat.'

'You can't spoil it for me, Gertrude. I know what happened. Come, Minty, we don't need this wet-blanketiveness.'

And with her dog faithfully at her heels, she stalked out.

'Silly old bat,' said Lady Farley-Stroud. 'Now, then, when I invited you to call, did I say anythin' about lunch?'

◆ ◆ ◆

It was that time of year and the nights were closing in. By the time we'd finished Miss Jones's delicious stew – with the dumplings I'd popped in while I reheated it – it was properly dark out. The fires and lamps were lit but it still felt gloomy, and I wondered aloud if we should pop down to the pub for a quick drink to brighten my mood a little.

'I was thinking exactly that myself,' said Lady Hardcastle. 'A glass of Old Joe's indifferent brandy and some cheery company would be just what the doctor ordered.'

And so, with our hats, coats and mufflers to protect us from the autumnal chill, we ventured down the lane to the village.

The blast of warmth, laughter and smoke as we opened the pub door lifted my spirits immediately, and the friendly greetings as we pressed our way to the bar completed the job. By the time we caught Daisy's eye I was feeling like myself again. There's nothing like the community and fellowship of an English pub to warm the cockles and restore one's faith in neighbours and friends.

'I wondered if we'd be seein' you two in 'ere tonight,' said Daisy. 'I said to Joe, I said, "Lady Hardcastle and Flo a'n't bin in for a few nights – I hope they's all right." And here you are.'

I smiled. 'I saw your mum and dad this morning at the shop. Didn't they tell you I was all right?'

'Didn't mention you. They just kept goin' on about Sir Hector's sister flirtin' with our dad. Our ma thought it was hilarious. Reckons the old girl must need glasses if she fancies that old lump.'

'That's when I was there – no wonder they didn't mention me.'

'You was there? What 'appened? Was it like our ma said?'

'Exactly like that.'

Once more I briefly told the tale of winking and suggestive comments, now adding Mrs Adaway's firm belief that Fred had been the one doing the flirting.

'That's precious,' said Daisy when I'd finished. 'You wait till I tells our ma. She'll love it.'

'Don't be too unkind, though,' I said. 'She's just a lonely lady. Are your parents here?'

'No, they's gone to see one of 'er old pals over Woodworthy. She's 'avin' a terrible time, the poor old love. Family troubles. They's gone to cheer 'er up.'

We ordered our drinks and stood for a while, listening to the chatter while scanning the room for an empty seat. That is to say, Lady Hardcastle scanned – I couldn't see over the crowd in the way she could.

As expected, the conversation around us was mostly about personal gossip, football, crop planting, and getting the animals in for the coming winter. There were jokes, reminiscences, and complaints about the government. Ailments, joys and inconveniences. And, here and there, I caught little snippets about the wild animal attacks and the deaths of Sid Hyde and Dick Durbin. But the panic had been replaced by resignation, as though the animal – referred to variously as a panther, a lion and, by one older man, as a 'hunky punk' – was now just another mundane threat to farmers' livelihoods, like the weather, vermin, insect pests, and blights.

With no seats in view, we turned back to the bar, where Daisy was 'drying' glasses with a wet tea towel.

'Have you seen any more of your giant rat?' asked Lady Hardcastle.

Daisy put down her glass. 'I knows you don't believe me, but I saw what I saw, and this mornin' I saw it again. Large as life. Larger. Biggest rat I ever seen.'

'Where was it?'

'Out in the yard. Bold as brass. Just sittin' there, lookin' about like it owned the place.'

'So you got a proper look at it?'

'I did.'

'And you're still sure it was a rat, despite its size.'

'A giant rat, yes. Like a rat had been crossed with a kangaroo. Like in that book you lent me, Flo, with that bloke on the island makin' all them what-d'you-call-'ems? Them Beast Folk.'

'*The Island of Doctor Moreau*?' I said.

'That's the one. Didn't sleep for weeks after readin' that. Well, imagine if that Dr Moreau fella had stitched a rat and a kangaroo together. That's what I saw in the yard.'

Lady Hardcastle frowned. 'I don't suppose you have paper and pencil back there?'

Daisy looked around. 'Nothin' handy.' She called to the other end of the bar. 'Joe? 'Ave we got paper and pencil?'

'What for?'

'Don't know. Lady Hardcastle wants it.'

Joe smiled toothlessly, nodded, and held up a finger in a cheerful call for patience.

He disappeared out towards the stairs that led up to the rooms he occasionally let out, and his own private accommodation beyond. I felt briefly guilty that we had driven him off, but then I remembered how much he relished an opportunity to disappear for a while, especially when the pub was busy. Mrs Arnold, his seldom-seen wife, probably also enjoyed an occasional bit of company.

Joe returned some minutes later with a few sheets of letter paper and the stub of a pencil.

'There you goes, m'lady,' he said. 'That what you's after?'

'It is, Joe, thank you,' said Lady Hardcastle. 'How's Mrs Arnold?'

'Can't complain, m'lady. She sends 'er regards.'

She took the paper and pencil with a smile and Joe went back to talking to his friends at the other end of the bar.

Lady Hardcastle handed the paper straight to Daisy. 'You've a talent for drawing, dear – we saw your drawing of Joe at the village exhibition. Can you sketch this fantastical hybrid?'

'I can give it a go.'

Daisy leaned on the bar and began work.

We sipped our drinks and waited, listening once more to the swirl of conversation.

A few minutes passed.

'There,' said Daisy, suddenly. 'It looked like that.'

We turned the paper round and looked at the drawing. It did, indeed, look like a cross between a rat and a kangaroo, but then it was bound to. If someone had just described something as a cross between a rat and a kangaroo and you asked them to draw it for you, it would have been something of a surprise if they didn't draw exactly that. It did, though, have one curious and unexpected feature.

'Tell me, dear,' said Lady Hardcastle, 'why did you add a smile?'

Daisy looked at her as though she thought her stupid. 'Because it was smilin' at me.'

On Tuesday, Lady Hardcastle did some pottering of her own and kept out of my way, so that when we sat down to lunch, it was the first time we'd spoken since breakfast.

'What have you been up to this morning?' I asked as she helped herself to pie.

'I have been hunting.'

'Hunting what? Big game? The thimble? The snark?'

'For a book.'

'Aha. And did you find it?'

'I did.'

'What was it?'

'Something I want to show Daisy. I'd like to go to the Dog and Duck after lunch if that's all right.'

'Of course.'

And so it was that, as soon as our meal was over, we bundled ourselves up once more against the nippiness, and tripped lightly down the lane to the village green and the pub beyond.

Lady Hardcastle marched up to Daisy and plonked her book – which I'd still not been allowed to see – on the bar.

'Have you seen any more of your rat?'

Daisy looked at her wearily. 'Don't you start. I've 'ad nothin' but rats from this lot since we opened.' She indicated the grinning faces of local rapscallion and part-time thief Mickey Yawn and his adoring girlfriend, Olive Churches. '"How's your rat, Dais?" "Sure it weren't a cat wearin' a disguise, Dais?" I saw what I saw, and what I saw was a giant rat.'

Lady Hardcastle flipped open the book to a page she'd marked with a folded piece of paper, and turned it round so that Daisy could see. 'Did it look like that?'

Daisy looked for a moment, then a grin spread across her face like the rising sun. She squealed. 'That's it. That's it right there. That's my giant rat.' She held up the book and showed it to the table of youngsters. 'See that, Michael Yawn? See? I wasn't imaginin' things. It's right there in Lady Hardcastle's book. One giant rat, or' – she turned the book back around so she could read the caption under the illustration – 'quokka. Wait a moment. Quokka? Are you 'avin' me on as well now, Lady H? I thought better of you. I thought you was my friend.'

'I like to think I am, dear.'

'There i'n't no such thing as a quokka.'

Mickey and Olive were looking over and smirking, but with Lady Hardcastle and me there, they decided to say nothing.

With a smile, Lady Hardcastle took the book back and showed Daisy the cover – *The Wildlife of Australia*. 'I assure you that there is a small marsupial in south-western Australia called the quokka. Your sketch matches the illustration perfectly.'

She unfolded the paper she'd used as a bookmark. It was Daisy's sketch from the night before and it was unmistakably the same creature as the one in the book labelled *Quokka – Setonix brachyurus*. I took the book and scanned the description offered by the – very boring, I quickly learned – author of the book. *Small marsupial. Herbivorous.* There was more but I didn't read it too carefully. It was a charming-looking animal, and I could see from further sketches in the book that it most definitely looked as though it were smiling. The one objection I kept coming back to, though, was geography.

'How far would you say it is to south-western Australia?' I asked.

Lady Hardcastle shrugged. 'From here? I don't know. Probably somewhere in the region of . . . what, nine thousand miles? Give or take.'

'By land?'

'Heavens no, Australia's an island. And so are we. Lots of sea between here and there.'

'Quokkas can't fly, I presume.'

'Not unless they steal an aeroplane, no.'

'I see.'

'They look wily, mind you, so I wouldn't put it past them.'

'Nor would I, to tell you the truth. But you can see where I'm trying to get to, can't you?'

'Of course I can, dear, but all I can think about now is a quokka trying to fly an aeroplane.'

I tutted and rolled my eyes.

'You're right, obviously,' she said. 'Finding a quokka in Gloucestershire is an extremely improbable event, but finding a rat the size of a house cat is, I posit, impossible. And when one has eliminated the impossible . . .'

'I'm not entirely convinced that you've tracked down all the improbables, but I'll let it pass. What do you propose we do?'

'I was hoping to catch it. We could put some food in a trap of some sort.'

Daisy had taken the Australian wildlife book and was reading. 'It says here they likes grass and leaves. There's plenty of grass on the green, so it won't be hungry.'

'It might not be hungry, as such,' said Lady Hardcastle, 'but I wonder if we might be able to tempt it with something a little more interesting. Everyone likes a bit of variety in their diet.'

'Might work,' said Daisy. She leaned in. ''Ere, d'you reckon they's valuable, these quokkas? Could I sell it?'

Lady Hardcastle laughed. 'I've assumed it belongs to someone, Daisy. We'll have to trace the owner.'

'Yes, but if you don't . . .'

'Well, yes, if we don't find its rightful owner then you can become a dealer in exotic animals with our blessing.'

'The drinks will be on me,' said Daisy with a grin.

'That's very kind of you, dear, I'll have a large brandy.'

'Will be, Lady H. *Will be*. I can't afford to keep you in brandy on my wages.'

'In that case, I shall buy you one. And Flo?'

'Brandy, please,' I said. 'Got to keep away the chill.'

'And I'll have a small cider, if I may,' said Daisy. 'Cheers.'

Later that evening we returned to the Dog and Duck with a cage Lady Hardcastle had built from chicken wire and assorted oddments from her studio. She had fashioned a spring-loaded door, which would close quickly but – she assured me – harmlessly when a creature as heavy as a quokka ventured inside, tempted – we hoped – by the tasty leaves and grass I had harvested from our back garden.

Under Daisy's supervision, we positioned the cage in the yard outside the pub near where the creature had last been seen.

We left it there and hoped for the best.

# Chapter Ten

We'd never set a definite time by which Edna and Miss Jones should arrive for work in the mornings – as long as Miss Jones was there to make breakfast and Edna got all her cleaning and other organizing done before lunchtime, we didn't much mind when they got to the house. Nevertheless, they had settled into a routine over the years, and usually arrived together long before they might really have needed to be there.

On that Wednesday morning, Edna arrived alone.

She called through from the boot room as she took off her coat. 'Hello, my lover. How bist?'

'Passing well, thank you, Edna. I'm just putting the kettle on. Tea?'

She bustled into the kitchen, rain-damp and bedraggled. 'I never says no to a cup of tea, m'dear – you knows that.'

She made herself comfortable in a chair with a weary sigh, as though she'd been hard at work for hours.

'Where's Miss Jones?' I asked as I warmed the pot. 'Is she all right?'

'She's on her way. Daisy called her over as we was passin' the pub but I shouldn't expect she'll be too long. Though I knows what you three are like when you gets together, so perhaps she might be a few minutes after all.'

'Is Daisy still on about her rat?'

'Rocker, is what I heard.'

'Quokka,' I said. 'At least, that's what Herself thinks. Although where she supposes it might have come from is anyone's guess – quokkas are Australian.'

'Then it'll have come from Australia,' said Edna, sagely.

'I can't fault your logic, but what I meant was—'

The back door slammed against the hammering rain, and a similarly bedraggled Blodwen Jones came dripping into the kitchen. 'Mornin', both. Sorry I's late. I had to have a chat with Daisy. Is the kettle on?'

'It is,' I said. 'Tea or coffee?'

'I'll have a coffee for a change if you're makin' one for Lady H. Give me a sec to get out of this wet coat and I'll be back. I've got news from the pub.'

I hadn't thought about Lady Hardcastle's starter breakfast, but a glance at the large clock on the kitchen wall showed that I ought to be getting on with it. I set about making some coffee to go with the tea and put a couple of slices of toast on.

'So, what's the news?' I asked when Miss Jones returned.

'Message from Dais. She said to thank you for the trap and to get round there as soon as you can, 'cos she's caught sommat and don't know what to do with it.'

'Did she say what sort of something?'

'A shocker, she said, but I thought it looked quite sweet, to tell the truth.'

'A quokka?'

Miss Jones laughed. 'That's not a word. A blocker, maybe? Docker? It was a bit small to be a docker, mind. Can't imagine one o' they little things unloadin' ships out at Avonmouth.'

'But you definitely saw it.'

'Greyish. About the size of a cat. Smiley little face.'

Edna suddenly sat upright. 'Cat? You don't reckon it's that thing what's been killin' everyone?'

Miss Jones laughed again. 'I can't imagine sommat that size killin' nothin'.'

'It might be a young one. The big one they seen in the woods might be its mother. She'll come lookin' for her cub and Daisy'll be for it.'

I held up my hands for calm. 'We have a witness who says the creature in the woods was a panther. And a scientist upstairs who's pretty sure the creature at the pub is an Australian quokka. No one's in any danger.'

'Well, it i'n't my place to be givin' no orders,' said Edna, 'but you and our resident scientist needs to get to the pub sharpish. If that thing's a danger, we needs to know about it.'

With a smile and a nod, I made up the starter breakfast tray and took it upstairs.

The sheet-covered beast in the bed stirred as I closed the bedroom door.

'Is that you, Flossie?' croaked Lady Hardcastle.

I put the tray on the bedside table. 'Out of curiosity, whom did you suppose it might be if it wasn't?'

The sheet flipped down. 'Wasn't you?'

'Yes. In your imagined world, who would awaken you with coffee and toast if not me?'

'I didn't know there was coffee and toast when I asked. You might have been an enterprising burglar out a-burgling.'

'Or a cut-throat busy occupied in crime, it's true. But, yes, it is I. I bring your starter breakfast and news from the Dog and Duck: our trap has been sprung and a beast captured.'

She struggled upright. 'Oh, that *is* good news. Was it a quokka?'

'Of that I can't be certain. I got the news second-hand from Miss Jones and she doesn't think "quokka" is a real word. But she did give a description and it certainly fits. Daisy asks that we attend her at the pub at our earliest convenience because she doesn't know what to do next.'

'Then we must make haste. Help me get dressed and we'll hurry down there before breakfast.'

◆ ◆ ◆

Twenty minutes later we were standing in the rain, knocking on the door of the Dog and Duck.

'We's closed,' came Daisy's less-than-patient voice from within.

'And we's wet,' came Lady Hardcastle's loud, clear voice from without. 'Open up, Daisy, there's a good girl.'

Bolts thunked and the lock clicked.

Daisy opened the door and peered out. 'Blimey, you are an' all. Get in quick, afore you catches your death.'

We hurried inside and dripped on the freshly swept floor.

'Blodwen Jones tells us you've captured your quokka,' said Lady Hardcastle as she looked around for somewhere to put her dripping umbrella.

I took it from her and put it with mine beside the coat stand in the corner.

'I've captured sommat,' said Daisy. 'But Joe still reckons it's a rat. It's all I could do to stop him from choppin' its head off with a meat cleaver.'

'Oh dear,' said Lady Hardcastle. 'That will never do. Where is the poor thing?'

Daisy beckoned us to follow as she set off towards the back of the pub.

In the storeroom, where they kept the skittles and other bits and bobs for occasional use, stood a table. On the table was Lady Hardcastle's makeshift cage.

Of Joe there was no sign, but the meat cleaver from the pub kitchen lay menacingly beside the cage.

Inside it was the most adorable little creature I had ever seen. It was exactly as described: greyish brown, a bit like a tiny kangaroo, about the size of a cat. The part I hadn't believed at any point during anyone's description – not even that of Mr Ambrose Tillotson, author of *The Wildlife of Australia* – was that the tiny marsupial was smiling. And yet there it was: round ears, eyes like black beads, a coat-button nose and . . . the warmest, most welcoming smile I had ever seen. And I'd seen many a happy smile – a lot of people are pleased to see me.

'Well,' said Lady Hardcastle, a delighted smile spreading on her own face, 'aren't you the most precious little thing. Hello, Mr Quokka. And how are you? I'm sorry we had to trap you in that nasty old cage, but we were worried about you.'

The creature didn't appear at all fazed by its incarceration, nor by the attention it was getting from three humans. It seemed merely curious.

'So that's definitely a quokka, then?' said Daisy as she reached out tentatively towards the cage.

The quokka regarded her with a smile and leaned forward to investigate the approaching hand.

Daisy flinched back.

Lady Hardcastle smiled. 'Don't worry, dear, it won't hurt you. Herbivore, remember?'

'I doesn't doubt it won't eat me,' said Daisy. 'But rabbits eats grass and I 'ad a nasty nip off one of them once.'

She maintained a safe distance.

I couldn't take my eyes off the delightful creature. 'I'm happy to accept that it definitely is a quokka, but an important question remains: where did it come from?'

There was an intake of breath from both sides as they prepared to reply, but I held up my hand.

'Before you answer, do please bear in mind that the first woman to say "Australia" will find out exactly what it's like to be punched forcefully on the nose.'

Lady Hardcastle leaned over me to speak directly to Daisy. 'I already know what it's like to be punched on the nose, dear. It would definitely be best not to say "Australia" if you can bear to hold it in.'

'Duly noted, Lady H,' said Daisy with a nod. 'But she's got a point, though, a'n't she? Where *did* it come from?'

'That, my dear Daisy, is what I intend to find out. I haven't forgotten our finders-keepers agreement and you're definitely in charge, but would you object if we took it off to the vet so he could give it the once-over?'

'If you wouldn't mind doin' it, I reckon that's a good idea. I'll try to find sommat more comfy for it to live in by the time you gets back. I don't reckon our ma will want it at the house, mind, no matter what you says about it not bein' a rat, but Old Joe will come round if I tell him you says it's safe.'

'Splendid. Then we shall pop back in a while with the Rolls and take him to see Mr Pinkard at his surgery in Chipping Bevington. I'm sure it will make a nice change from farm animals and pampered pets.'

We left Daisy feeding carrot leaves to the inquisitive quokka and returned to the house for breakfast.

◆  ◆  ◆

The rain had stopped by the time we arrived at the vet's surgery on the outskirts of Chipping Bevington. Lady Hardcastle was driving while I sat in the passenger seat with the improvised quokka cage on my lap. The animal itself – warm, dry, and full of carrot tops – had fallen fast asleep.

Lady Hardcastle parked with her customary abandon and hopped out. I waited for her to come round to my door to help me out with the cumbersome cage, and then we made our way to the door together. I felt quite protective towards the vulnerable little chap so I carried the cage, leaving Lady Hardcastle with her Australian book.

We knocked, and were greeted by a handsome woman of about Pinkard's age who I assumed, with no evidence whatsoever, to be his wife.

'Good morning, welcome to Pinkard and Partners. How can we help you?' She noticed the cage in my arms. 'Is it this little chap?'

'Good morning,' said Lady Hardcastle. 'Yes, it is. A friend of ours found him in Littleton Cotterell and we wondered if Mr Pinkard would be good enough to take a look at him for us. We've no real concerns, we just want to check that he's unharmed by his ordeal.'

'Of course, come in.'

She led us through a hallway into what seemed once to have been a sitting room, but which was now lined with chairs and served as a waiting room. I had been expecting to find it full of poorly puppies and mewling cats in wicker baskets, but it was empty.

The woman smiled and gestured for us to sit. 'The vet will see you shortly.'

She retreated back to the hall and disappeared, closing the door behind her.

'This is an adventure,' said Lady Hardcastle. 'I've never been to a vet's before.'

'Nor have I,' I said. 'I'm not sure what I was expecting.'

'I thought it might be busier, certainly,' said Lady Hardcastle. 'But as for its appearance . . . it's essentially just a doctor's surgery for animals, so I suppose it oughtn't to surprise us that it looks exactly like a doctor's waiting room.'

'I suppose not.'

A door opened somewhere beyond the hall. Polite goodbyes and a thank you. Human footsteps and the snicking of claws on the tiled floor suggested that a dog and its owner were being shown out.

The door opened and a handsome head appeared.

'Would you care to come thr— Lady Hardcastle and Miss Armstrong. What a pleasant surprise. I had no idea you were pet owners. Come into my office, do.'

We stood and followed Mr Pinkard out into the hall. I carried the still-sleeping quokka through another door into a white painted room – formerly the dining room, I fancied – lined with cupboards, and a workbench filled with bottles, jars and a microscope. In the centre of the room was a waist-high examination table.

'Just pop our little friend on the table and we'll have a look, shall we? What seems to be the trouble?'

I did as he asked and he leaned in to look through the chicken wire into the cage.

He hmm'd. 'I confess I'd been expecting to see a rabbit. But that's not—' He looked again. And hmm'd again. 'How long have you owned this intriguing little creature?'

'Oh, he's not ours,' I said. 'Daisy Spratt – the barmaid at the Dog and Duck – found him hiding in the pub yard. He's a long way from home so we wanted to make sure he was all right.'

'Well, yes. Quite. Would you mind . . . ?'

He gestured to the cage door and I opened it for him. He reached in and grabbed the creature gently but firmly, pulling it out on to the table. I put the cage on the floor.

The quokka stirred slightly but didn't wake.

Pinkard examined it, lifting a limb here, pressing muscles there. He looked in its mouth and opened one of its eyes. He hmm'd as he worked. Still the quokka remained contentedly asleep.

Eventually his examination was complete. 'Well, ladies, I have to thank you. I've never seen anything quite like it. What you appear to have here is a small, female marsupial of some kind, but I'm blowed if I know what kind.'

Lady Hardcastle offered him the book. 'We think it's a quokka.'

He read the indicated pages and hmm'd a little more. 'Well I never. Yes, I agree with you – it definitely does appear to be a quokka. You found it at the village pub, you say?'

I nodded. 'Daisy found it, yes.'

'And you've no idea where it came from? Apart from Australia, of course.' He laughed.

'None whatsoever,' said Lady Hardcastle. 'That little mystery aside, though – is she well?'

'She appears perfectly healthy. She might be a little underweight, but I confess I have no idea how much fat a quokka should be carrying. For all I know they could be lean little beasts and she might be exactly the right size. She's uninjured, certainly, and I can see no obvious signs of disease.' He smiled and gently scratched the fur around her ears. 'She's a remarkable little creature. What do you intend to do with her?'

'For now we'll return her to Daisy,' I said. 'She'll take care of her at the pub.'

Lady Hardcastle nodded. 'And in the meantime, we shall make some enquiries. It's unlikely she made her own way to England, so someone will be missing her.'

'They will indeed. A rare animal like that would have cost someone a pretty penny.'

'Do you think so?' I asked.

'The trade in exotic animals is a lucrative one, Miss Armstrong, yes. I don't have much experience of it myself, but I know that they can change hands for small fortunes. It's usually larger, fiercer animals, of course. Or reptiles. Or colourful birds. But something as endearing as this would almost certainly be in demand. I can imagine a doting father buying one for his daughter as a birthday gift. If he had the oof, of course.'

'That raises the stakes a little,' said Lady Hardcastle. 'I don't like the thought of a young girl losing her precious pet. She must be heartbroken. We shall make every effort to track her down.'

'You're very kind,' said Pinkard. 'I hope you find the owners soon.'

'Thank you.' She gave him her card with a smile. 'I'm grateful for your expertise and reassurance. Please send me your bill and I'll make sure to pay it at once.'

'Nonsense,' he said. 'I did nothing but a little prodding and poking. It's not as though I'm rushed off my feet.'

'We noticed the empty waiting room,' I said as I slid the dozing quokka back into her cage.

'Indeed. Farmers are grateful for any veterinary help they can get and will gladly accept a new practitioner. Pet owners, though . . . I started a small animals surgery a few weeks ago and I've seen perhaps one or two each time. It takes people a while to get used to the idea of a new vet. At least I hope that's what it is.'

'I'm sure they'll warm to you,' said Lady Hardcastle. 'We shall certainly be singing your praises.'

'I say – thank you. Between that and the chance to examine such an unusual animal, I'd say you've definitely paid for what limited services I offered today.'

There was another round of thank-yous, followed by some goodbyes and hopes that we might all meet again soon, and then we were back in the Rolls and heading for Littleton Cotterell.

◆ ◆ ◆

We pulled up outside the Dog and Duck to find that Daisy had just finished setting up a large rabbit hutch on a trestle table in the pub's yard.

Lady Hardcastle and I clumsily disembarked and carried the small cage to the table to introduce our tiny friend to her more luxurious accommodation.

'Hello again, ladies,' said Daisy, looking down at the sleeping quokka. 'What did the vet say?'

I unlatched the cage and lifted her gently out. 'He said she's fine as far as he could tell, but that he doesn't really know very much about marsupials.'

'She?'

'Yes,' said Lady Hardcastle. 'What you have there is a seemingly healthy lady quokka. And a very sleepy one.'

Daisy nodded. 'Well, she's nocturnal, i'n't she?'

It was my turn to be surprised. 'Is she?'

'It says so in your book.'

I hadn't read the whole page. 'Oh, yes, of course it does. I'm sorry. Yes. Nocturnal.'

Lady Hardcastle rolled her eyes. 'That's a fine quokka palace you have there, Daisy.'

'Me and our Wilf used to have a pet rabbit each, and they lived in this in our back garden. Our ma kept it when they died, "just in case we ever needs it again". I reckon she was more upset by their passin' than we were.'

'Well, it's a good thing she did – this will be perfect for little . . . little . . . actually, that's a point, what *is* she called?'

'Well, I thought she was a boy so I've been thinkin' of her as Alfred. You know, after that Australian tennis player.'

'Dunlop?' I asked.

'That's the one. But now I know she's a girl I reckon we ought to call her . . . oh, I know: Matilda.'

'A fine Australian name for a beautiful Australian girl,' said Lady Hardcastle.

Daisy held the hutch door open while I placed Matilda on to the straw with which Daisy had thoughtfully lined the sleeping compartment. We checked that the water and food were within reach if Matilda should wake from her sleep in need of refreshment, and left her to snooze.

Back inside the pub, Daisy resumed her post behind the bar and we took up our customary positions propping up the other side.

'Do you have any sandwiches, Daisy dear?' asked Lady Hardcastle.

'We gots beef, ham or cheese. But I don't recommend the cheese – it's gone quite 'ard. And the ham is fatty.'

'Two beef, then, if you please. Do you want a drink, Flossie?'

'I'll have a cordial,' I said. 'Whatever you have, please, Dais.'

'We gots lime, elderflower, or some grim-lookin' sarsaparilla like always. We've 'ad it for years and nobody drinks it. Oh, there's ginger beer, o' course.'

'Actually, that sounds good. I like your ginger beer.'

'Joe just made a fresh batch. It's very popular. Your pal's drinkin' it.'

'My pal?'

'Your newspaper pal. Good-lookin' posh lady. Dresses like she's goin' to the Grand for lunch with the mayor.'

'Dinah Caudle?'

'That's her. I knew she was Dinah but I kept wantin' to say Corker.'

'Has she been here long?' asked Lady Hardcastle.

'Not long, no. She come in askin' for you just afore I went out to see to the 'utch. She's in the snug.'

We took our drinks through to the snug, where the impeccably dressed Dinah Caudle was leafing through her notebook, a glass of ginger beer on the table in front of her. She had the small room to herself.

She looked up as we entered. 'Ah, there you are. I've been looking for you.'

'Hello, dear,' said Lady Hardcastle. 'Sorry about that – we've been to the vet's.'

'So Daisy said. She told me some improbable story about a rat who looks like a kangaroo and won't stop smiling at her. I've heard her tall tales before so I didn't take her entirely seriously.'

'In this instance at least,' I said, 'she was telling the unembellished truth.'

We sat and quickly recounted the tale of the quokka. We also confirmed Daisy's assertion that it seemed to be smiling all the time.

Miss Caudle made some notes. 'How utterly enchanting. You must let me see it later.'

'She's asleep outside,' I said. 'We can pop out after lunch. Have you eaten?'

'I ordered a ham sandwich some while ago but it has yet to arrive.'

'Excellent choice,' said Lady Hardcastle.

'I hope so. Daisy said it was nice and fatty. But fatty ham and' – she looked down at her notebook to check the word as though she, too, didn't believe it was real – 'quokkas aren't the reason for my visit. I belatedly come in response to your summons of last week.'

'It was hardly a summons, dear. We just thought you might like the inside gen on the local murder story.'

'Always. And what do you have for me there? Sim has given me the official version, but his stories can be a bit dreary sometimes. He's always full of equivocation and "in my capacity as police surgeon". I love him dearly and I can't wait to marry the stupid man. But . . . I mean. Really. He has no sense of drama.'

Between us, Lady Hardcastle and I ran her through the salient details of the killing of Sid Hyde, and added some colour by describing the attack on Dick Durbin and Felix Kiddle.

Miss Caudle seemed pleased. 'That's more like it. Simeon just wittered on about wound patterns and made some jokes about Ollie Sunderland that I didn't understand. He did talk about a mint-flavoured dog, but I'd lost patience with his foolishness by then.'

I laughed. 'Mrs Adaway's dog – the one who was guarding the injured gamekeeper – is burdened with the name Lady Araminta Fluffikins. Minty to her friends.'

'Ohh,' said Miss Caudle. 'That makes a great deal more sense. I'm sure I can fashion all this into a much more engaging story. Thank you, ladies.'

'Entirely our pleasure, dear,' said Lady Hardcastle. 'Keep our names out, though, would you?'

'As you wish. Though our readers would very much enjoy reading more about your exploits. You're quite the celebrities in Bristol, you know.'

'I do know. And that's the problem. It was a lark when we first came out to Littleton Cotterell. Amateur sleuths bringing justice to rural n'er-do-wells and all that. But since my brother tempted us back into working for the SSB I can't help but feel we ought to keep a lower profile. It's hard to keep the work of the Secret Service Bureau secret if its officers are in the newspapers all the time.'

'You make a compelling point. I shall omit you as much as I can. Unless you do something exciting and heroic, of course.'

Lady Hardcastle smiled. 'You must do what you feel is best, dear, of course. One wouldn't want to be accused of trying to control the press.'

'There is another point of view,' I said. 'You could see our local notoriety as a perfect cover. We've become known as two amateur detectives, getting into scrapes and helping the rozzers bring criminals to justice – no one would ever suspect that we were working for the government. Isn't that how you used to work with your husband? While he was busy being a diplomat, you were the flighty socialite hosting all the parties and being seen at all the right places. And all the while you were spying for the Crown.'

'She makes a compelling point, too, Emily,' said Miss Caudle. 'No one would ever suspect what you really get up to.'

Lady Hardcastle sighed. 'I suppose so. But if you do have to mention us, don't go overboard.'

'Duly noted, darling. But you do get into some entertaining scrapes.'

Daisy brought our sandwiches just as two farmers' wives joined us in the snug, and we switched to less private topics of conversation as we ate.

We were contentedly munching our doorstops when one of the wives leaned over towards our table.

''Scuse me, Miss Armstrong, but do you have any idea why Joe's got a rabbit hutch out in the yard? He's not goin' to be servin' rabbit, is he? Be cheaper to get my Benny to shoot him some. They's a right nuisance on our land – diggin' up all our cabbages.'

'It's Daisy's,' I said. 'She thought there was a rat in the yard but it turned out to be a rare Australian animal called a quokka. She's taking care of it until we can find its owner.'

Both women laughed.

'A what-a?' said the other one. 'You's 'avin' us on.'

'No,' I said. 'That's really what it is. We had it confirmed by Mr Pinkard in Chipping Bevington this morning.'

'Well I never,' said the first. 'It's all strange animals round 'ere these days, i'n't it? First there's the tiger—'

'Panther,' said her friend.

'What did I say?'

'Tiger. They's the ones with the stripes. This'n was black.'

'A black tiger? Don't talk daft.'

'Not a black tiger, a panther.'

'Oh. I see. Well, first there's the *panther*, then this quokka thing. And last night my Geoffrey and his little pals was playin' out over by the woods t'other side of Toby Thompson's place. You'll never credit what he says they saw.'

'And what was that?' I asked.

'A dragon.'

Lady Hardcastle almost choked on her sandwich. 'A dragon?'

'He swears it. I told 'im not to go makin' up stupid stories, not when people have died, but he's adamant. "Ma," he says, "I know what we seen, and we seen a fire-breathin' dragon." To be fair to the lad, he's not usually one for makin' up stories, so I reckon they did see sommat up there.'

# Chapter Eleven

When we finally finished lunch it was almost two o'clock. We took Miss Caudle to the yard to show her Matilda and she made appropriate cooing noises.

'She's quite the most enchanting little thing, isn't she? I wish we had an illustrated edition – I'd have a photographer out here like a shot. If we had a photographer.'

We left the quokka to her quokka-ing and started to think about going home, but found ourselves in a familiar pickle with the car. Miss Caudle had left her own car at the house so we all needed to get back there, but the three of us wouldn't fit into the two-seater.

The solution was obvious – we would walk home together and then Miss Caudle would bring one of us back to the pub to collect the Rolls. It involved more faffing than I would have preferred – I was certain I'd be the one to have to fetch our car – but it was nice to see Dinah again so perhaps it was worth it.

As we passed the post office, Lady Hardcastle touched Miss Caudle's arm and brought us all to a halt. 'How do you fancy another mystifying tale of village life? You could make a series of it.'

'I do love a quirky story,' said Miss Caudle. 'What do you have for me?'

'Come into the post office and meet Bessie Talbot.'

We found the postmistress dejectedly sorting through a pile of letters on the counter.

She looked up as we entered. 'Good afternoon, ladies. What can I do for you? More misdelivered post, is it?'

'Actually, no. At least I don't think so. Although we did leave the house before Wilf arrived so I can't be certain. Actually, I'd like to introduce you to a friend of ours. Bessie, this is our good friend Miss Dinah Caudle of the *Bristol News*. Dinah, this is Mrs Bessie Talbot, Littleton Cotterell's new postmistress.'

The two women how-do-you-do'd and shook hands.

'Please feel free to tell me I'm wrong,' continued Lady Hardcastle, 'but I thought you might be interested in telling Dinah about the strange goings-on here at the post office. I wondered if making the story public might help you get to the bottom of it. Or at least make it stop.'

Bessie thought for a moment. 'That's a kind thought, but I's worried it might reflect badly on us. It's bad enough the people of the village knowin' we can't get the post right every day, without the whole of Bristol knowin' it, too. Head Office might not look too kindly on us if they finds out we's been messin' things up so badly.'

'That's always a worry,' said Miss Caudle. 'But why don't you tell me the story so far and I'll see if there's a way of telling it without making you look bad? If I can't, there's no need for me to print anything. Honestly, Mrs Talbot, with the murder, the animal attacks and Daisy's peculiar marsupial, I've quite enough already to fill a couple of weeks' worth of columns. And that's before we even get to the dragon in the woods.'

'Dragon?' said Bessie.

'Oh, it's nothing,' said Lady Hardcastle. 'Just a fancy a few of the local boys dreamed up.'

Miss Caudle nodded. 'Almost certainly. But if I *can* think of the right way of telling your story, it might work just as Emily says: it might help to put an end to . . . whatever it is.'

Bessie looked momentarily confused as she tried to work out who this Emily character might be, but Lady Hardcastle's encouraging smile helped the penny to drop.

'Well,' she said, 'it all started last Monday . . .'

For the next few minutes, Bessie outlined the events surrounding the Mixed-Up Post of 1912. She explained how everything had been sorted properly, then delivered to entirely the wrong addresses. She told Miss Caudle about the complaints from the villagers – some of which had been rather rudely expressed – and about the repeated changes she had made to her working habits in an effort to stop the errors. She dismissed the idea that Wilf, the local postman, might be incompetently messing things up – he took too much pride in his work to do anything like that. Finally she included the purely speculative suggestion that it might be disgruntled local grocer Hilda Pantry, who had wanted to take over the post office herself.

'. . . she's a grumpy old girl, but I don't reckon she'd stoop to this. I still think it's local kids messin' about, but I'm at my wits' end trying to work out how they's gettin' away with it.'

'What a palaver,' said Miss Caudle. 'You have my every sympathy. For the moment, I'm not certain it will make a good newspaper story. Our readers will expect the explanation in the final paragraph, you see? They'll not be patient enough to wait a week or more for the rest of the story to unfold. But if you do come up with a solution, it will make a splendid little piece. Everyone loves a peculiar story like that.'

Lady Hardcastle had been thinking. 'I'm sure you've already considered it, Bessie, but is there no way you or Mr Talbot could keep an eye on the post until it's time for Wilf to put it in his trusty bag?'

'We've done our best, Lady Hardcastle, we really has, but there's always so much else to do. Eventually one of us has to leave it unattended, and then whoever it is sneaks in and works their mischief. I just doesn't know what to do.'

I, too, had been thinking. 'If you'd be prepared to supply me with a flask of tea and a round or two of sandwiches, I'd be more than happy to spend the night hiding in here somewhere and keeping an eye on things. I'm sure I'll be able to spot the culprit.'

'That's very generous of you, m'dear, but the post don't get here from Chippin' till about four in the mornin'. That's when it all happens. You'd be sat there all night for nothin'.'

'Not for nothing. If I came over at four when the post arrived, I'd be seen by whoever's doing this. But if I'd been here since before bedtime, no one would suspect a thing. I'd be Johnny-on-the-spot, as my American friend says, and I'd catch them in the act.'

'You'd do that for us?' said Bessie.

'Of course. I'm as keen as anyone to find out what's going on here. But, as I say, it'll cost you tea and sandwiches.'

'I'll throw in a slice of cake if you solves it for us.'

With that, it was agreed. We made the arrangements and then took Miss Caudle back to the house.

Miss Caudle stayed with us for a couple of hours, chatting, drinking tea, and, I strongly suspected, just hiding out to avoid having to go back to the office. Still, it was nice to catch up and we made some important arrangements for the future.

Lady Hardcastle's birthday was a few weeks away so we extracted a promise that Miss Caudle and her fiancé, Dr Gosling, would come to dinner with us at our favourite Bristol restaurant, Le Quai. I'd already been in touch with Inspector Sunderland's wife, Dolly, and she had assured me that she would be coming, as had our friend Lady Bickle. They were each in charge of ensuring that their husbands would also be present – there was never any point in trying to arrange these things with the men themselves.

With these important arrangements made, and all gossip properly shared, we finally bid Miss Caudle farewell.

'Do you want a lift into the village to collect your car?' she asked.

I shook my head. 'No, I think I'd rather we left it by the pub. I might be glad of it in the morning.'

She pootled off in her little red Rover 6 and we went back inside, where we set about making our plans for the evening.

Dinner was in hand – Miss Jones had made a mutton pie – so it only remained for us to make preparations for my night at the post office.

'You'll need to be warmly dressed,' said Lady Hardcastle. 'I'll wager the post office can get a bit chilly in the wee small hours, especially if you're sitting still.'

'I have an extra cardigan and woollen stockings.'

'Splendid. And you'd benefit from something to sit on.'

'I imagine the Talbots could spare a kitchen chair for someone keeping watch on their post.'

'A nice cushion would make it more comfortable.'

'It would. And I could take that travel rug we never remember we own.'

She smiled. 'You'll be so snug you'll fall fast asleep and miss everything.'

'It wouldn't be the first time. Do you remember when we were trying to catch that chap in Paris? I was off in the land of Nod by the time he showed up to break in to the embassy.'

'But we still caught him. I say, are you armed?'

I frowned. 'I don't think Hilda Pantry will put up much of a fight. And I'm sure people would think badly of me if I should start throwing knives at the local youngsters.'

'But still. One never knows. It might be neither of those. It might be a big, burly farmer armed with a shotgun.'

I rolled my eyes. 'Or a panther. Or a drink-addled quokka, bent on revenge against the GPO for losing her birthday cards. I'll make sure I have a blade up my sleeve.'

'That's a good girl. Can you do some mashed potato to go with that pie, please?'

◆ ◆ ◆

After pie, mash, peas and gravy, I packed a Gladstone bag with some essentials and strapped a sheathed knife to my right forearm. We sat together in the drawing room, speculating endlessly and pointlessly on recent events until finally it was time for me to leave.

I pulled on my overcoat and slipped out into the cold October night.

Bessie Talbot welcomed me with the promised flask of tea and two rounds of sandwiches wrapped in greaseproof paper. She even gave me the cake she'd promised, then she and Jimmy retired for the night to leave me to my lonely vigil.

Between us we had built a hide for me from packing crates in the corner of the room behind the counter. I had an excellent view of the counter itself, and of the pigeonholes behind it, and there I sat, on one of the Talbots' kitchen chairs, grateful for my cushion and my travel rug, and trying not to fall asleep.

I mused for a while on the unjust world that always saw me as the one to sit alone in the dark, watching for things that might not happen, and wondered when the revolution might come.

My next ponderings were on the wisdom or otherwise of having forty winks. On the one hand, staying awake might enable me to see if anyone sneaked into the room before the post arrived – it would explain why Bessie never heard anyone enter, if they came in while the Talbots were asleep. On the other hand, the mischief couldn't be mischiefed until after the post had first been sorted, so it would be just as useful, if not more so, to be rested and wide awake by the time the delivery arrived from Chipping.

I went over and over this quite a few times and reached no satisfactory conclusion. But suddenly Lady Hardcastle was leading a revolutionary army of panthers and drunken quokkas, while Mrs Adaway was harangued by a giant Bichon Frisé who was outraged at being known as Minty and wanted to go by her real name, Dr Véronique Plouffe of the Société astronomique de France.

If I'd been awake, I'd have known I was dreaming.

I woke with a start when Bessie unbolted the post office door, but a quick glance around the room showed that there were no intruders and that nothing had been interfered with.

She returned with a sack of mail and brought it back through the hatch to the space behind the counter.

Our agreement had been that she wouldn't acknowledge me in any way once I was concealed, so that anyone keeping an eye on the place wouldn't be aware I was there. Still, it seemed odd to ignore her, so I gave her a little wave and she smiled in return.

I opened the flask and poured a cup of tea, which I sipped gratefully. I was surprisingly hungry, too, and ate a little of the sandwich and cake while I watched Bessie carefully but quickly sort the post into the pigeonholes. It took about twenty minutes and there didn't seem to be any major problems. Once she was finished, she took a large ledger from under the counter and made entries on several pages.

Her work done, she settled on a stool and sat for a while drinking her own cup of tea. This is what we'd imagined she would do – sort the post and then keep an eye on things until Wilf the postman arrived to bag it and deliver it.

But then came the interruption she'd talked about. Husband Jimmy appeared at the office door behind her and asked for some help. She got up and went with him, leaving the post unattended.

I watched.

A clock ticked. Somehow I'd not noticed it before, but now I could hear nothing else.

*Tick.*

*Tock.*

Then another sound. Another sort of ticking, but out of time with the steady beat of the clock.

I had a good view of the whole area and was quickly able to locate the source of the new sound.

A scarlet macaw was making its way along the work surface that ran beneath the pigeonholes, its claws clicking on the wood as it went. Its movement was calm and unhurried, and it seemed very much at home.

The parrot strutted coolly along the shelf, stopping occasionally to look about as though checking that all was in order. Then, using its beak to pull itself up, it climbed the rack of pigeonholes and began systematically pulling the sorted letters out and dropping them on the worktop.

With this first task completed, it hopped down and began picking up the letters one by one and putting them back in the holes.

It took a while, especially as it insisted on climbing rather than flying, but after about a quarter of an hour the letters had all been re-sorted, and the parrot, clearly considering it a job well done, rewarded itself with one of the walnuts from Bessie's bowl. It cracked the nut with its bolt-cutter beak, ate the wrinkled kernel, and then strutted off once more to its hiding place behind some directories in the corner of the room.

I came out from my own hiding place and followed the bird's path to the directories. It was not, as I had thought, a hidden nest, but a hidden hole in the wall, which the macaw was using as its own private door to the post office.

I bent to look out through the hole and saw a bead-like eye looking back in.

'Good morning, Mr Parrot. Would you care to come back in and introduce yourself?'

The eye disappeared briefly, only to be replaced by the other eye. It regarded me curiously.

'Come on, Mr Parrot. You've been working so hard. I'd like to meet you.'

The parrot cocked its head. 'Bradley and Stoke's.'

'I beg your pardon?'

'Beg your pardon. Bradley and Stoke's.'

I'd heard talking parrots before, but this was oddly disquieting. Bradley and Stoke's was the name of the circus that Lady Hardcastle's friend Colonel Dawlish had taken over in 1908.

'Do you know Colonel Dawlish?' I asked.

The eye just looked at me. It blinked.

I wanted the bird to come back in, but it clearly wouldn't respond to my verbal commands. I needed something to tempt it.

I looked around and noticed the bowl of walnuts. It had already helped itself to one, so it clearly liked them. Perhaps it wasn't too full to want another.

I picked up a nut and held it within view of the hole in the wall.

'Can I interest you in a walnut, Mr Parrot?'

'Lovely nuts, all the way from Brazil.'

'Actually, I think they grow here in England but you'd have to ask Lady Hardcastle – she's the one who knows about trees.'

I continued to hold up the nut, and the parrot continued to look at me and my tempting treat.

Eventually it seemed to decide that free food was free food, regardless of the provenance, and hopped up to return through the hole. It came towards me, not cautiously as I had expected, but with quiet avian confidence. Even by the dim lamplight I could see it was a beautiful creature. Its head and chest were bright scarlet and its face white. The red feathers across its shoulders gave way to yellow, then blue at the tips of its wings. Its long red tail dragged along the shelf behind it.

It took the nut. 'Thank you.'

It seemed odd at first that it could talk with its mouth full, but then I supposed it wasn't really 'talking' at all. Once again it cracked the nut and helped itself to the kernel.

While it was eating, I took the opportunity to grab another nut. I was distracted briefly by a memory of one of Lady Hardcastle's lectures where she'd explained that walnuts weren't nuts at all, but seeds. The seeds of drupes, she'd said. In the same conversation I'd also learned that tomatoes were berries but that strawberries were not. She did tell me what they were, but my mind had drifted long before the explanation.

Mr Parrot had finished his walnut.

'Would you like another?' I asked, holding it up.

He walked towards me and I positioned my forearm between us. He hopped on as though I were a perch. His claws looked sharp, but he was resting on the knife sheath beneath my sleeve so I couldn't feel them. He was surprisingly light, and surprisingly willing just to sit there.

I stood and we made our way towards the office door.

'Godspeed,' said the parrot.

'Thank you,' I replied. 'And to you.'

I knocked and opened the door with my free hand.

'I'm sorry to interrupt,' I said, 'but you have a visitor.'

I walked in and the Talbots, who had been poring over a pile of densely printed forms together, looked up.

'Oh, my word,' said Bessie. 'What have you got there?'

'That's a scarlet macaw, that is,' said Jimmy. 'A parrot. Do you remember old Mrs Dunlop? She used to live across the street from our ma. She had one – her son brought it back from Brazil. He was in the merchant navy, see?'

'Well I never.'

Jimmy looked at me. 'Can it talk?'

I nodded. 'I believe it can. It told me about Brazil nuts and wished me godspeed.'

'Godspeed,' said the parrot.

'You see? It seemed to say something else, but I'm not sure quite what it was. It *sounded* like something very familiar, but I can't believe it really was that. I think my mind must have just made some unintelligible sounds into words for me.'

They looked at the parrot. The lamps were less bright in the parlour-cum-office, but even so, we could all see how magnificent the macaw was.

'Oh,' said Bessie suddenly. 'But who's guardin' the post? You's in here with our parrot friend, so what's happenin' to the post?'

'I don't think you need to worry about the post while I have Mr Parrot with me. This' – I held up the bird on my arm – 'is the mysterious mail mixer-upper.'

They both looked at me blankly and I told them what I had just seen.

They continued to look at me blankly.

'I have no idea why, but it seems to be very keen on the idea of taking letters out of the pigeonholes and then putting them back. Mr Parrot has been quietly re-sorting your post for almost two weeks.'

'But how did it get in?' asked Bessie.

'There's a hole in the wall behind some big books in the corner. He just hops in and out through there. Is that an outside wall?'

'No,' said Jimmy. 'That goes through to the storeroom. I saw someone had knocked a hole through there when we moved in. I been meanin' to fix it, but I thought p'raps they done it for a reason. I couldn't think what, mind, but no one knocks holes in walls for fun. That's the door to it over there, look.' He pointed to the corner of the room. 'Your parrot there must have found its way into the storeroom from outside, then come through to investigate. It's a beautiful bird, i'n't it?'

Bessie tutted. 'Beautiful or not, it's been causin' me no end of trouble this past couple of weeks. You keep it here while I goes and sorts the post again.'

She bustled through to the post office, leaving Jimmy and me to admire the parrot and speculate on where it might have come from. It was perfectly happy to sit on my arm and seemed very interested in our conversation.

I didn't want to leave the mischievous bird unattended while Wilf came to collect the post, so I waited with the Talbots until I thought Edna might have arrived at the house, then asked if I might use the telephone to call her.

The telephone rang for a long while.

Eventually someone picked up the earpiece. 'Hello,' said an only dimly familiar woman's voice. 'Lady Hardcastle's residence.'

'Edna?' I said. 'Is that you?'

'Oh, Miss Armstrong,' said Edna in her normal voice. 'Thank gawd. It is me, yes.'

'What was that voice you were doing?'

'What voice?'

'When you answered the telephone. I didn't recognize you.'

'I thought you might be someone important. I didn't want to give the wrong impression. You knows I hates these things.'

'I'm glad you answered it, though. Thank you. I want you to do a couple of things for me, please. I'm at the post office with Bessie and Jimmy, so I shan't be able to prepare Herself's starter breakfast. Can you take care of that for me?'

'Of course I can. What else?'

'Do you by any chance know anyone who has a parrot cage?'

'A what? It's a bad line. I thought you said "parrot cage".'

'I did. Do you know anyone who has one?'

'I does as a matter of fact. Why?'

'Can you fetch it and bring it here?'

'I reckon so. What should I tell Lady H?'

'Tell her I've solved the mystery and that I'll see her soon.'

Bessie made me some toast and tea while we waited for Edna, and both she and Jimmy continued to be effusive in their thanks. I didn't point out that either of them could have done what I'd done – it was nice to be appreciated.

It didn't take Edna long to find whoever it was that owned an empty parrot cage, and she was soon knocking on the door.

I could hear her from the parlour.

'Hello, my lover. I gots a parrot cage for you like Miss Armstrong said. What do you want it for?'

'Come this way,' said Bessie. There was a pause while Bessie led Edna through, then she said, 'We wants it for the parrot.'

I held up the amiable bird, who regarded Edna quizzically for a moment and then said, 'Tickets three shillings.'

'Well I never,' said Edna.

'He's a cheerful soul,' I said, 'but he does like to play with letters, so I think we ought to find him somewhere else to live until we can discover who he belongs to.'

'Whom,' said the parrot.

I raised an eyebrow. 'Don't you start. I get enough of this at home.'

'Come home, Bill Bailey.'

'Talkative little fella, innum,' said Edna.

'He does seem to enjoy a chat,' I said. 'Shall we?'

I gestured to the cage with my free hand and Edna opened the door.

The parrot gave a little flap of his large wings in response and craned towards the cage.

I moved my arm towards it, and as soon as he was able, he hopped inside and closed the door behind him with his beak.

'Night night,' he said, and pulled himself up on to the perch.

'Well I never,' said Edna again.

I smile-frowned. 'That was easier than I was expecting. But let's not look a gift parrot in the beak.'

'What's he doin' here?' asked Edna as the parrot started preening.

Bessie and I told her the story of his capture, and she chuckled along as we described the chaos caused by one troublesome bird.

'If I'd had a million years I'd never have guessed it was a parrot doin' it,' she said when we were finished. 'I thought it was Hilda Pantry.'

'You weren't alone,' I said. 'But it turns out it was this colourful chap.'

'Pretty colours,' said the parrot.

I could see that the Talbots, though extremely grateful, were also keen to be left alone to get on with their parrot-free work.

I patted my thighs and stood. 'Well, we'd better be going. Thank you for the tea and toast, Bessie and Jimmy, we'll leave you to get on. I hope it'll be more straightforward with this troublesome little chap out of the way.'

'Thank you for findin' him, m'dear,' said Bessie. 'I shan't know meself without him interferin' with my sortin'.'

'I shan't know meself without the missus endlessly complainin' about the sortin',' said Jimmy with a grin.

'Cheeky blighter.'

I followed Edna to the door.

'Bye, m'dears,' she said.

Outside, she started to walk towards the lane.

'The Rolls is just there,' I said, pointing towards the car parked outside the pub. 'No sense in carrying our feathered friend all the way to the house when we can all ride in comfort.'

'Oh. In the motor car? Do you know, in all these years I a'n't never been in your motor car.'

I stopped and turned. 'What about that time I took you home because Dan was poorly and you wanted to get him his lunch?'

'Oh, yes. I'd forgotten that.'

'Or that time I drove you to Chipping to pick up that cloth you wanted for your curtains?'

'And then, too.'

'Or—'

Edna laughed. 'Turns out I've been in it quite a lot.'

'Apparently you have, yes.' I indicated the cage and its contented occupant. 'Will you be all right with that on your lap?'

'I reckon.'

As we neared the Rolls, we were passed by Mickey Yawn and Olive Churches. They gave us a cheery good morning.

'And good morning to you, too,' I said. 'You're out and about early.'

Mickey grinned. 'Got a job, a'n't I? Labourin' for Sam Hardiman again. He's doin' some buildin' work over t'other side of the village.'

'I thought you were working for Angelina Goodacre and her bicycle business.'

'I am, but things gets quiet this time of year so she don't 'ave so much for me to do. I'm takin' on labourin' work to keep the wolf from the door, like.'

'Sounds like you're working hard.'

'I'm savin' up. Want to set up me own bike shop.'

'Good for you. I wish you the best of luck with it.'

'And I's his moral support,' said Olive.

'Immoral support, more like,' said Edna under her breath.

Mickey didn't seem to hear. 'What you got there?'

'It's the parrot who's been causing all the trouble at the post office,' I said.

He came to look closer. 'I bet he's worth a few bob.'

'I bet he is,' I said. 'So we're going to try to find out who he belongs to – they'll be missing him.'

Mickey was intrigued, but Olive was hanging back. 'Come on, Mickey, we gots to go. Don't want to be late on your second day.'

With a grin, Mickey allowed himself to be dragged away.

Once they were gone, we boarded the Silver Ghost and drove the half a mile to the house with both Edna and the bird chattering to me. If anyone had asked, I'd have been hard-pressed to say which of them made the most sense.

I parked neatly on our improvised drive and helped Edna from the car.

As we approached the front door, she said, 'I don't think I've ever gone in through your front door.'

'What about—'

She was laughing as I led her inside.

'We're home,' I called.

Lady Hardcastle emerged from her study and stood admiring the handsome macaw.

'I say. What a magnificent bird.'

'Godspeed. Beautiful bird,' said the parrot.

'Beautiful indeed,' said Lady Hardcastle.

Edna put the cage down on the table.

'Thank you for your help,' I said. 'I'm not sure what I'd have done without the cage.'

'My pleasure, m'dear. You don't mind if I gets on now, though, do you? I gots to get the upstairs cleaned today.'

'Of course, Edna dear,' said Lady Hardcastle. 'But you'll be mentioned in dispatches for cage acquisition above and beyond the call of duty.'

'It belongs to our neighbour. She had a cockatoo. Lived more than fifty years, it did. Got it from her uncle when she was a little girl. She was devastated when it passed but she don't want another one 'cos it would outlive her. She keeps the cage to remind her of her old pal.'

'And she shall have it back with our grateful thanks as soon as we've worked out what to do with the bird.'

'There's no need to rush. I reckon she'll be glad it's bein' put to good use.'

'Good use indeed. Our guest seems to be quite contented there. Are you comfortable, Mr Parrot?'

'Bradley and Stoke's. Comfortable seats. Only three shillings.'

Edna had just set off for the kitchen, but stopped and turned. 'Wasn't that the name of the circus that came to the village in '08? Your friend Colonel Dawlish, wasn't it?'

'It was indeed. Bradley and Stoke's Circus. I say, Flossie, you don't suppose . . . ?'

'I've started wondering the same thing. But shall we discuss it over breakfast? I'd like to get washed and changed before we eat – I feel like I've slept in these clothes. Mostly because I have.'

'Of course, dear. I'll draft a telegram to George asking him if he's lost a parrot. Though goodness alone knows how it would have got here.'

'Perhaps it's a homin' parrot,' said Edna over her shoulder. 'Flew away and come back to a place where it was happy. We had a grand old time when the circus came to the village.'

'Apart from all the murders,' I said.

'Ach, there's always murders. You has to take the rough with the smooth.'

With that she was gone.

I went upstairs for a much-needed wash and brush-up while Lady Hardcastle wrote her telegram.

Feeling restored, or so I thought, I came back down for breakfast and volunteered to take Lady Hardcastle's telegram to the post office as soon as we'd finished – I was keen to let the Talbots know we were already trying to find out where the parrot had come from.

Lady Hardcastle, though, took one look at me and declared me unfit for duty, and ordered me to go straight back to bed.

'Edna can drop the telegram form off at the post office on her way home,' she said. 'You need forty winks. At least. More like fifty, from the state of you.'

I acquiesced.

A couple of hours later, invigorated by sleep and another wash, I came down to see if there was anything to eat. It was too late for breakfast and too early for lunch, so it would have to be brunch.

As I sat down to eat the sausage sandwiches made for me by a bemused Miss Jones – she had spent some time talking to the parrot and was very taken with him – Lady Hardcastle suggested we take another journey over to Chipping Bevington to see Pinkard and get his opinion on the health of the bird.

'He seems perfectly well to me,' I said as I munched enthusiastically on the sandwich. 'Is it really worth bothering him?'

'No one minds being bothered by things that involve being paid for their time, dear – it's how they make their money. And I feel we owe it to the owners to ensure their precious bird is well cared for.'

'As you wish. And if he does belong to Colonel Dawlish, I'm sure he'll appreciate our taking proper care of his parrot for him.'

'Exactly.'

With sandwich and coffee consumed, and hat and coat re-donned, I was ready for our return to the vet's office. I persuaded Lady Hardcastle to drive, arguing that I was still too sleepy to be entirely safe on the road.

Mrs Pinkard let us in again. She gave the caged macaw a bemused look, but made no comment, instead politely inviting us to take seats in the waiting room.

Mr Pinkard seemed equally entertained to see us.

'Good morning, ladies,' he said. 'How splendid to see you both again. And with a bird this time. You're becoming quite the collectors of zoological exotica.'

Lady Hardcastle smiled. 'Good morning, Mr Pinkard. Yes, we do appear to be, don't we? This is another unexpected recent arrival at Littleton Cotterell. We wondered if you'd care to give him a quick once-over to make sure he's well enough to withstand a week or two in our care while we search for his owners.'

'It would be entirely my pleasure. It makes a definite change from quivering lapdogs and lame cattle.'

The parrot exited the cage with the same graceful calm with which he had entered, and stood patiently on the examination table while Pinkard looked him over.

'A male bird,' he said. 'I would estimate about twenty years old. He seems used to being handled, and he's very obviously been well looked after. I see no signs of any disease or malnutrition. Where exactly did you find him?'

'He was sorting letters at the post office,' I said.

Pinkard smiled. 'Was he, indeed? I admire an enterprising individual who's prepared to work for a living. Was he eating?'

'Stealing walnuts from the postmistress.'

'Resourceful, too.' He finished his examination. 'Not the best diet for him, but it's kept him going. He might need a little more to drink, but other than that you have a very healthy bird on your hands.'

'And what *should* we feed him?'

'Fruit and vegetables would be his natural diet. And a few walnuts now and again since he seems to like them so much. Avoid mushrooms, onions and beans.'

'That sounds straightforward enough,' said Lady Hardcastle. 'Thank you.'

'As I said, my lady, it's entirely my pleasure. He's a spectacular bird. I should think—'

'Bradley and Stoke's. Spectacular shows. Tickets from sixpence.'

'Good heavens. What was that all about?'

'We're wondering if he might belong to a friend of ours at Bradley and Stoke's Circus,' said Lady Hardcastle. 'He certainly seems to know the ticket prices. All the way from sixpence to three bob, apparently.'

'Best seats, three bob,' said the macaw.

'You see? The problem is that the circus overwinters in Dorset, so we've no idea how he can have come this far north.'

Pinkard chuckled. 'Well, parrots *can* fly.'

'That's the only explanation we've come up with so far. But we shall see. I've sent a telegram to my friend and we'll keep Mr Parrot at the house for the time being. Even if he's not from the circus, someone will be missing him.'

'Much like your quokka.'

'Indeed.'

'And how's she?'

'She seemed well enough when we dropped her back at the Dog and Duck. Perhaps we should open a temporary menagerie at Littleton Cotterell.'

Pinkard smiled. 'Perhaps you should at that. And what about Mrs Adaway's little Minty?'

'We've not seen her for a couple of days, but I'm sure she'll outlive us all. They probably both will.'

I opened the cage door and, once again, the parrot strutted inside and closed the door behind him.

'Remarkable,' said Pinkard. 'Such clever birds.'

'Clever boy,' said the parrot.

We thanked Mr Pinkard for his expert advice and made our way back out on to the street, having first asked Mrs Pinkard to be sure to send us their bill.

Time for home and another nap.

# Chapter Twelve

I was dozing in the drawing room, dreaming about my desperate need for a nap, when I became aware of a ringing sound. Quite pleasant at first, but then more insistent, as though the bell were annoyed with me.

It was the sound of the front door and women's voices that woke me.

Edna appeared in the drawing room. 'Sorry to disturb you, Miss Armstrong, but Mrs Adaway has called for Lady Hardcastle. But Herself's in the orangery and I doesn't like to go in there. Would you mind . . . ?'

I was still struggling to full wakefulness, but I managed to stand. 'Of course. Show her in here and get the kettle on, would you? I'll nip out and tell Herself we have company.'

Edna returned to the front door while I scooted out through the boot room to the orangery.

Lady Hardcastle had set up a photographic studio in the orangery when we first moved in, and used it to make what she called 'animated moving pictures'. Things had been rather hectic for the past year, so progress on her latest project was slow, but she had clearly taken advantage of my nap to sneak off and do some more work on it.

I opened the door and called out. 'Are you in here? We have a visitor.'

There was a clatter, a thud, and some extremely fruity language before Lady Hardcastle appeared, dressed in her workman's overalls and with a diagonal smear of purple paint right across her face.

'A visitor? A friend visitor or a put-on-some-decent-clothes-you-slattern visitor?'

'It depends. Where do you rank Joyce Adaway on your visitor scale?' I looked at the paint smear. 'And are you all right? There was a lot of clattering. I didn't startle you?'

'I'm fine, dear. I knocked a tin of paint over while I was trying to reach something on a high shelf.'

'Purple paint?'

'Yes, how did you know?'

'Lucky guess.'

'And as for dearest Joyce . . . I think she's a one-ought-to-be-properly-dressed visitor, but I also think there'll be amusement to be gained from scandalizing her with my overalls.'

'And the—'

'And the what?'

'Nothing. Still waking up. Not quite with it yet.'

I followed her back into the house and straight through to the drawing room, where Mrs Adaway and Minty were waiting.

'Good morning, Joyce dear,' said Lady Hardcastle. 'Sorry not to be able to greet you when you arrived – I was a little busy.'

Mrs Adaway looked her up and down. 'So I see. Did you know you have—'

Lady Hardcastle laughed. 'Workman's overalls on? One could hardly miss them. It can get a bit messy out in the studio sometimes.'

Mrs Adaway frowned. 'One can only imagine.'

We settled ourselves down just as Edna came in with the tea.

I poured.

'It's so very kind of you to call on us,' said Lady Hardcastle.

Mrs Adaway sipped her tea. 'Thank you, m'dear. I worried my visit might be an imposition.'

'Not at all. One might not think it, but we get very few callers. It's nice to see someone.'

'Splendid. But I'm afraid my visit isn't without ulterior motive.'

'Oh?'

'I understand you know Fred Spratt.'

'We do. He and Eunice are wonderful people – they bring a lot to village life. Their daughter Daisy is a good friend, too.'

Mrs Adaway smiled. 'So I gather. You see . . .' She reached down to scratch Minty's fluffy ears. 'Well . . .' She shifted in her seat and took another sip of tea. 'The thing is . . .' Another scratch of the patient dog. 'I don't really know how to say this. Perhaps I should just come straight out with it.'

*Perhaps you should*, I thought. *I actually do have all day, but I hadn't anticipated spending it doing this.*

Lady Hardcastle was more generous. 'Take your time, dear. We're all friends here.'

Mrs Adaway sighed. 'I'm in love, gels. I'm in love with the village butcher. There. I said it.'

We, on the other hand, said nothing.

'I know you think I'm being foolish – Gertie certainly thinks so. Actually, I think her exact words were "That's the most asinine thing you've ever said, and that's quite an achievement – in a lifetime of asininity it faces some very strong competition." She's never liked me. But I do love him, I really do. And I truly believe he feels the same. It's in the air every time he speaks to me.'

Still, neither of us said a word.

Apparently she interpreted our stunned silence as rapt attention and carried on. 'But I need to be certain, d'you see? And I need to know how to progress things with him. So I've come to you, my dear friends, for advice on how to proceed with darling Fred.'

Lady Hardcastle smiled kindly. 'I don't wish to pour cold water on your dreams, dear, but Fred and Eunice are very happy. They bicker and tease each other mercilessly, but I've seldom seen such a devoted couple. Are you absolutely sure you're reading the signals correctly?'

'He flirts with me every time I go in there.'

It was my turn to give an encouraging smile. 'He's a butcher, Mrs Adaway – they flirt with everyone. I'm sure it's part of the apprenticeship. A nod and a wink here, a suggestive remark there. His cheerful, familiar manner is all part of the business of selling his wares.'

'I understand what you're saying, m'dear, but you've not seen the way he looks at me. And I honestly don't know what he sees in dull old Eunice. As I've said before, she's not good enough for my Fred.'

'How about this?' said Lady Hardcastle. 'We shall undertake to speak to Fred and ascertain the lie of the land for you. As it happens, Florence is an expert mediator in matters of the heart and she'll be able to sound Fred out without tipping your hand. She'll be able to discern Fred's true feelings and we can let you know the best way to proceed. How does that sound?'

Mrs Adaway beamed. 'That's almost precisely what I'd hoped you'd say. Would you do that for me, Florence dear? Would you intercede on my behalf?'

'I'm more than happy to speak to Fred,' I said. 'He and I have been on good terms since we first moved to the village.'

'Oh, how wonderful you both are. Thank you. Thank you. Minty, don't do that. No! I'm so sorry, I fear I shall have to cut my visit short. Minty is usually such a well-behaved house guest. I really must apologize.'

She said her goodbyes as she scooped up the dog, and I showed her to the door with renewed promises to speak to Fred Spratt.

I returned to the drawing room.

'"An expert mediator in matters of the heart"?'

'You're an expert at many things, Floss. She just wanted someone on her side.'

'I'm easily swayed by empty flattery, though, so you probably did the right thing. I'll pop out to the butcher's in a little while and try to find a way of explaining things to Fred and Eunice.'

'You see? I knew I could rely on you. My next task, though, is to get myself out of these overalls and into something more suitable for a lady spending the afternoon at home.'

'You do that and I'll go into the village.'

It was about two in the afternoon when I arrived at the butcher's, and both Fred and Eunice were there, chatting amiably away. I could hear them from outside because their voices were raised, though not in anger. Eunice had been slightly hard of hearing for a while, and Fred often feigned deafness when he didn't want to be bothered, so between them they usually spoke a good deal more loudly than you might otherwise expect.

They were attuned to the sound of the shop doorbell, though, and both looked up as I entered.

'Good afternoon, Flo,' said Eunice. 'What's he forgotten this time?'

I smiled. 'Nothing at all, Eunice. And the beef was delicious.'

'Nothin' but the best from Spratt's, m'dear,' said Fred. 'We prides ourselves on it.'

'And rightly so,' I said.

'So what can I do for you today? We got some lovely lamb chops. And we just had a couple of ducks come in from our supplier. We'll have venison in a couple of weeks, an' all. Oh, I tell you what, how about some sausages? I made 'em this mornin'. Go delicious with some mashed spuds, they will. Some onion gravy. Maybe some carrots and runner beans. Larry's got some choice veg this week.'

Lawrence Weakley was the local greengrocer and we already had a larder full of his delicious wares.

I smiled. 'Honestly, Fred, we have plenty of meat and veg this week – Blodwen keeps a well-stocked larder and you gave me some sausages the other day. I'm actually here on a . . . well, on a slightly delicate matter.'

Eunice leaned forward on her stool behind the till. 'Delicate?'

'Indeed. You remember when Joyce Adaway came in the other day for some meat for her dog?'

'I remembers it well. I a'n't never seen no one buy such a choice bit of meat for a dog afore. Those steaks would 'ave made someone a lovely dinner they would.'

'It's a pampered little dog and no mistake. Do either of you remember the conversation you had with her?'

Eunice suddenly sat upright. 'Why? What's she been sayin'? We wasn't rude or nothin'. We treated her proper.'

I smiled again. 'No, nothing like that. You remember how we thought she had an eye for Fred?'

'I remember teasin' 'im rotten about it.'

'Well, it turns out that she's smitten.'

This provoked a hearty guffaw from Eunice and a proud smile from Fred.

'You 'ear that, Freddie? You's got yourself one o' they admirers. You've always wanted admirers.'

Fred shook his head, but he was still smiling. 'You's both as daft as each other. 'Course she i'n't smitten.'

'I'm afraid it's true,' I said. 'She came to the house to tell us so, and to beg me to intercede on her behalf.'

Eunice laughed again. 'And is that what you's doin' now? Intercedin'? She's come a-wooin' for 'er snooty friend, Freddie.'

'Obviously I haven't. That's just what we told her I'd be doing so as not to upset her. She can be a bit . . . abrasive, shall we say?'

'She can be downright rude if you gets on the wrong side of 'er. I overheard her 'avin' a right old set-to with Lady Farley-Stroud one Christmas.'

'I don't think it would be indiscreet of me to reveal that those two don't get along.'

'Common knowledge, m'dear.'

'Actually, I thought it might be. But what I was saying is that, although she can be a bit forthright, she's not a bad old stick underneath it all. And she's a lonely old lady. And when Fred switched on his usual charm—'

'He could charm the birds out of the trees, our Freddie.'

'Well, quite. But she saw that as a sign that he has a pash for her.'

'That's rich, that is. You hear that, Fred?'

'I hears more than you thinks,' muttered Fred.

'What?'

'Nothin', dearest.'

I rolled my eyes. I'd thought this was going to be awkward, but I hadn't reckoned on how long it was going to take to make my point.

'So,' I said, trying to herd them back towards the main purpose of the conversation, 'what I was thinking was if you could close the valve on the charm a little—'

'I don't think he can do that, m'dear – he was born that way.'

'—and not do anything to encourage her, we might be able to let the whole thing blow over. Please don't be unkind – as I said, she might be a bit of an old bat, but she's just lonely. We'll try to manage things from the other side as best we can and we should see an end to it all without anyone getting hurt.'

Eunice smiled. 'Of course we will, won't we, Freddie?'

Fred nodded earnestly. 'Course.'

'We gots to look after each other,' said Eunice. 'I might be a lonely old widow one day—'

'Oi!'

'You drinks too much and you eats too many of Sep Holman's pies.'

'Fair dos. But we'll take care of your Mrs Adaway like Eunice says. I'n't nobody likes to be mocked.'

'Thank you,' I said. 'We'll have a word with her and try to steer her away, but she might come over before we get the chance – she does love to spoil that dog.'

'We'll look out for her,' said Eunice.

'We will,' agreed Fred. 'And are you sure I can't get you anythin'? We got some lovely lamb I could mince up if you fancies a shepherd's pie.'

'Dinner is in hand, thank you,' I said. 'But I might mention it to Blodwen for later in the week. She makes a lovely shepherd's pie.'

We said our goodbyes and I strolled back to the house.

I arrived in time to be greeted by a freshly washed and dressed Lady Hardcastle.

'All done?' she asked.

'As done as can be,' I said. 'They know what she's thinking now and they'll let her down gently.'

'Splendid. Can I ask you something?'

'Anything.'

'Why did you let me greet Joyce with a gigantic smear of purple paint across my face?'

'Was there? It wasn't obvious.'

'It was an inch wide from cheek to jaw.'

'I'm sure she didn't notice – she had other things on her mind.'

'Hmm. Well, I'm going to write some letters. See you for dinner at seven?'

'I look forward to it.'

◆　◆　◆

I was still discombobulated from my sleepless night so I took another nap that afternoon. By the time I went downstairs to put the finishing touches to the dinner Miss Jones had prepared for us, I was feeling fully revived, if a tiny bit concerned that I might not be able to sleep at bedtime, having had so much extra sleep during the day. I'd deal with that later, though – for now it was time to eat.

Lady Hardcastle was full of the joys of . . . something or other when we sat down. Possibly spring. It was spring in Australia, after all.

'Have you had an enjoyable afternoon?' I asked as she poured the wine.

'Most invigorating. You remember my friend Alice Austin-Walter? She was in the year below me at Girton. Particularly gifted physicist.'

'Is she the one with the psychopathic Siamese cat?'

'Albert, yes. She and I have been corresponding for a while on the implications of Dr Einstein's special relativity.'

'You mention it often.'

'I do. It's fascinating. We've begun speculating upon the possibility of releasing almost unimaginable amounts of energy, if only we could fathom a way of disintegrating large, unstable atoms.

I'm not sure it can be done, but it's interesting to talk about. I also wondered if energy might be released if we could find a way of smashing two small elements together to make a larger one.'

'To what end?' I asked.

'To provide power for all our needs. Heating, lighting, transport – everything.'

'Would this energy be released slowly?'

'No, fantastically quickly.'

'Like an explosive, then.'

'That's a drawback we've considered. Such a development could well be used to make a devastating bomb.'

'Every silver lining has a cloud, eh? And how's the cat?'

'Still a nightmare. Alice has fresh scars on her arm from when she tried to remove him from the laundry basket.'

'Nasty.'

'Indeed. We had two telephone calls while you were asleep, too. Inspector Sunderland called to bring us up to date with his progress on the Hyde case.'

'And? What progress *has* he made?'

'None whatsoever.'

'That's disappointing.'

She shrugged. 'He was very apologetic but, yes, it's disappointing. It's nearly two weeks since Hyde was killed. Eight days since we learned it was murder. And no one has anything to show for it. I'm getting itchy to start investigating it properly for ourselves.'

'We've already spoken to most of the runners and riders, though. What more would you have us do?'

'I've no idea at present, but I'm keen to do *something*. Every time I think I might have time to give it some proper consideration, along comes another distraction. What with panthers, quokkas, parrots, amorous sisters-in-law, bewildered butchers and corrupt railwaymen, I've not had a moment to sit and cogitate.'

'Don't forget the dragon.'

'And then there's the dragon, yes.'

'What was the other one?'

'The other what?'

'The other telephone call. You said we'd had two.'

'Ah, yes. Dinah wanted to know if we'd found out anything more about the quokka.'

'So she was disappointed, too.'

'At first, yes, but the post office story has become interesting now we know it was the parrot. She said if we can find out anything more about its origins – and the quokka's – she'd be keen to write a "Strange Creatures in Gloucestershire Village" story, leading with the postal chaos and ending with the endearing marsupial. But we're getting nowhere on either of those.'

'You've written to Colonel Dawlish about the parrot. It's not as though we've been idle.'

'Well, yes, but even if the parrot does have something to do with George, we've no idea even where to begin trying to find out who owns the quokka.'

'You've considered placing notices in the newspapers, of course?'

'I have, but which ones? There are more than half a dozen in Bristol alone, and who knows how many in Somerset and Gloucestershire. We'd have to think about South Wales, too. And possibly Wiltshire. One would also have to include the nationals, of course, and after spending a small fortune on announcements there's still no guarantee that the quokka's owner reads any newspaper at all. Dear old Sherlock just bunged an announcement in *The Times* and all his problems were solved. Well, once he'd astounded Watson with arcane knowledge he'd acquired while writing a monograph on the spatter patterns of spilled oolong tea on German-made hearth rugs, obviously.'

'Obviously.'

'So consider it considered and rejected.'

'What are we to do, then?'

Lady Hardcastle shrugged. 'I suggest moping and grumbling. Perhaps some sighing.'

'That's the spirit. What about some music as well, though? Or a hand or two of cards? You never know – being relieved of even more of your enormous fortune might focus your mighty brain.'

'It might well. Are you going to eat those carrots?'

With dinner over and the fires burning brightly, Lady Hardcastle's spirits were lifted by the evening's activities – we opted for music and cards over her proposed moping and grumbling – but we made no firm decisions about our next course of action. Still, it wasn't as if we were actually *supposed* to be doing anything, so I couldn't summon the energy to be especially concerned about our 'failures'. It would be interesting to find out what had been going on, but it wasn't our job and I was happy to let the information come to us whenever it felt the urge to reveal itself.

We retired at around eleven, with Lady Hardcastle having lost an absolute packet and me, against all fears, utterly exhausted and ready for sleep. I checked on the parrot before I went up and made sure he had food and water in case he woke before us feeling peckish.

◆ ◆ ◆

I rose early on Friday feeling refreshed and invigorated, and went straight to the kitchen. My plan was to check that the range was still lit and put the kettle on to make myself a pot of tea before my exercises.

The room was icy cold, and I sighed at the thought of having to go out to get more wood for the range.

But the range was warm.

The window was open.

I lit a lamp and inspected it.

I was certain it had been closed when I went to bed – I hadn't wanted our avian guest to get cold. So how had it opened? Had Lady Hardcastle come down in the night and opened it? Was one of us a sleepwalker? The glass was intact and there were no other obvious signs of burglary, but who would have broken in through the window anyway? The back door was locked – as with the front door, I couldn't break my London lock-the-door habit – but it was never bolted. Edna and Miss Jones each had a key so they could come and go as necessary whether we were there or not. Nevertheless, it would be the easiest point of entry for an enterprising burglar, and there were no signs of illicit entry there, either.

It was a mystery.

There was something else strange, too, but it took me a little while to realize what it was. And then it struck me. I had checked the window at bedtime so that the parrot wouldn't get cold . . . but where was the parrot?

Not only was the window open, so was the cage door, and the bird was gone.

I closed the window and looked around the house, but of the parrot there was no sign. It must have flown out through the open window.

There was nothing to be done – I certainly wasn't going to walk up and down the lane in my exercise togs calling out for a lost parrot – so I carried on as usual.

When they arrived, I told Edna and Miss Jones what had happened.

'That's a shame,' said Edna. 'I quite liked 'avin' the old chap in 'ere with us. Talkative, weren't he?'

'He was,' said Miss Jones. 'And not rude like some. My great-aunt had a parrot and it swore like a navvy.'

I smiled. 'They're not really talking – they can only repeat sounds they've heard.'

'Well, that would explain it. Aunt Hilda swore like a navvy herself.'

Edna laughed. 'I dreads to think what a parrot would learn in our house. But I 'spect he'll come back. They always knows where the food is.'

'Actually, that's a good point,' I said. 'He might have gone back to the storeroom at the post office. He seemed happy there and he had a constant supply of walnuts.'

I made Lady Hardcastle's starter breakfast and took it up to her.

She was already sitting up and writing in her notebook. 'Good morning, Flossie. And how does the day find my tiniest servant?'

'I'm uncommonly well, thank you, aged employer. But I bring bad news with the toast and coffee.'

'Bad news? Oh dear. Who's been murdered this time?'

'No one's been murdered, but the parrot is missing.'

'Missing?'

'The kitchen window was open and so was his cage. And he's nowhere to be seen. I've searched the house.'

'No signs of burglary?'

'None.'

'Well,' she said, 'this is a pickle. He was very adept at getting into the cage and closing the door behind him. Perhaps he's mastered the skill of opening it, too.'

'Perhaps. But what about the window?'

'An intelligent bird who can open cage doors and sort post might easily be able to work the latch on a kitchen window. I'm prepared to wager he's gone back to the Talbots.'

'I confess I thought the same. What do you say we have our breakfast and go up to the post office to see if he's there?'

'I'd say that sounds like a splendid idea.'

# Chapter Thirteen

It was another chilly day, but the sun was out and we decided to walk into the village.

'Oh, I completely forgot to tell you,' said Lady Hardcastle as we strolled between the hedgerows. 'One of my letters yesterday was from Jasper Laxton's solicitors. He wants to sell the house and he's giving me first refusal.'

Lady Hardcastle's old friend had built the house for himself and his young family, but a business opportunity had arisen and he had moved out to India soon after it was completed. He had only intended to be away for a year, and had rented it to her at a favourable rate to prevent it from standing empty while he was away. A year had turned into two, and the family had settled into life on the subcontinent, leaving us to enjoy life in a house far bigger than we needed. But now, it seemed a decision had been made and the house was soon to be up for sale.

'Did they say why?' I asked. 'Are the Laxtons not returning or do they just have other plans?'

'There were no other details, I'm afraid. Just the offer.'

'What will you do?'

'Well, that's rather why I wanted to talk to you. What do *you* want to do?'

I thought for a moment. 'I confess there was a certain appeal in knowing the move to Littleton Cotterell was temporary. Even if we enjoyed our quiet life in the country, we might have to move out at any moment and find somewhere else. But the truth is that I love living here. It's a beautiful village, and for some reason we've been accepted. The locals are friendly – even the murderous ones – and we've both made good friends here. If you want to buy it I'd be happy to settle down, I think.'

'I'm so glad you said that. I ran through all the possibilities in my head and the thought of having to leave made me rather sad. So, if you want to stay, too, I shall make Jasper an offer.'

'As I always say, the only thing I miss from our time in London is electricity. And gas, of course. But we'd have to move into Bristol to get those.'

'I should love electricity – especially in the studio. Think of the photographic effects I could achieve with proper lighting. I wonder if we could construct an outbuilding at the end of the garden and install a generator. It must be possible – Hector and Gertie have a generator at The Grange.'

'Lord Riddlethorpe's men might be able to come up with something.'

Lord 'Fishy' Riddlethorpe owned a motor racing team, but he and his engineers were always excited by a technical challenge, even one that didn't directly involve motor cars.

'What a good idea. I shall write to him as soon as I've replied to Messrs Philtrum, Hallux and Uvula, or whatever they're called.'

As we approached the post office I caught sight of Daisy coming out of the pub yard. She saw us and waved us towards her.

'I wonder what she wants,' said Lady Hardcastle.

'If we're lucky, she's found the parrot,' I said as we quickened our pace.

Daisy didn't wait. 'Matilda's gone.'

'Oh dear. Dead or missing?' said Lady Hardcastle as we drew near.

'Missin'. But she could be dead an' all, for all I knows. I come out to change her water and give her some carrot tops before she turned in for the day and found her cage door open. No sign of 'er.'

I looked at Lady Hardcastle. 'Both gone? That can't be a coincidence.'

'Both?' said Daisy.

'I went to the kitchen this morning to find the parrot missing,' I said.

'Parrot? I didn't know you 'ad a parrot.'

'I caught it at the post office yesterday. It had been interfering with the post. I assumed you knew – you always know everything.'

'Nope. No one's told me nothin'.'

'Well, it's gone. Window open, cage open, parrot gone. We thought he'd masterminded his own escape, but if Matilda disappeared at the same time, it's looking more as though someone took them.'

'But who'd want to steal a parrot and a quokka? Don't make no sense.'

'We've always assumed they were quite valuable,' said Lady Hardcastle. 'I imagine they'd fetch the prettiest of pennies if one could find the right buyer.'

'Yes, but who—?'

'Someone who overheard our conversation in the pub and knew Daisy was taking care of a valuable creature,' I said. 'Someone who's not above a bit of petty larceny if there's a few easy bob to be made.'

'Oh dear,' said Lady Hardcastle. 'Not young Mickey Yawn? I was sure he'd turned a corner – I had such high hopes for him after Angelina took him on as her apprentice. Did he know about the parrot as well?'

I nodded. 'He and Violet saw it when Edna and I were getting into the Rolls. They were both very curious. I could easily be wrong – I hope I am – but it would be self-indulgent to overlook the most obvious suspect just because we have a soft spot for him.'

'I gots to say I agrees with her,' said Daisy. 'He's a nice enough bloke but he a'n't ever been what you might call honest. Even if he has "turned a corner" I reckon the temptation to nick anythin' that i'n't nailed down would be too strong for little Mickey. It's in his blood. And as for that Olive of his . . . everyone knows what a load of villains her family are.'

'It would be a shame if it were true,' said Lady Hardcastle, 'but you're right: we need to talk to them. Where might we find him?'

'He's labouring for Sam Hardiman on the other side of the village, he told me,' I said.

'But I thought he was working for Angelina Goodacre.'

'He is, but bicycles don't sell so well in the winter months or something, so things are a bit quiet. He's taken on some extra work so he can save up to open his own bicycle shop.'

Lady Hardcastle frowned. 'I'm even less inclined to suspect him in that case – he seems to have discovered his métier.'

'Even so . . .' I said.

She sighed. 'Even so, yes. So, where is Hardiman working?'

'Sam's doin' up a couple of cottages up Badger Lane,' said Daisy. 'Over beyond the village hall. Derelict they was. He got 'em for a song. I reckon he'll make a few bob there.'

'Then we should go up and see him,' said Lady Hardcastle. 'Even if it's only so that we can eliminate him from our enquiries.'

◆ ◆ ◆

Lady Hardcastle and I skirted the green towards the village hall.

'Since you're in a house-buying mood,' I said. 'Have you given any more thought to a pied-à-terre in London? Oh, oh, or a swanky flat in Bristol?'

She laughed. 'You're very free with my money.'

'We talk about it all the time. Sooner or later you're going to have to make up your mind, even if it's just to say no.'

'I'll see how traumatic the experience of buying the house turns out to be, and then revisit it.'

'And can we give it a name?'

'The flat-in-town conundrum?'

'That offer of a punch on the nose still stands. No, silly, the house. We've been calling it "the house" for four years. Our address is just "Littleton Lane".'

'It's been bothering me, too, but we couldn't do anything because it wasn't our house.'

'Hence my question about finally naming it. So when it *is* your— *our* house, we can call it whatever we want.'

'How exciting. Something bafflingly pretentious in Latin?'

'Or scandalously obscene in Welsh?'

'Or just something utterly ghastly? Dunspyin or Chez Emily.'

'It needs more thought, I feel.'

'I cannot but agree. I hear the sounds of toil ahead – I think we've found young Master Yawn's place of work.'

Sure enough, we rounded the next bend and saw Sam Hardiman's wagon outside two dilapidated cottages. As we drew nearer I saw a plume of cigarette smoke, under which lurked the louche and lanky form of Mickey Yawn. He was sawing an enormous piece of timber.

By his side, gazing at him adoringly, was Olive Churches.

He looked over at us as we opened the gate. 'Mornin', Lady H. Mornin', Miss A. What am I accused of nickin' this time?'

'Good morning, Mickey,' said Lady Hardcastle. 'You're accused of nothing, dear, but we would like a quick word if you have a minute.'

He held up the saw he'd been using. 'All right, but I'm supposed to be workin', mind.'

'He's supposed to be workin',' said Olive.

I smiled. 'We won't take up much of your time. But you're right – a couple of things have gone missing and—'

Olive sneered. 'And you thought you'd come over 'ere and accuse him of nickin' 'em.'

I tried not to sigh. 'No, but as before when we wanted to talk to you about a similar matter, you both associate with the sort of people who might know something about it, even if you've turned over a new leaf.'

Mickey gave a little chuckle. 'All right, I'll bite. What's been taken? Jewellery? Clocks? Old army medals?'

'The quokka and the parrot,' said Lady Hardcastle.

Mickey's chuckle gave way to a full laugh. 'Well, you did say they was valuable.'

'Valuable and vulnerable,' I said. 'Notwithstanding their financial worth, they both take a fair bit of looking after. We need to get them back before they come to harm.'

'Notwithstandin', eh? You sounds like my brief. He always 'ad big words like that ready to drop in to the conversation to try to impress people. Didn't help him get me off, though.'

'Is that because you were actually guilty?'

'Well, yes. But you expects a decent brief to get you off notwithstandin' your actual culpability.'

It was my turn to laugh. 'Do you know anything about the stolen animals or not?'

'Our dad reckons there's someone round 'ere stealin' all sorts of animals,' said Olive.

'I intend no disrespect to your father, dear,' said Lady Hardcastle, 'but he always says something like that. There's always a mysterious "someone" up to no good. Have you heard anything specific?'

'No,' said Olive, sullenly.

Mickey carefully placed the saw on the half-cut beam. 'Tell you what we'll do, Lady H. You i'n't wrong – we do know some scoundrels. And I liked the look of both them animals – don't want to see 'em come to no harm. So we'll keep our ears open, and if we 'ears anythin', we'll come knockin' on your door. How does that sound?'

'It sounds like exactly what I was hoping for. Thank you. Now you'd better get back to your work or Sam Hardiman will be after us for wasting your time.'

'Oh, he won't say nothin'. He's skivin' off hisself. There's a widow in the next street who always needs odd jobs doin' this time of day.'

'*Odd jobs*,' said Olive with a giggle and a wink.

Lady Hardcastle smiled indulgently. 'Yes, dear, we get it. But we'd better let you get on, anyway. Thank you for your time.'

We left them to their work and returned home via Holman the baker's. No one should have to track down missing animals without the aid of doughnuts.

Back at the house I asked Miss Jones to make some coffee and put the doughnuts on plates. It turned out I did have standards after all. We'd bought enough for her and Edna so I called her down, too, and they settled down for a break while I took the tray through to the drawing room.

Lady Hardcastle wasn't there.

I went back out into the hall.

'There's coffee and doughnuts if you want them,' I called. 'Where are you?'

'Dining room, dear.'

I went through and, sure enough, there she was at the dining table with her sketchpad and pencils, drawing a beautiful portrait of the missing parrot.

I set the tray down and poured the coffee. 'He's going on the crime board, then?'

'He is. He's the victim of a crime, after all.'

'I suppose he is, yes. It's a bit of a mess, though, don't you think? Animal attacks, a murder, railway corruption, and now some stolen pets.'

'You're right, of course. But the alternative is to have four crime boards. You make enough fuss over fetching one down from the attic – I'm not sure I could cope with the moaning four would provoke.'

'You could always help. It's much harder to hear me complaining about having to haul heavy things about the house on my own when I'm not actually on my own because someone's helping me.'

'One is reminded of the old idiom about keeping a dog and barking oneself.'

The doorbell rang and I rose to answer it. 'Always the dog in these things.' I went out into the hall. 'Never a pretty cat or a fluffy bunny rabbit. I'd settle for a fierce lion.' I opened the door. 'But no, always a dog.'

The telegram boy looked puzzled. 'It's not a dog, miss, it's a telegram.' He handed it to me.

'Thank you. Do you need to wait for a reply?'

'No, miss. But I wouldn't say no to a 'andsome tip. For me trouble, like.'

'A tip? I'll give you a tip: never work for someone who keeps using canine metaphors to describe you.'

'Er, right you are, miss.'

I gave him a penny, too.

'Thank you very much, miss. Good day.'

I closed the door and returned to the dining room.

'Hawkers? Rag and bone men? Knife sharpeners? Beggars?'

'A telegram boy,' I said. 'With a telegram. For you.'

She took it and read it through.

'Good heavens,' she said. 'Well, that's a turn-up for the books. It's from George. *In receipt of your letter. Stop. Astonishing coincidence. Stop. Scarlet macaw stolen from circus. Stop. Used to do a post office skit. Stop. Named him Brigadier Aubrey Godspeed after a commanding officer from the old days. Stop. Occupational hazard these days. Stop. Animals stolen all the time. Stop. Rival lost a black panther recently. Stop. Hang on to the bird and will send a chap up to have a look. Stop. Might even come myself. Stop. Yours and all that caper George. Ends.* He's not the most efficient telegrammer – I dread to think how much that rambling missive cost him – but I think I'm beginning to see at least a small justification for keeping at least some of these things on the same board.'

'You think ours is the stolen panther?'

'One can never be certain of anything without evidence, but one would get pretty long odds on it being a different one, don't you think? I mean, how many panthers do we suppose there are roaming about the English countryside?'

'And the quokka?'

She just looked at me.

'Right,' I said. 'Sorry. But where does that leave us?'

'Well, at least two of the stolen creatures have been re-stolen while in our care, so I'm going to begin with the assumption that the thief—'

'Or thieves.'

'Or thieves is—'

'Or are.'

'I'm not above a spot of rhinobattery myself, you know. I'm going to begin with the assumption that they're local. It was a fair assumption anyway, given that the escaped creatures were all spotted locally, but last night's events make that more likely, I feel.'

'And whom do we suspect?'

'Who, indeed?' She tapped her teeth with her pencil for a moment.

She seemed about to speak, but instead took out a clean sheet of paper and began drawing the quokka.

It took a while, but I knew that sketching was one of the ways she cleared her mind when she needed to think, so I left her to it. And the doughnut was delicious so it wasn't as though I didn't have something pleasurable to do in the meantime.

A good few minutes passed while she sketched and shaded the small marsupial, but eventually she put down her pencil and smiled.

'Well?' I said.

'I think I have it.'

'Excellent. Who is it? Should we tell Sergeant Dobson?'

'I think we shall need to tell Inspector Sunderland.'

'About the animal thefts? Surely that's a local matter.'

'About everything. But first we need to investigate little Geoffrey's dragon.'

'You jest, of course.'

'Indeed no.'

'I can think of at least three good reasons why there's no dragon loose in the woods, the first being that there's no such thing.'

'Your Welsh ancestors will be turning in their graves to hear you denying their national emblem. Your scepticism notwithstanding, we shall take ourselves over to the woods to see if we can see the mythical beast for ourselves. After lunch, though – there's no rush.'

# Chapter Fourteen

The sunshine had been only brief, and by lunchtime the sky was overcast. But there was no sign of rain and the temperature had crept up a tiny bit, so it wasn't unpleasant as we pootled along the lanes in the Silver Ghost towards the woods on the other side of Toby Thompson's dairy farm.

It was in a clearing in those very woods that we had found the body of Frank Pickering during our first week in the village. I confess I thought we had more hope of seeing poor Frank's ghost than of glimpsing a dragon, but Lady Hardcastle had the bit between her teeth and I knew that any objections I might raise – no matter how rational and well expressed – would simply be ignored.

'They're big woods,' I said. 'How will we know where to start?'

She took a left turn down a rutted track. 'If I'm right, it'll be obvious.'

She drove on for a while, the Rolls-Royce's suspension soaking up the lumps and bumps with ease. The track clearly hadn't been used for a long time and was almost overgrown in places, but Lady Hardcastle eased us through, and our progress, though bouncy, was merely slowed by overhangs and undergrowth rather than completely impeded.

'Aha,' she said suddenly and glided swiftly to a halt. 'Let's hop out and take a look around.'

I prefer to imagine I climbed out with lithe, athletic grace rather than hopped, but the effect was the same: I found myself standing in soft – though thankfully not squelchy – mud beside a gap in the hedgerow. I followed Lady Hardcastle through.

We were at the top of a steep bank, which led down to a broadish flat area and then up a similarly steep bank on the other side. The banks stretched off in both directions. To our right they disappeared around a gentle curve, while to our left our bank tapered down to join the flat bottom of the miniature valley. The other side sloped much less and opened out to what seemed to be a broad, weed-strewn, gravelled plateau, with the edge shored up with heavy timber to form a platform.

If it hadn't been for those little details I might have thought we were looking down at a dried-up riverbed. But all that, as well as the glint of railway tracks through the weeds and the hefty buffers at the end of the line, meant we had found a disused railway siding.

Rather than slither down the treacherous bank, we walked towards the left and then crossed over to the more easily negotiated gentle slope, to reach the buffers.

'We've been living in Littleton more than four years now,' I said, 'but I had absolutely no idea this was here.'

'Nor did I,' said Lady Hardcastle. 'It looks as though it was abandoned quite a while ago.'

We crossed and scrambled up the shallower bank on the other side and looked around.

'Over there, said Lady Hardcastle. 'A quarry, do you think?'

We walked on a little way in the direction she had pointed, and sure enough found ourselves at the top of a disused quarry. A track led away through trees to our left, while access to the old working faces was by a gently sloping switchback cart track.

'Limestone,' I said, confidently.

'I say, well done you. You can't tell a lime tree from a laburnum, but there you are identifying rock like a skilled geologist.'

I pointed to a faded, broken sign: . . . *erell & Woodworthy Limestone Quarry, Ltd.*

She laughed. 'That would do it. Can't you just imagine it in its heyday? Quarrymen toiling below. The sound of picks on stone. Shouts. An explosion and the clatter of falling rock. Men hoisting rough-hewn boulders on to wagons. Mighty horses drawing them slowly up the long, winding track to be loaded on to railway wagons and hauled off to build . . . everything.'

'It's quite a romantic place when you put it like that. It's quite sad to see it abandoned and neglected.'

She pointed to the narrow roadway that led off in the opposite direction to the railway. 'Not entirely abandoned. Those cart tracks look reasonably fresh.' She turned towards the area that formed a sort of railway platform. 'Those weeds have been trampled recently, too. And did you see the railway tracks?'

'I certainly did. I saw them glinting. Oh. I saw them glinting. They're not rusted and unused – they've been polished by wheels. There's been more than one train along here in the past month or so.'

'That's my interpretation, certainly.'

I smiled. 'No sign of a dragon, though.'

'Not at the moment, but it's been a few nights since Geoffrey and his little pals saw it. Maybe if we come back after dark we might be lucky enough to see it for ourselves. We'll have to be stealthy, though. For all their terrifying size and fierceness, dragons can be shy creatures, so we'll have to make sure not to be seen.'

I sighed and shook my head. 'You really are the most infuriating woman. You could just tell me what you've worked out.'

'I could, dear, but where would be the fun in that? We'll come back tonight and see what we can see.'

'And if we see nothing?'

'Then we'll come back tomorrow night. And the night after. The dragon will show itself eventually.'

There was no point in arguing with her.

We took one last look around and then returned to the car.

'Have you given any thought to how we might get out of here?' I asked as Lady Hardcastle started the engine. 'I've no idea where we might end up if we follow this track forwards. It ought to follow the railway siding and come out by the loading platform but you never know. And I'm not certain we'll be able to get much further along it, even if it does take us in the right direction. The vegetation looks much thicker ahead.'

'I know. I've been weighing up our options and I can't help but think we have no choice but to drive out the way we came.'

'Backwards?'

'Unless you've seen a place where we can turn round then, yes, backwards.'

'Then we should put the roof down – you can't see anything out of that little rear window.'

I hopped – or rather climbed out with lithe, athletic grace – and set about lowering the Silver Ghost's folding roof. It was the work of a moment – or a few moments, at least – and I was soon back in the passenger seat and waiting to be dumbfounded by Lady Hardcastle's amazing driving skills.

Unusually for her, she set off slowly and carefully. I had been expecting automotive carnage as we bounced at a ridiculously inappropriate speed between the weeds and bushes, always less than a second from wedging the car so badly into the undergrowth that we'd have to walk home.

But from those first few seconds, it seemed as though everything was going to be all right.

The first real test came when the track kinked slightly.

She turned the wheel the wrong way and pushed the rear of the car very firmly into what I was subsequently told was a hawthorn bush. Colourful swearing ensued and I was grateful that Brigadier Aubrey Godspeed wasn't with us – he'd never be welcome back at the circus if he learned to talk like that.

She extricated us from the bush and tried again.

Slowly, foot by foot, she managed to reverse all the way to the metalled lane, and we were free to speed home.

◆　◆　◆

After dinner that evening, we changed into black clothes suitable for a bit of late-night snooping. I packed a flask of coffee and some sandwiches and we set off for the disused railway siding.

We were less than half a mile from home when Lady Hardcastle turned round to go back so I could also get some cake.

We finally got going again, and were both in reasonably high spirits as we drove through the lanes. I wasn't hopeful that we'd actually see anything, but it felt good to be active at last.

As is always the case, the journey to our chosen surveillance spot seemed to take much less time than it had the first time, and we came upon the turning on to the overgrown track so quickly that I almost missed it. Lady Hardcastle made the turn in time, though, and we cautiously threaded our way between the bushes and weeds in the pitch black with only the Rolls-Royce's headlights to guide us. To be fair, they were rather good headlights, and we managed to follow the track to the gap in the hedge without getting stuck, but it had still been much easier in the daylight.

The engine purred to a stop. The only sounds were the distant barking of a fox and the ticking of cooling metal as the Rolls settled down for a nap.

'Now what?' I said. 'Do we just sit here and wait for the dragon?'

'That was my plan. We'll give it an hour. Perhaps two.'

'Righto. At least we have sandwiches.'

'And cake,' she said. 'Don't forget the cake.'

We sat in silence for a while.

A pair of tawny owls began a long-distance chat, hooting back and forth.

'What do you suppose those two are talking about?' I asked.

'Just catching up on the woodland gossip. Did she hear about the young badger who got into a scrap with the fox? She did, but what about those noisy jackdaws who came into the woods this afternoon? She hopes they're not going to visit often – she could hardly sleep with all the racket they were making.'

'In reality he's asking if she'll agree to be his paramour, isn't he?'

'Boringly, yes. It's the season for it.'

We sat quietly for another half an hour.

I poured coffee from the flask and offered Lady Hardcastle a sandwich.

And then there was a new noise. An entirely familiar noise.

It was the puffing of a locomotive.

I sat up straight. 'I take back all the uncharitable things I said about your plan to spend the evening sitting in the dark.'

'What uncharitable things? You didn't say any uncharitable things.'

'Did I not? I certainly thought them. Horrible, rude, impatient things. Your name was mud. I thought this was going to be a monumental waste of our time and the only result would be coldness and disappointment. But here comes a train.'

'Here, as you say, comes a train.'

'I mean, it's not a dragon, but a train's better than nothing.'

'O ye of little shoes. Let's get out and watch.'

I put the cups away and clambered out to follow her through the gap in the hedge.

The puffing came slowly closer.

Suddenly, she pointed. 'And there, my dearest, doubting Flossie, is your dragon.'

As the locomotive lumbered towards us, the hot, orange sparks from the chimney were illuminating the smoke and making it look as though it were a stream of liquid fire. Creative young boys could easily imagine it to be a dragon. Except . . .

'But it's so obviously a locomotive,' I said.

'It is to us, yes. But the village is a long way from the main railway lines, so they've probably never seen one in the dark. And even if they did make the connection, where would they think it could be going? The quarry closed long before they were born and this siding was abandoned. Unless they stumbled upon them one day, they wouldn't know there were tracks here. So it couldn't possibly be a train. And, as Mr Holmes always says, once they'd eliminated the impossible, whatever remained, no matter how improbable, must be the truth. And that meant it absolutely had to be a fire-breathing dragon.'

I shrugged – a pointless action in the dark. 'That makes a haphazard sort of sense, I suppose. But it leaves another question unanswered: why is there a locomotive on this abandoned siding?'

'Let's follow and find out.'

The locomotive was pulling a short train of unmarked wagons, their doors bolted shut.

We waited until the last wagon had passed us and then, keeping to the shadows, followed it to the buffers. The train was moving scarcely above walking pace on the old, overgrown tracks, so it was easy to keep up.

A red lantern swung from a barely seen hand at the end of the line, and the train puffed to a sedate stop, brakes squealing softly.

There were shouts from the platform and we heard the sound of wagon doors being unbolted and slid open.

Still in the shadows, we positioned ourselves so that we could see the activity on the platform. Four men had been awaiting the arrival of the train, and by the light of the lanterns they had set on the ground they were unloading several large crates from the wagons. They were heavy, and the men were handling them very carefully. *Stolen animals*, I wondered? I also remembered Old Roberts's speculation about stolen artwork – there'd been an art theft in London recently, after all.

They worked quickly and quietly, first loading the crates on to a trolley, and then moving them to a large, heavy farm wagon pulled by two enormous horses.

They lifted the crates on to the farm wagon, then closed and locked the railway wagons. One of them handed the train driver a package and the engine immediately puffed to life and began backing out of the siding.

Lady Hardcastle began tapping her fingers on my hand and arm – the silent signals we used in the field. I replied with the same code and we quickly agreed that we would follow the farm wagon on foot.

We had found the mysterious dragon, and we might yet catch some thieves.

With their lanterns swaying, the horses clopping, and the iron-bound wheels grinding, it was easy to follow the farm wagon at a safe distance. Our snooping outfits included rubber-soled plimsolls, so there was little chance of our being heard as we walked slowly behind the men and their crates.

With no real idea where we were going – nor, I was forced to concede, any strong idea of where we'd started out from – the journey seemed endless. We stepped lightly along unfamiliar lanes with nothing to focus upon but the clinking of horse tack and the occasional muttered comments between the four men. Despite the distance between us and the cover provided by the racket the horses and wagon were making, it didn't feel safe for us to talk to each other, so we carried on in silence, seemingly for miles.

After an absolute age – but probably more like a quarter of an hour – we emerged from a particularly winding lane on to a main road. More than that, it was a *familiar* main road, and I suddenly knew where we were. I tapped a message on Lady Hardcastle's arm and she responded in the same way. She knew where we were, too.

And it wasn't long before we knew for certain where we were going.

Yard by yard the giant horses plodded along the road, getting ever closer to Bottom Farm.

As they approached the main gates, two more lanterns appeared from behind the barn and moved towards the gates from the inside. By the time the wagon arrived, we were close enough to see that the two men opening the gates and ushering the wagon in were farmer Jonathan Rood and vet Robinson Pinkard.

They waited at the gate until the horses and wagon were in the yard, then carefully closed the gates behind them.

Lady Hardcastle and I stayed in the shadows on the other side of the road until all the lights had disappeared behind the barn, and then crossed and hopped over the gates as silently as we could.

Once inside, we could see that the barn was the first of several large outbuildings, and I pointed out a pathway that ran behind it and would allow us to get closer to the others without having to cross the yard in the open. We inched along, careful not to trip over anything and give ourselves away.

As we cleared the end of the barn, we found ourselves behind some machinery at the edge of the yard. Ahead of us, the wagon had stopped and the two horses were being taken out and led away by one of the men, to be unharnessed. Meanwhile the other three men, supervised by Rood and Pinkard, were unloading the crates and placing them with great care on to the cobbled yard.

By the light of the lanterns it was now possible to see that the crates had holes drilled in their lids, though the labels were still unreadable from where we had concealed ourselves.

Finally the wagon was unloaded and, one by one, the crates were placed on a trolley and wheeled into a second barn.

As the lanterns illuminated the interior of the building, it was just possible to make out some storm damage, some of which had been patched and repaired. The repairs were not to an especially high standard, as though the work had been done in a hurry, and there were still sections of roof covered with tarpaulin.

Once everyone was inside with the final crate, Lady Hardcastle and I ventured closer to the building, to a gap in one repaired section of the wall through which light was streaming. We stood on a small pile of rubble and peered in.

The building was full of crates of various sizes, as well as several substantial iron cages on wheels. They were very familiar to someone who had grown up in a circus – these were the sorts of cages in which we used to transport our animals.

I scanned the room more carefully. As well as the large cages, one of which was home to a sleeping tiger, there were several smaller ones, though it was impossible to see what was in them in the dim light.

Ominously, a large, empty cage similar to the one housing the tiger appeared to have been damaged, probably when one of the roof beams fell on it during the recent storms. The bars were slightly askew and the cage door hung open. If anything had been inside, it would have been terrified by the storm and the falling beam and would have fled as soon as the door popped open.

I tried to attract Lady Hardcastle's attention so I could check that she'd seen it, too, and as she shifted her weight to turn towards me, one of the bricks she was standing on slipped free and clink-clonked down the pile.

Inside, Pinkard turned at once towards the sound.

We froze.

It seemed as though he was looking straight at us, but we were in the shadows outside the barn and there was no way he could see us. He muttered something to one of the men, who picked up a lantern and cudgel and strode purposefully towards the door.

Time for us to evaporate.

As carefully, quietly, but above all as quickly as we could, we moved away from the hole in the wall, taking ourselves further from the yard and the first barn. Once we judged we were a sensible distance away, we crossed the weed- and rubble-strewn dead ground to the farm wall and lay low in the shelter of a pile of old timber.

Just as we ducked down, the man rounded the side of the building and made a half-hearted search of the area immediately around the hole. He raised his lantern and I could see him peering out into the gloom, back towards the yard and the main barn.

'There's nothin' 'ere, Mr Pinkard. Prob'ly a fox or sommat.'

We waited until he had returned inside and then slithered over the wall and on to the main road.

Once we were well clear of the farm and heading in the right direction, I pulled a flashlight from the pocket of my overcoat and switched it on, feeling very pleased with myself and hoping Lady Hardcastle would be impressed by my forethought. And I'm sure she would have been, had she not at that very moment switched on a flashlight of her own.

'Great minds,' she said, pointing hers at her grinning face. 'Now, do you remember where the quarry track comes out?'

'Just along there,' I said, 'after the tree with the massive trunk.'

We found the opening and, now we weren't having to keep eyes and ears on the wagon, I saw the remains of the old quarry gates, half covered by bushes.

From there it was a simple matter of following the track to the railway siding.

'How confident are you of your ability to reverse along that track in the dark?' I asked.

'I'm not sure, dear. It was hard enough in the daylight.'

'Then why don't we explore the track from this end and see if we can just drive straight through?'

After a little bit of exploring, we discovered the point where the track began, and we followed it until we reached the Rolls. A couple of spots would require a little care but it seemed passable enough, and was definitely preferable to trying to back out the way we had come.

It wasn't too long before we were back out on the main road and heading for home.

◆ ◆ ◆

It was gone midnight by the time we arrived back at the house, and I was more than ready for cocoa and bed.

Lady Hardcastle, though, had other ideas, and picked up the telephone earpiece as soon as we got through the door. 'Hello, yes, can you put me through to the Bristol Police, please. A Division at the Bridewell . . . No, it's not an emergency . . . No, everything is fine, I just want to talk to someone from CID . . . I'm aware of the time, but they work through the night, you know . . . No, I wouldn't prefer to wait until morning . . . Thank you so very much . . .' She rolled her eyes and shook her head as she waited, but refrained from saying anything that might antagonize the operator. She was soon connected. 'Hello? I wonder if Inspector Sunderland is on duty . . . Yes, I'm well aware of the time, the telephone operator has just told me . . . No, I know he has to go home sometimes, but I also know he sometimes works the night shift. He rather enjoys it, he tells me . . . A friend . . . No, not that sort of friend . . . No, really, if he were having an affair he could do much better than me, I can assure you . . . Yes, his wife is a lovely woman. We're having dinner with them both soon . . . No, I don't want to invite him to dinner. I want to leave a message for him . . . No, it's not a personal message, it's in connection with a case he's working on . . . That's right. Can you tell him that Lady Hardcastle telephoned, please— . . . Yes, I'm afraid so. Hello, Sergeant . . . Yes, we're interfering again . . . I know, but we can't stop ourselves. Can you tell him I telephoned and that we believe stolen exotic animals are being held at Bottom Farm in Littleton Cotterell . . . Animals, yes. He'll understand the significance . . . Thank you, Sergeant. Good night to you, too.'

'Sergeant Massive Beard?' I asked when she had hung up.

'The very same.'

'Just one of those things sent to try us.'

'Unlike towels.'

'Don't say it. Cocoa before bed?'

'Yes, please, Floss. With brandy. I think we've earned it.'

# Chapter Fifteen

When I took up Lady Hardcastle's starter breakfast the next morning, she was already awake and, once more, making notes in her notebook.

'Ah, the redoubtable Floss Armstrong,' she said, peering over her reading glasses. 'How delightful to see you.'

'It can't have come as a surprise,' I said. 'I bring you coffee and toast every morning at about this time.'

'You do, but I'm always pleased to see you and I never take you for granted.'

'I'm pleased to see you, too. And surprised to see you awake and vertical at this hour for the second time this week.'

'Things to do, places to go, dear thing. Do you think Miss Jones might be able to prepare breakfast a little earlier today? I'd like to get moving as soon as we can.'

'I'll go and ask. Where are we off to?'

'Some daylight snooping is required, I feel.'

I wanted to question the good sense of this, but I decided that could wait. I might be able to dissuade her while we ate, but if I couldn't and we went anyway, I didn't want to be the one responsible for our late departure. I left her munching and sipping and went back downstairs to ask Miss Jones to prepare an early breakfast.

She accepted the need for urgency – I think she found it slightly glamorous to be playing a part in helping with our investigation – and was more than capable coping without my offered help. Instead I returned upstairs to assist Lady Hardcastle, who was not.

Half an hour later she was dressed and presentable and we sat down in the dining room together to tuck in to our usual morning feast.

She helped herself to grilled mushrooms. 'You look as though you have something on your mind.'

'And I'm sure you can guess what,' I said. 'Do you think it's altogether wise to go back to Bottom Farm? In the daylight? What do you imagine we can achieve? Inspector Sunderland will get your message as soon as he arrives for duty – shouldn't we just leave it to him?'

'He might be on late turn – I didn't press the sergeant for details of his shifts. And he might be busy anyway. If he can't get out here until later – or even tomorrow – I'd like to be able to give him as much information as possible. It will make his life so much easier.'

'And ours so much more difficult. What do you think we can see by day that we haven't already seen or surmised by night?'

She speared a sausage and waved it at me as though wagging a sixth finger. 'I have no idea, dear – that's precisely the point. A conviction relies on sound evidence and reliable witnesses. Let's suppose that Rood and Pinkard take a scare and decide to do a moonlight flit with all the animals. Sunderland might be happy to arrest them on our say-so, but a decent brief would tear our testimony to shreds. "You say you saw a caged tiger? And you were looking through a hole in the barn wall? At night? Are you entirely sure? Might it not be possible that you were mistaken?" If we've seen it all in the daylight, we'll be much less easy to discredit.'

'I suppose. But there might be fisticuffs.'

'I've never known you flinch from a punch-up.'

'True, but there's a tiger. And who knows what else?'

'As long as there are no cows in there, I think we'll be fine.'

I hmm'd but relented. This was a disagreement I clearly wasn't going to win.

With breakfast eaten, we shod ourselves for the great outdoors and Lady Hardcastle packed her satchel. As usual she had a sketchbook and pencils, but the main reason for the large bag was the Mauser she'd taken to carrying.

'What's wrong with your little Colt?' I asked.

'As I said before, I'd like something with a little more oomph. The Colt is accurate and deadly, but if I'm facing a frightened tiger I'd prefer something more substantial. Preferably something I can shoot from a decent way away. I'm not sure I can justify carrying a hunting rifle, but with the shoulder stock this isn't a bad compromise.'

I nodded. I wasn't keen on guns, but she was the expert and if I had to face an angry tiger I'd much rather she was confident of her weapon.

I made sure I was properly armed, too – sometimes a biff on the conk wasn't enough – and also popped my new toy in my pocket. My friend Ellie Wilson had sent me one of the brand-new Vest Pocket Kodak cameras from America, and I thought a few well-chosen snapshots might bolster the evidence we were hoping to collect.

We were packed and out the door by eight.

◆　◆　◆

It was my turn to drive, and I set off on a route that would take us directly to Bottom Farm.

'Not this way,' said Lady Hardcastle. 'I think it would be better if we approached the barns on foot. Let's go up to Top Farm and park out of sight – we can cross the fields from there and sneak up on them from the other side.'

'Oh, that's a good plan,' I said, and turned off to hit the hill road from the other side.

Audrey Lock saw us as we drove past Chapel Farm but we didn't want to delay ourselves by stopping to chat, so we gave her exaggerated smiles and waves and drove on.

The farmhouse at Top Farm was shuttered, and there were no signs of life. Lady Hardcastle got out and unlatched the gate to the farmyard so that we could drive the Rolls in off the road and leave it out of sight among the outbuildings.

She slung her heavy satchel over her shoulder and we set out across the late Sid Hyde's fields towards the boundary hedges.

'What's the rest of your plan?' I asked as we walked.

'If I'm to be forced to be completely honest, dear, I don't really have much of a plan beyond sneaking in to that damaged barn and looking for evidence that the animals are stolen. If we can find something – anything – to indicate that Rood and Pinkard came by the animals illicitly, we'll have a motive for Hyde's murder.'

'And if we can't? All we have on that score so far is Colonel Dawlish's cable saying that the parrot *might* be his and that someone he knows has lost a panther.'

'Quite. But while I confess I'm unclear on the law regarding the buying and selling of exotic animals, I'm sure the keepers of dangerous beasts must have to take reasonable steps to ensure the safety of others. At the very least someone has to answer for negligently allowing a wild animal to escape and kill Dick Durbin the poacher, as well as severely injuring Felix Kiddle and mutilating that sheep.'

'So proof of theft and proof the panther escaped from the barn, then.'

'Yes, please. Now, you're the expert on stealthy approaches – how do you propose we proceed from here?'

We had taken a broad, circuitous route to the farm boundary, partly so we could avoid being seen from the road, but also so we could get as good a view as possible of Bottom Farm to try to establish who was about and where they were. Four farmhands were working in a distant field with a machine which I assumed, entirely without evidence, to be the seed drill Rood had talked about.

I pointed them out to Lady Hardcastle.

'Ah, yes,' she said. 'I presume those are the chaps we saw last night.'

'I haven't seen any sign of Rood himself, mind you. We need to be careful around the barns.'

'Of course. He could be anywhere, though – I'm not inclined to call things off at this stage.'

The hedgerow dividing the two farms was tall enough to conceal us as we walked along the boundary back towards the road and the Bottom Farm barns. It wasn't long before the storm-damaged barn was looming over us and we had to make a decision about when and where to squeeze through the hedge.

I soon spotted a tiny gap. 'What about there?'

She laughed. 'You jest. I can't get through there.'

'Of course you can. Look, one of our badger friends has dug a little trench underneath. I've done this sort of thing before – it's larger than it looks.'

'Yes, but I'm not a badger.'

'Those white streaks in your hair tell a different story. Would you like me to push or pull?'

She sighed. 'Very well. You go through first to prove it can be done, then pull me through if I get stuck.'

I got down on my front and wriggled through the gap easily. There was plenty of cover on the other side so I gave a low hiss to signal it was safe for her to come through.

Her satchel appeared first and I pulled it clear. Hands and arms appeared next, then a head and a grumpy face. More wriggling ensued and soon her torso was clear.

She stopped. 'I thought you were going to pull me through.'

'I thought I was only going to do that if you got stuck.'

'I *am* bally-well stuck.'

'You don't look stuck.'

'That's because you can't see the hawthorn branch poking me in the derriere. Just bloomin' well heave me out, there's a good girl.'

Obviously this was Lady Hardcastle so the language was a good deal more fruity than that, but the sentiment was the same.

I pulled.

She emerged.

She dusted herself down and tutted.

We found cover behind some rusting farm equipment and took stock of our surroundings.

There were no obvious signs of activity in the yard but we could definitely hear animals in the storm-damaged barn.

It was time to make a decision: should we back out and return to the car, or should we press on and investigate the barn in the daylight?

It wasn't a difficult choice, and at Lady Hardcastle's signal we rose carefully and approached the rear of the barn. As we drew close I saw that a large hole in the wall had been hastily patched with a sheet of board, which was already coming loose. Surely we could remove that without making too much noise and then put it back once we were done.

I indicated my intentions to Lady Hardcastle, and together we gave the board an experimental tug. It came free easily. I hoped Rood's farmhands were better farmers than they were carpenters.

We entered the rear of the barn through the hole in the wall, and pulled the board up behind us to mask the hole again.

Inside was a menagerie to rival any I had seen before. By lantern light through a hole in the wall the night before, I had gained an impression of cages and crates, but I'd had no idea of the extent of the collection.

There were more cages than I had imagined, and as well as the tiger I could see a huge brown bear, a kangaroo, and a number of small monkeys – probably macaques of some sort. A pair of zebras looked forlornly at us from a pen far too small for them.

The smell was almost overpowering. So many animals in a large but confined space created quite an odour.

Still, there was no need for silence – there were enough grunts, snorts, rumbles and screeches to cover any noise we might make – so we felt able to explore the barn.

We quickly found Matilda the quokka and Brigadier Godspeed, who welcomed us to Bradley and Stoke's Circus.

I made Lady Hardcastle wait while I took several photographs, trying to capture the full extent of the operation. When I was done, I signalled that we could carry on.

At one side of the large open space was a walled-off room – our next target.

Inside we found a food preparation area, as well as a file containing feeding and mucking-out schedules along with care instructions for a variety of creatures. A quick scan of a ledger showed an astonishing list of animals, with columns showing dates of arrival and departure as well as coded information which I hoped might be evidence of the places from which the creatures had been stolen and the identities of their buyers. It was only vaguely incriminating on its own, but it was certainly suggestive that the entries weren't in plain text. I was sure that once Inspector Sunderland began contacting other forces around the country, the rightful owners would be traced and their identities linked to the coded lines in the ledger.

There was a noise outside. Not an animal noise – this was the sound of iron on iron, of a barn door being unlocked.

I signalled to Lady Hardcastle and we hurried out.

The cages and crates were large enough and plentiful enough to conceal us as we made our way back to the hole in the wall, and we were outside in the fresh air without being seen. We replaced the board and retreated to the cover of the rusting machinery to contemplate our next move.

Belatedly, we realized that trying to wriggle back through the tiny gap in the hedge in broad daylight would be a foolish risk that would leave us badly exposed to capture. By now, we strongly suspected Hyde had been killed when he got too close to the operation, so the consequences of being caught were potentially terrible. Still, no one knew we were there, so we had plenty of time to think of a better plan.

We heard an ominously familiar click.

'Out!'

Lady Hardcastle and I rolled our eyes at each other and stood up from behind the dilapidated clout raddler or whatever rusting farm junk it was that had been hiding us so well.

Jonathan Rood was standing a few yards away, shotgun cocked and pointing straight at us.

'The lads warned us about you two when we started the business,' he said. '"Watch out for they ladies from t'other side of the village," they said. "They's a couple of interferin' la-de-dahs," they said. "They'll be on to you if you doesn't watch out." But then I met you. You couldn't be no threat. Like the boys said, just a couple of la-de-dahs playin' at bein' detectives.' He swung the shotgun to indicate that we should move. 'And yet here you are. In my yard. Pokin' about in my business. Get goin'.'

I didn't know whether to be more offended that he was pointing a gun at us or that he'd called me a la-de-dah. I decided that this wasn't quite the time or place for an argument about my background and current place in the social hierarchy, and just followed Lady Hardcastle out into the open.

Rood gestured again. 'Keep movin'.'

He clearly didn't have a great deal of experience as a taker of prisoners, and it hadn't occurred to him to check us for weapons. On the other hand, why would two interfering la-de-dahs be armed? And even if they were, he had a shotgun.

We plodded on into the fields.

'One doesn't like to appear too inquisitive,' said Lady Hardcastle after a while. 'Our curiosity got us into this mess in the first place, after all, but would you mind awfully telling us what you intend to do?'

He was behind us so of course I couldn't see, but from the tone of voice I imagined his little laugh was accompanied by a sneer. 'I should-a thought that were obvious.'

'Again, one doesn't wish to antagonize the man with the shotgun, but if it were obvious, one wouldn't have had to ask.'

'You's goin' to be another tragic victim of the Beast of Littleton Woods. It got nosy old Sid Hyde, and it'll get you two busybodies the same way.'

'So you're not going to shoot us? I must say, that's a relief. One always imagined a slightly more glamorous and romantic end than being shot to death in a Gloucestershire field by an animal smuggler. What do you say, Armstrong? Is death by panther a suitable way to go?'

'I confess I'd been hoping to die in bed at an advanced age, surrounded by loved ones after saying something at once profound and hilarious, but "Here Lies Florence Armstrong – Mauled by Panther" would look good on a gravestone.'

'Is it well trained, this panther?' asked Lady Hardcastle.

'Of course it's not, you stupid woman,' said a new voice.

We stopped and turned. It was Pinkard. With his gumboots and his tweed trilby, and carrying a medical bag, he looked every inch the country vet. The only jarring note was that he was wearing some sort of knuckleduster which covered the index finger and pinkie on his free hand.

'I say, there's no call for that,' said Lady Hardcastle. 'Kill us if you must, but do let's try to keep things civil.'

Pinkard laughed. 'You're every bit as pompously witless as I thought you would be.' He opened his knuckleduster hand to reveal four iron, claw-like blades. 'Do you know what this is?'

'I do,' I said. 'I saw one in India. It's a *bagh nakh* – a tiger claw. Is that how you faked the injuries on Sid Hyde's body?'

'Who's a clever little lady's maid? Yes, that's exactly what it is, and exactly what I used it for. Hyde was as nosy as you, but he worked things out a good deal more quickly so he had to go. I'm really rather disappointed in you two, to be honest. People round here speak so highly of your crime-solving abilities – I was afraid you'd have fathomed it all out days ago. Still, here we are at last.'

I frowned. 'And you expect us to stand here and let you attack us with the claw? Have you heard nothing else about us?'

'Oh, I know you're a feisty little one – there are all sorts of stories about the grown men you've bested. But no, I don't expect you to stand there and let me maul you – I like to think we're a good deal more sophisticated than that.'

While Rood kept us covered with the shotgun, Pinkard crouched down and opened his bag. He produced a hypodermic syringe, already loaded with a clear, yellowish liquid.

He brandished the syringe. 'Here's how it works. You will each allow me to inject you with this animal tranquillizer. If you do not, Rood here will shoot the other one. And we wouldn't want that, now would we? It would be messy and inconvenient for me and horrifying and unpleasant for you, so I recommend we do it my way. The tranquillizer will send you into a blissful sleep – it will be happy and painless. While you're under, I shall open you up with the *bagh nakh*. Your wounds will be fatal, of course, but you'll know nothing about it, and the dim-witted authorities will chalk you up as two more victims of the Beast of Littleton Woods. I think we should have one of Rood's men discover your mutilated corpses once he and I are far enough away to be beyond suspicion.'

'All this to protect a little bit of animal smuggling?' said Lady Hardcastle.

'My dear lady, you clearly have no idea how insanely lucrative this "little bit of animal smuggling" is. People pay a fortune for the sort of creatures we're able to acquire—'

'Steal,' I said.

'If you insist. But the sums of money involved would make your head swim – I'm more than happy to end a few pointless lives to protect that. I—'

He turned suddenly as a snarling black shape appeared, as if from nowhere, and flew at Rood. It sunk its claws into his chest and knocked him to the ground. The shotgun went off as he fell, startling the panther, who let his prey go. It was terrified. Looking around, it briefly turned its attention on Pinkard, who was already fleeing across the field as fast as his gumboots would carry him.

'One is reminded of the old saying about frying pans and fires,' said Lady Hardcastle as she frantically rummaged in her satchel for her Mauser.

The panther spun round, apparently noticing us for the first time. It crouched and seemed to be trying to decide whether we were a threat.

Lady Hardcastle continued to fumble in her satchel and swear at the recalcitrant gun.

For some reason, this noise and frantic fidgeting seemed to persuade the panther that actually *I* was the threat.

It pounced.

As well as packing my exciting new camera and making sure I had my trusty knife strapped to my forearm, I had also taken the precaution of making sure I was carrying the blowpipe and drugged dart we had liberated from the Hungarian assassin in Paris. As the panther wound up for its strike, I drew the blowpipe from my sleeve, put it to my lips, and let loose the dart.

It struck the panther in the chest but it was already flying towards me.

It hit me, knocking me to the ground. I braced myself to fight it off but it just let out a rather sad whine and went limp.

Lady Hardcastle, finally armed with the Broomhandle Mauser, looked over at me and the snoring panther.

'You've got something on you, dear.' She mimed brushing at her own front. 'Just there.'

# Chapter Sixteen

I moved the unconscious cat's head so I could turn towards Lady Hardcastle. 'You could offer a little help.'

She smiled. 'Of course. What do you need?'

'Do you think you could get this panther off me?'

Between us we managed to roll the animal into a safe resting position, and I stood up.

I brushed myself down. 'How's Rood?'

Lady Hardcastle knelt to examine him. 'It looks like he's another one who caught his head on something as he went down. A rock this time. He's breathing, but unconscious. These claw gashes will need proper cleaning but they look more messy than they really are – he's not losing any more blood. We should get Dr Fitzsimmons up here.' She rolled him on to his side. 'I think we can safely leave him here for the time being. Our priority should be to get this panther locked away before she wakes up and does herself or others any more damage.'

Between us, we managed to carry the panther back to the barn. She only weighed about nine stone but she was long and floppy, and that made her seem a great deal heavier. Added to the awkwardness was the worry that she might wake up at any moment, grumpy and frightened, and savage us as we tried to get her to safety.

In the barn we quickly located an empty cage and put her inside. I found a water bowl in the feeding area and put it in with her in case she was thirsty when she came to. I had no idea what effects the sedative on the dart might have, but on those occasions when I'd been drugged unconscious and put in a cell, I always welcomed a cup of water when I woke up.

Back out in the yard we were surprised to see Sergeant Dobson, red-faced and perspiring, dismounting his bicycle.

'Good morning, Sergeant,' said Lady Hardcastle. 'Your arrival is as fortuitously well timed as ever.'

The sergeant was still panting. 'Inspector Sunderland telephoned the station. He said you might be about to do sommat foolish and I should get out to Bottom Farm as quick as I could.'

'He's a poppet, isn't he? I'm afraid he was entirely correct – we did do something foolish, but we seem to have got away with it. Thank you for rushing over here.' She saw him bending down. 'Ah, actually, please don't remove your bicycle clips. Jonathan Rood has been mauled by the panther, you see. He's not too badly hurt, but he will need the ministrations of a trained physician. Would you be an absolute treasure and cycle into the village to fetch the doctor?'

Poor Sergeant Dobson stood slowly upright and tapped the brim of his police helmet with a weary finger.

'Of course, m'lady. I'll be as quick as I can.'

He mounted up and cycled back out of the yard.

Just at that moment, Phillis Rood emerged from the farmhouse wiping her hands on a flour-dappled apron.

She walked towards us. 'Would you be good enough to explain what you's doin' on our property? You can't just go wanderin' about on people's farms, you know, no matter who you thinks you are.'

Lady Hardcastle smiled her most infuriating smile. 'Ah, Mrs Rood, good morning to you. We bring good news and bad. The good news is that the escaped panther has been recaptured. The bad is that she mauled your husband before we could incapacitate her. The good news is that he's going to be fine – he just needs Dr Fitzsimmons to clean and dress his wounds. The bad is that the jig is well and truly up.' She indicated the barn. 'We know about the stolen exotic animals. The good news is that they will soon be returned to their rightful owners. The bad is that you and your husband will soon be going to gaol.'

'I didn't 'ave nothin' to do with it. It was all that Pinkard's doin'.'

'The possible good news is that that will be for the courts to decide. Who knows, they might agree with you. The bad is that Pinkard has done a bunk, so you two might have to face the music on your own.'

'Where's Jonny?'

Lady Hardcastle pointed. 'Over in the field. We ought to get back to him. He was unconscious when we left him—'

Phillis began walking towards the field. 'Unconscious? You said he was all right. What did you leave him out there for if he was unconscious?'

Lady Hardcastle followed her. 'You'd allowed a dangerous wild animal to escape. We decided that getting it back into a cage before it harmed anyone else was more important.'

I set off after them.

'The storm did that,' said Phillis as she strode on. 'A roof beam fell on its cage.'

'So we saw. But if you're going to steal dangerous animals, you need to take responsibility for them.'

'I didn't steal nothin'.'

We walked out into the field, until Phillis saw Rood and started running towards him. Lady Hardcastle tutted, so I ran after Phillis and left Herself to catch up in her own time.

Phillis had reached her husband and he seemed to be stirring.

She knelt down and took his hand. 'Oh, my poor Jonny. Look at the state of you.' She turned to me. 'How could you leave him like this?'

'To be fair,' I said, 'he got off rather lightly – he's lucky Lady Hardcastle didn't shoot him. He was pointing a shotgun at us.'

Phillis saw the gun lying on the ground and made a lunge for it.

I reached it first and stepped on her hand. 'Please don't do that, you'll only get hurt.'

Lady Hardcastle strolled up and took charge of the shotgun. She broke it open and removed the unspent cartridge.

'Now,' she said. 'Do you have some sort of handcart so we can get him back to the house?'

'There's one in the main barn,' said Phillis, sullenly nursing her bruised hand.

'Excellent. Armstrong? Would you mind?'

Once more I walked back to the yard and towards the main barn.

As I approached, a familiar police-issued motor car pulled in through the main gates and drew up in front of me. Inspector Sunderland got out, accompanied by Constable Hancock and a man I didn't recognize.

'Miss Armstrong,' said the inspector. 'I rather thought you might be here. Where's Lady Hardcastle?'

I pointed back towards the field. 'Over there with Mr and Mrs Rood. He was attacked by the panther.'

'Good lord. Is he all right?'

'Some nasty gashes to his torso and a bit of a bump on the head, but he'll live. We've sent for Dr Fitzsimmons.'

'And the panther?'

'Safely caged with the other stolen animals in the barn. She's been tranquillized so she might be a bit groggy, but she seemed in good health when we captured her.'

'You *captured* her?' said the other man.

'We did. And you are . . . ?'

'My apologies,' said the inspector. 'Miss Armstrong, this is Dr Michael Saunders of the Bristol Zoological Society. I've asked him to come and take charge of the . . . menagerie. Dr Saunders, this is Miss Florence Armstrong, a highly skilled, thoroughly trusted, unofficial assistant of the local police.'

We how-do-you-do'd.

'Where are the animals?' asked Dr Saunders.

I pointed again. 'In the second barn.'

'Do you mind if I take a look, Sunderland? Or do you have to do police things first?'

Inspector Sunderland smiled. 'These *are* the police things, Dr Saunders. Please – go ahead.'

The zoologist headed off towards the barn.

I watched him go, then turned back to Sunderland. 'If you'll excuse me for a moment, Inspector, I've come in search of a handcart so we can bring Rood back to the farm.'

'I'm sure we can help you with that, can't we, Hancock?'

'Of course, sir. Do you have any idea where to look, miss?'

I seemed to be spending most of my time pointing at things. 'Mrs Rood said there was one over there in the main barn.'

'Fetch it, would you, Constable,' said the inspector. 'Miss Armstrong and I will make our way out to the stricken man. Meet us there.'

With another 'Yes, sir', the constable loped off.

Inspector Sunderland and I started walking in the opposite direction, back to the field.

'I knew you two would get yourselves in trouble,' he said. 'Captured the Beast of Littleton Woods, eh? That'll earn you top billing in one of Dinah's newspaper stories.'

'Captured the Beast and avoided being murdered by Robinson Pinkard.'

'Pinkard was here?'

'He was. He took off when the panther showed up.'

'Any idea where he might have gone?'

'None, I'm afraid. He lives in Chipping Bevington, though, so you might start there.'

The inspector sighed.

By the time we reached the others, Rood was awake. Phillis was comforting him, but taking occasional breaks to berate Lady Hardcastle for leaving him out in the field.

She looked up as we approached. 'I thought you was gettin' an 'andcart to take poor Jonny back to the 'ouse.'

'It's on its way,' I said. 'This is Inspector Sunderland. He wants a word with you.'

'I knows who he is. He come round 'ere t'other day askin' his questions. What do you want now?'

'I'm here to arrest you both on suspicion of theft and illegally keeping dangerous wild animals. You do not have to say anything, but anything you do say will be taken down and may be given in evidence.'

'Rood was also involved in the murder of Sid Hyde,' said Lady Hardcastle.

'Was he, indeed? Then I shall add that to the list of possible charges.'

'It weren't me,' croaked Rood. 'It was all Pinkard's doin'.'

Lady Hardcastle tutted. 'You were standing right there pointing a shotgun at us while Pinkard told us how you helped him. You didn't deny it then.'

'What, and have 'im do me in an' all? Of course I kept me mouth shut.'

I confess I thought he made a good point but, as with everything else, it was for the courts to decide.

By now, Constable Hancock was lumbering across the field pushing a handcart.

'You seem to have things well in hand, Inspector,' said Lady Hardcastle. 'Would you mind awfully if we left you to it?'

The inspector smiled. 'Not at all, my lady. I'll get everything squared away with these two and then come to see you at home. I'll need details and explanations.'

'Of course.'

She picked up her satchel and we trudged back across the field once more to Bottom Farm, and then the road up to Top Farm where we'd parked the Rolls.

◆　◆　◆

We arrived home just as Edna and Miss Jones were leaving.

'Did you find anythin'?' asked Edna. 'I couldn't 'elp overhearin' you at breakfast, like. Has Jonny Rood been smugglin' animals? Is 'e the one what done for Sid?'

Lady Hardcastle laughed. 'All in good time, Edna dear. We need to let the police do their work first. I promise we'll tell you everything as soon as the inspector says we can.'

Edna looked disappointed. 'But it was 'im, wasn't it? I never trusted 'im. Nor 'is missus, neither. Too good-lookin' for her own good, that one.'

'I promise we'll explain it all later. But for now could you keep it under your hat?'

'You can trust me, m'lady. You knows I won't say a word.'

They left and I put the kettle on for a pot of tea while I made some sandwiches for our lunch.

'It'll be all round the village before we've finished these,' I said as I put the tray on the dining table.

'And all over Gloucestershire by teatime,' agreed Lady Hardcastle. 'But we did our best. I say, you've made rather a lot of sandwiches. Are you trying to fatten me up for winter?'

'You don't need my help there, m'dear. But actually, no. Inspector Sunderland will be here soon and I've never known him turn down the offer of free food.' The doorbell rang and I went to answer it. 'It's as though he can smell it.'

It was, as I'd predicted, Inspector Sunderland, but as I let him in I saw Sergeant Dobson sweating along the lane on his bicycle. We waited for him to dismount and remove his bicycle clips, then I led them both through.

'I'm so sorry,' said the inspector. 'I seem to have interrupted your lunch.'

'Not at all, Inspector dear. There's plenty for everyone. Sit down and help yourself. You, too, Sergeant, if you'd like to.'

Sergeant Dobson smiled. 'I a'n't never been known to turn down the offer of food. I don't s'pose there's any more tea in that pot?'

'I'll make some more,' I said. 'Give me a moment.'

I returned a few minutes later with another cup and a fresh pot of tea to find them already talking about the case.

'. . . magistrates in the morning. Ah, Miss Armstrong. I was just explaining that we have Rood under guard at Fitzsimmons's place and his wife in the cells at the village police station.'

'Splendid,' I said. 'And the animals?'

'All in the tender care of Dr Saunders. He's in his element there. He'll be inventorying that lot for hours yet. I got the impression he'll be sad to see them returned to their rightful owners – there

265

are one or two specimens he'd very much like for the zoological gardens down in Clifton.'

'Perhaps after all this, some of their owners might decide that's the best place for them,' said Lady Hardcastle. 'One wonders how many of them were being kept legally in the first place.'

'Well, quite,' said the inspector. 'But we've kept you waiting long enough, Sergeant. You have news, I take it?'

'Indeed I does, sir. I just had a call from Old Roberts over Chipping station—'

'Old Roberts?'

'The stationmaster,' I said.

'Ah. Sorry, Sergeant, do carry on.'

'Thank you, sir. Well, he calls me, all excited like, 'cos he thinks he's caught a wrong'un. Fella at the station was buyin' a ticket to Aberdeen, if you please. Well, that i'n't sommat they sees every day, so of course Young Roberts—'

'Old Roberts's son,' I said. 'Works in the ticket office.'

The inspector smiled and nodded his thanks.

'That's right,' continued Sergeant Dobson. 'So Young Roberts has to look things up in their book – make sure he's got the right fare and can tell the fella all the connections he needs to make. But the fella's getting impatient, see? He don't want to hang about and he starts gettin' nasty. Tells Young Roberts his good friend Mr Billen the regional controller will have a thing or two to say about the shoddy way they runs their station. So, of course Old Roberts, 'e won't stand for no one talkin' to his staff like that – 'specially not when it's his own son, like – so he goes over to have a word with the fella. He's a bit suspicious when he hears Billen's name, an' all. He don't like Billen, see? Reckons he's up to no good—'

'We reckon Billen's up to no good, too,' said Lady Hardcastle. 'We'll fill you in later.'

Another nod and a smile from Inspector Sunderland.

'I don't know the man meself,' said the Sergeant, 'but if Old Roberts reckons he's a wrong'un, that's good enough for me. Anyway, then he notices that the fella don't have no luggage. That's a bit strange for someone goin' all the way to Aberdeen, he thinks. Now he's already asked the fella to calm down, but he's still givin' Young Roberts the benefit of his opinion about the state of Chipping Bevington station. He's gettin' hisself all hot and bothered. Agitated, like. So he takes a handkerchief out of his pocket to mop his brow, and out falls this strange knuckleduster thing with sharp blades on it. And Old Roberts don't like the look of that. But he pretends he hasn't seen it, and instead he apologizes to the fella again and helps Young Roberts with the ticket. When they's done, he directs the fella to the First Class waitin' room and invites him to make himself comfortable while they gets him a complimentary cup of tea. Only they a'n't got no First Class waitin' room and he's actually locked him in the broom cupboard. That's when 'e called me.'

'Good lord,' said Inspector Sunderland. 'When was this?'

Sergeant Dobson took his watch out of his pocket. 'Well, I reckon he telephoned me about twenty minutes ago. So give him a few minutes to collect his thoughts and get the call put through . . . maybe half an hour? I didn't think there was any rush – sounds like this fella could do with coolin' off a bit. An' after what you just told me, it sounds like it's that fella Pinkard, so I reckon he needs to get used to bein' locked up.'

Inspector Sunderland gave a chuckle. 'You may be right, Sergeant. Even so, I'd better get over there and arrest the man properly. Will you have room for him if I bring him back to Littleton while we wait for transport to take everyone into Bristol?'

'There's a cell ready and waitin' for him, sir.'

The inspector stood. 'Splendid. Thank you. Well, I'd better be on my way.'

'Call on us on your way back, please, Inspector,' said Lady Hardcastle. 'We can fill you in on all the missing details.'

'Of course – I shall see you later. Um . . . would you mind if I took another of those delicious sandwiches with me?'

I wrapped some sandwiches in greaseproof paper for the sergeant and the inspector, and we sent them on their way.

# Chapter Seventeen

While we waited for Inspector Sunderland's return, Lady Hardcastle retired to the darkroom in her orangery studio to develop the photographs I'd taken of the animals in the barn. I put my feet up with a cup of coffee and read the newspaper.

Four o'clock came, and I made some tea and a few more sandwiches. And because I thought we deserved it, I also cut some cake. And then, because I knew the inspector would be coming, I made more sandwiches and cut more cake.

I'd just come back from telling Lady Hardcastle that tiffin was served – once again thinking we should have some sort of intercom system to save me the trip out into the garden – when the doorbell rang. It really was as though he could smell the food.

I sat the inspector down in the dining room with the tea, sandwiches, cake and crime board, and went off again to try to hurry Lady Hardcastle along. I met her in the kitchen.

She smiled. 'I heard you, dear. These things can't be rushed. Everything has to be timed to the second, or the photographs won't work.'

'I wasn't rushing you as such, but I thought you'd want to know that Inspector Sunderland is here.'

'Splendidly splendid. Lay on, McFloss.'

We entered the dining room together and the inspector stood. He waved, then indicated that his mouth was full.

'Hello again, Inspector dear,' said Lady Hardcastle. 'Do sit down.'

He swallowed his bite of sandwich. 'Good afternoon, my lady.'

Though we had all been friends for more than four years, and had often dined or been to the theatre with Inspector Sunderland and his wife, Dolly, neither of them would ever dream of using the other's given name. Dolly called us Emily and Flo, and we called her Dolly. But though she referred to her husband as Ollie, he was always 'the inspector' and Lady Hardcastle was always 'my lady'. I could never put my finger on exactly why, but somehow this conscious formality seemed warm and friendly. Warmer and friendlier, perhaps, than had they been entirely chummy. It might have been the mutual respect it evinced. Or the almost quaint old-fashionedness of it. I had no idea.

Lady Hardcastle began piling her plate with sandwiches. 'Are all the miscreants behind bars?'

'They are, indeed. Young Hancock is still with Rood at the doctor's place – Fitzsimmons wants to keep him under observation for another couple of hours to make sure there are no lasting ill-effects from the knock on the head. Phillis Rood—'

'I believe her full name is "the Gorgeous Phillis Rood",' interrupted Lady Hardcastle.

'She's a strikingly attractive woman, certainly. But for now no one can admire her – she's in one of the cells at the village nick, with Mr Robinson Pinkard in the other.'

'Did he come quietly?' I asked.

'I should jolly well say not. He was furious. He ranted on about missing his train, about the awful state of the railway, and about how appallingly he'd been treated. He absolutely did not appreciate being locked in a broom cupboard for more than an hour and assured us that his good friend Bernard Billen would hear of this. I let him fume and jab me in the chest with his finger for a little while – I thought he might be more tractable if he let off a bit of steam – and then told him he was under arrest for murder, theft, and whatever charges we could think of regarding keeping dangerous animals without a licence.'

'We wondered about that,' said Lady Hardcastle. 'Does one need a licence?'

'I have absolutely no idea. It's never come up before and they certainly didn't cover it in my training. We'll find out in due course, I'm sure. Sadly, this enraged him even further and he loudly protested his innocence while I cuffed him and led him to the car. Apparently I'll be hearing from his MP. They're good friends, he says.'

'I'm sure the local MP will cut all ties once news of his crimes hits the newspapers,' I said.

'It will be as if he never knew him,' agreed the inspector.

Lady Hardcastle held up a finger as she remembered something. 'We must call Dinah. I promised her the exclusive story if we got to the bottom of everything.'

'By all means,' said the inspector, 'but would you be good enough to explain it all to me, first?'

'Of course. We can't prove *everything* but I believe we have enough of the story that getting the evidence shouldn't be too difficult. So, obviously, Pinkard is a dealer in exotic animals, and doesn't much mind where he gets them. It could well be that he's part of a larger criminal gang, but we shall have to leave that to you. We have no idea when he started – he was probably involved in the scheme while he was still living in London – but at some point after moving to Chipping Bevington, he met Jonathan Rood. Rood is an arable farmer, but he has a few animals so he would have needed the services of a vet. Pinkard needed somewhere to house his stock of stolen beasts and Rood had a large additional barn, so one imagines

Pinkard sounded him out, found that he wasn't above a bit of shady dealing, and they went into business together.'

The inspector was taking notes. 'That doesn't sound unreasonable.'

'It's pure conjecture, but it fits what we know. Now, Pinkard is friends with Bernard Billen, the regional controller of the railway, and Pinkard recruited him as traffic manager. He needed to move his stock about, and Billen knew of a disused quarry siding not too far from Rood's farm. Perfect. But how would they get the trains on to a disused siding? Easy. Billen bribed a signalman at Littleton Junction to divert the trains as necessary and everything fell nicely into place. It all ran smoothly until the signalman, now flush with bribe money, decided to retire to the coast, leaving no one to divert the animal trains. At first Billen tried to recruit Old Roberts at Chipping Bevington station. One wonders if the disused siding idea turned out to be riskier and less convenient than they first thought. Perhaps a wheeze involving the railway station itself might have been safer? I don't know. It was all academic, though, because dear Old Roberts turned out to be incorruptible. So they reverted to plan A and turned the new signalman, Wilf Dunmead. They were back in business.'

'I'm going to need to speak to Billen and Dunmead,' said the inspector. 'And do you know the name of the original signalman? They'll all face charges.'

'Jimmy Brown,' I said. 'He moved to Brean.'

'It's all right for some. Though I prefer Weston.'

'It's the donkeys, isn't it?'

He laughed. 'Probably, yes.'

Lady Hardcastle took a sip of her tea. 'Everything was grand until the storms struck a few weeks ago. They caused a lot of damage to buildings in the area – including, unfortunately, Jonny Rood's second-best barn. One suspects it wasn't particularly well maintained. Some of the wall planks were blown out, roof tiles were ripped off, and a roof beam fell into the barn itself. It struck a cage housing a beautiful female panther, bursting open the door, and the poor, terrified creature fled for her life. Frightened and hungry, she hid out in Littleton Woods, eating whatever she could catch. Then two weeks ago, she took one of Sid Hyde's sheep. Sid Hyde was a bright man, and it could well be that he was already suspicious that something was going on at Bottom Farm. When he lost one of his best ewes, he decided to investigate. Pinkard proudly boasted to us that he'd drugged Hyde and then ripped him open with the *bagh nakh*—'

'The what?'

'*Bagh nakh*. The knuckleduster weapon with the four blades. It's Indian. The name is Hindi – it means "tiger claw". Pinkard spent time in India so he must have picked it up there – probably just as an interesting curio. But when the time came to get rid of Hyde, he knew exactly how to make it look like a panther attack.'

'The weapon was still in his possession when I arrested him. He probably cleaned it, but if anyone can find traces of blood on it, Gosling can. I think we have a reasonably solid case for murder there.'

'Don't forget Dick Durbin the poacher,' I said. 'He was killed by the panther, and she badly wounded Felix Kiddle. If it hadn't been for Rood and Pinkard's negligence, she'd never have been roaming free. They're indirectly responsible for both attacks.'

'There's certainly a case to be made,' said the inspector.

'There certainly is,' agreed Lady Hardcastle. 'Meanwhile, we got sidetracked – or so we thought – by Daisy's giant rat and the mystery miscreant who was mis-sorting the letters at the post office. But the giant rat was a quokka, and the post mucker-abouter was a scarlet macaw, and they'd both escaped at the same time as the panther. We caught them both and took them to Pinkard to be checked over. But he couldn't risk having us trace their owners, so he promptly stole them back and returned them to Bottom Farm. Then we put it all together—'

'*You* put it all together,' I said. 'I was nowhere near it this time.'

'You're too kind, dear. So I put it all together when my friend George Dawlish – you remember George? He owns Bradley and Stoke's Circus. They came to the village in '08.'

'I remember,' said the inspector.

'Of course. It was rather memorable, wasn't it? Anyway, George wrote to me to tell me he'd lost a parrot, and it all fell into place. That was when Flo and I went to the farm to make sure of our facts before you became properly involved. There are ledgers and paperwork in the barn—'

'We have them – thank you.'

'Excellent. And Flo took some photographs of the barn. The prints are drying in the orangery. Then Rood held us at gunpoint while Pinkard foolishly confessed all, and we'd probably be dead if our dear friend the panther hadn't savaged Rood and frightened Pinkard away.'

'I've been meaning to ask: how *did* you capture her?'

'Blowpipe,' I said. 'Fast-acting tranquillizer. Ancient South American recipe. Caught her square in the chest. She was already asleep by the time she hit me.'

He chuckled as he finished making his notes. 'The court case will be an entertaining one. I think I have the full picture now. There's plenty of documentary evidence, and if we can't get Rood or the Gorgeous Phillis to turn on Pinkard, we still have your testimony. Billen might wilt under pressure, too. I foresee a pleasing round of convictions. Pinkard might even swing – especially as he tried to kill you two as well.'

Lady Hardcastle shrugged. 'If I could have got my bally gun out of my stupid bally satchel I might have saved you the bother.'

'I'm glad you didn't – it would be easy to argue self-defence but it would have muddied things. It's all much neater this way.'

'I suppose. Would you like some more tea?'

He put away his notebook and pencil. 'No, thank you, my lady. I'd better be getting back. And you have a newspaper reporter to call. I'll never hear the end of it if you don't.'

'Why ever would you get it in the neck, Inspector dear?'

'If you don't tell Dinah, she'll moan to Gosling. And then he'll complain to me for not reminding you. It'll be better all round if you telephone her straight away and tell her the full story.'

'I shall do precisely that.'

'Marvellous. Well, thank you for your help, ladies, I shall bid you farewell. If I don't see you before, Dolly and I will see you for dinner at Humphrey's next Tuesday evening.'

I showed him out.

◆　◆　◆

Miss Jones had prepared a pie for us, as well as peeling some carrots and potatoes. All I had to do was get everything cooking, and make a red wine sauce in the frying pan she'd used to brown the beef and had left unwashed for that very purpose.

Lady Hardcastle's telephone call to Dinah Caudle at the *Bristol News* had taken quite a while, and I wondered if it might have been quicker to drive into town to tell her in person.

The paper was still only published on Mondays and Fridays, and Miss Caudle was confident that such an important, exclusive story would appear in the Monday edition. She was, apparently, extremely happy and grateful.

Over dinner we decided that the villagers ought to know what had been happening before the *News* appeared in the newsagent's on Monday, and the best way to do that would be to go to the Dog and Duck. Actually, the absolute best way would be simply to tell Edna, who could spread news quicker and more widely than any newspaper, but she'd already gone home. There was a chance that Constable Hancock, another noted gossip, had already given them the gist, but he wouldn't have all the details and we wanted to make sure the full story got round.

So, after dinner, we strolled up to the pub to set the story straight.

There was an unexpected hush from the drinkers near the door as we stepped inside. Then, as people further inside started to notice us, applause broke out. By the time we reached the bar, the whole place was on its feet and we were being offered congratulations and thanks from all sides.

Lady Hardcastle, never one to hide her light under a bushel, was beaming.

She raised her hands for silence. 'Thank you, dear friends. I take it word of our encounter with the panther has spread—'

'Saved us, you 'as.'

'Wait, I thought it was a lion.'

'I can finally let the cat out. Poor little fella's absolutely burstin'.'

She waited until the hubbub had subsided a little. 'In celebration . . . the drinks are on me.'

The place erupted again, and we had to wait a while for the rush to die down so we could talk to Daisy.

Eventually, she was free and came over to us. 'Did you find Matilda?'

'We did, dear,' said Lady Hardcastle, 'but I'm afraid she's in the care of the man from the Bristol Zoological Society now. He'll be tracking down her rightful owner.'

Daisy sighed. 'Ah well. I didn't really have a chance to get to know her. But she was so adorable-lookin'. I'll miss her.'

'She was a lovely girl. The postal parrot—'

'Mail-sorting macaw?' I suggested.

'The psittaciform . . . no, I can't think of anything. Anyway, we found the parrot, too, and I strongly suspect we also know his owner: our friend George Dawlish.'

'Him from the circus?'

'The very same. But the main thing is that the panther is back in captivity and the suspected murderer is under lock and key. He and the Roods should be down at the Bridewell in Bristol by now, and they'll be up before the magistrates tomorrow.'

Over the next half an hour – with everyone asking questions it took much longer than it had with the inspector – Lady Hardcastle explained everything that had been happening over the past couple of weeks. She spared them no details, in the hope of reassuring them that they were, indeed, safe now. At the end, glasses were raised and our health toasted.

We stayed a while, answering questions and accepting metaphorical pats on the back – no one was forward enough to actually pat us – before Lady Hardcastle left instructions with Old Joe that he should chalk up the rest of the evening's drinks to her account and send the bill at his earliest convenience.

We slipped quietly out while the villagers continued to celebrate the end of the Panther Menace, and sauntered back to the house.

◆　◆　◆

I carried the brandy-laced cocoa through to the drawing room, where Lady Hardcastle was playing a piece I vaguely recognized.

I put the tray down on a side table. 'What's that?'

'"Marche royale du lion" from Saint-Saëns's *Carnival of the Animals*. I couldn't find anything about panthers. There's a bit about kangaroos later – that might do as a tribute to dear little Matilda.'

But she stopped as soon as she'd finished the introduction and came to join me beside the fire.

'I do enjoy playing, but I sometimes wonder if we ought to get a gramophone. Then we could listen to music while I have a nice sit-down.'

'I'm surprised you haven't bought one already,' I said.

'I am, too. It's most unlike me not to embrace new technology. And the gramophone isn't even new. We should see what they have in the music shops in Bristol.'

'We'll need something to do now the village is safe once more.'

'We shall, indeed.' She raised her cocoa cup. 'Here's to us and another successful case.'

'To us,' I said. 'Everything is wrapped up nicely.'

'Everything except saving poor Fred Spratt from Joyce's misguided attentions.'

'You'll think of something. You always do.'

'I'm not sure that's entirely true, but I shall put my thinking cap on and try to come up with something. We should go to The Grange tomorrow.'

# Chapter Eighteen

Sunday morning was a relaxed affair. I allowed Lady Hardcastle an extra half-hour's lie-in before taking up her starter breakfast, and we ate a most leisurely breakfast in the dining room once she was finally up and dressed.

The post arrived while we were eating and I got up to fetch it.

'It all seems to be for us,' I said as I sat back down and handed Lady Hardcastle's letters to her.

Silence followed as we each read our own mail.

My twin sister Gwen was well, but with the baby due in less than two months she was now, so she complained, the size of 'an ammunition wagon'. I didn't fully understand the reference. Given her husband Dai's connection to the Royal Artillery, it was obviously something to do with field guns, but beyond that I didn't really have much to go on. She'd made references to hippos before, so I took it to mean that she was feeling uncomfortably large. Meanwhile, in Maryland, Ellie Wilson was still frustrated with her family, still playing the piano, and still writing constantly to Skins Maloney. So no change there, but it had been less than two weeks since her last letter, so perhaps it was a little ambitious to expect any. I made a mental note to write back with news of our recent adventures, possibly playing up my prowess with the blowpipe since Lady Hardcastle was so determinedly not mentioning it in her own accounts.

The lady herself opened another letter and read for a few seconds. 'Oh, how lovely.'

'Good news, I take it?'

'The best. It's from Lavinia. She's expecting another child in the spring.'

'Another nephew or niece for you to spoil and lead astray.'

'I know. I'll have my work cut out with two of them. This is most gratifying.' She read on. 'Oh, and Harry twisted his ankle playing golf.'

'How on earth . . . ?'

'Caught it in a rabbit hole, apparently. He can't drive and he's hobbling around with a stick.'

'Poor Harry.'

'Poor Lavinia – she's the one who'll have to look after him. My dear brother is a terrible patient.'

I smiled. 'I'd better get this stuff cleared up. When did you plan to go to The Grange?'

'I thought we might drop in for elevenses. I'll telephone Gertie while you do maidly things.'

Lady Farley-Stroud had been only too pleased to invite us for coffee and buns, and we had driven up the hill to The Grange to arrive at exactly eleven o'clock.

The spaniels were tearing about in front of the house, with little Minty doing her best to keep up. As we pulled to a stop outside the front door, all four dogs sprinted over to us to make sure we really were who we seemed to be. The Rolls was familiar, but the people inside might be different, after all.

As soon as they saw us getting out of the car and were able to confirm our identities, we were greeted enthusiastically and led towards the house. Minty seemed not quite to understand what the game was but was willing to join in anyway, and we approached the door with an honour guard of gleefully bouncing dogs.

Jenkins led all six of us through to the library, where Sir Hector, Lady Farley-Stroud and Mrs Adaway were already sitting comfortably and tucking in to the promised coffee and buns.

Sir Hector stood as we entered. 'Hail the conquering whatnots. O frabjous day and all that, what?'

'Hello, Hector dear. Not so much a vorpel blade going snicker-snack, more Flo's blowpipe going *pftht*. And we didn't leave it dead, either – we gently carried it unconscious to Rood's second-best barn and put it in a cage. There was some galumphing on the way back, though, I suppose.'

I was forced to rethink – I *was* getting credit, after all.

Sir Hector chuckled. 'Nevertheless, m'dears, you rid the village of the dread monster. Well done, you. Sit ye, sit ye.'

'Yes, well done,' said the seated sisters-in-law together.

We sat on the sofa with Lady Farley-Stroud. At her invitation, I poured two cups of coffee and helped myself to a piece of Mrs Brown's celebrated lardy cake.

'Dear Minty will be safe in the grounds now,' said Mrs Adaway. 'She's still terribly grateful to you for saving her life. She tells me often.'

'I'm glad you've both recovered from your ordeal,' said Lady Hardcastle. 'And speaking of recovery, how's Felix Kiddle?'

'Very much on the mend,' said Sir Hector. 'Strong as an ox, that fella. Rarin' to be back at work. Told him to take it easy, though – we can afford to keep payin' his wages till he's properly fit to muster again.'

Mrs Adaway tutted. 'The lower orders will never learn their proper place if you keep coddling them, Hector. You're storing up trouble for yourself, you mark my words.'

'Could be the exact opposite, Joycey, old horse. When the workers rise up against their bourgeois capitalist oppressors, they'll say, "No, don't put old Hector up against the wall and shoot 'im. He was a good sort. Paid a fair wage, treated his workers well."'

Mrs Adaway tutted again and took a bite of her scone.

'Got in touch with m'solicitors, too, and set up a trust for Dick Durbin's son. Chap might have been a poacher, but he didn't deserve to die like that. We'll make sure his family's looked after.'

Mrs Adaway tried to tut for a third time, but the scone prevented her. She settled for a scowl instead.

'The other news,' continued Sir Hector, obliviously, 'is that I'm talkin' to Hyde's brother. Chap's Hyde's only livin' relative. I'm plannin' to buy Top Farm and rent it to Louis Finch. It's a good farm – he should be able to make a decent livin' off it.'

Mrs Adaway was itching to say something, but Lady Farley-Stroud spoke up before she could clear her mouth of another bite of scone.

'Are you still both available to help with the arrangements for the Christmas dinner and concert?'

'I certainly am,' I said. 'I love that you feed and entertain the village at Christmas.'

I oughtn't to have been so proud of causing Mrs Adaway's face to turn that entertaining shade of red, as she struggled to swallow her mouthful and give Lady Farley-Stroud the benefit of her opinion on feeding villagers at Christmas.

'What about you, Joyce?' asked Lady Hardcastle. 'Will you be joining us again? It was so lovely to see you here for the yuletide festivities.'

Mrs Adaway was finally free to speak. 'If I'm invited. I can't say I entirely approve of the Boxing Day bean-feast – a lot of scroungers and hangers-on coming up for a free meal – but one does like to be with family.'

'There's the concert, too,' I said. 'All the villagers doing their party pieces.'

'Actually, yes, that is rather charming. With dear Fred Spratt on violin. Which reminds me – Minty needs more steak if she's to return to full health after her ordeal. I need to get down to the butcher's shop.' She grinned. 'If I'm lucky, that dreadful Eunice creature will be out and I'll have dearest Frederick to myself.'

I was trying to decide whether to say that his name was actually Alfred – it wasn't, but the thought amused me, anyway – when I saw Lady Hardcastle start to smile. So expressive was her face sometimes that I could have sworn you could actually see the thoughts forming.

'Actually, dear, I don't think he's there today. We saw Daisy at the pub last night and he's left her and Eunice in charge while he goes to a Labour Party meeting in Chipping Bevington.'

Mrs Adaway spluttered on her coffee. 'Labour Party?'

'Oh, yes. He's a staunch supporter. Has been since before we moved here.'

'Oh, this will never do. I had no idea. Why did no one tell me? You let me moon after a Marxist. That's it, then. I can have no more to do with the dreadful man if he's one of them. Eunice is welcome to him.'

'Oh, come now,' said Lady Hardcastle, 'I'm sure—'

'No, that's the end of it.' She stood. 'Minty! Come! We shall have to see what Mrs Brown has in the kitchen for you.'

She and the dog swept out.

'Ha!' barked Sir Hector. 'Well done, Emily. Wish I'd known it was that simple.'

'Yes,' said Lady Farley-Stroud. 'Well done. I'm not sure what we'd do without you.'

# Acknowledgements

As always, I am indebted to my editor, Victoria Pepe, whose skilful blend of kind encouragement and 'Yeah . . . don't do that' helped to turn my story ideas into something everyone might enjoy (rather than just me – I always think I'm a hoot).

Once the manuscript was written, Laura Gerrard's perspicacious insights once again encouraged me to turn an okay story into a good story.

I am, and will always be, immensely grateful to them both.

# Author's Notes

Unusually for a Lady Hardcastle Mystery, this story is set entirely in the fictitious area of Gloucestershire around Littleton Cotterell and Chipping Bevington. Littleton Junction does not exist, nor is there a marshalling yard there. There are several pubs in the real-life area with 'Railway' in their names, but the Railway Arms is as made up as the Dog and Duck.

Lady Hardcastle was partly correct about the donkeys at Brighton. The beach there is pebbly and wholly unsuited for donkeys, but there are many photographs and accounts of donkey rides. The photos usually show the Lower Esplanade, and this is backed up by several online reminiscences.

The first citation of the word 'cryptozoology' in the Oxford English Dictionary is from 1968. The cited text mentions the word and credits its invention to Ivan T. Sanderson. Hardcastle and Flo have form for making up new words, so it amused me to have Flo make one up that subsequently came into general use when it was coined by a real person.

Banjo Patterson's song 'Waltzing Matilda' was written in 1895 and first published in 1903. It quickly became very well known and is often now referred to as 'Australia's unofficial national anthem'. But it was first recorded in 1926 by a British man, John Collinson. Born and raised in Wallsend, Northumberland, he moved to

Australia shortly before the outbreak of World War One and served with the Australian Army in Gallipoli and France. He was badly wounded at the Battle of the Somme and was sent to the Australian Auxiliary Hospital in Harefield, Middlesex. After one of the twenty-seven operations he endured to repair his arms and legs he began singing 'Waltzing Matilda' while still groggy from the anaesthetic. Nurses encouraged him to take part in a concert at the hospital, where his talent was recognized, and he was recommended to Sir Henry Wood (of the Proms fame), who took him under his wing. With Wood's support, Collinson attended the Royal Academy of Music in London in 1919, and from there his musical career took off. He performed all over Britain and, in 1926, became the first person to record 'Waltzing Matilda'. The recording was released by Vocalion Records.

Although I tend to think of it as a modern word, it turns out that 'brunch' has been in use since at least 1895 and was probably popularized (though almost certainly not coined) by Guy Beringer, who used it in an article in *Hunter's Weekly* that year.

Lady Hardcastle and her fictional friend, Alice Austin-Walter, speculate on the possibilities of nuclear fission around thirty years before Enrico Fermi and his team succeeded in operating the first nuclear reactor at the University of Chicago, in 1942. Fusion, Lady Hardcastle's other idea, still isn't a viable source of energy, but the first fusion bomb was developed by Edward Teller, Stanislaw M. Ulam, et al., and was first tested in 1952 at Enewetak Atoll in the Marshall Islands. As always, there's no reason for Lady Hardcastle to do any of this other than my own amusement.

Though it may be rare, and confined to particular types of engine, many videos exist online showing the glowing smoke effect produced by some steam locomotives at night-time.

In Britain, the process of attaching a harnessed horse to a cart – referred to in the US as 'hitching' – is called 'putting to', while un-attaching it is 'taking out'.

Obviously a fast-acting, non-lethal sedative that would work in tiny quantities on the tip of a blowpipe dart is entirely fanciful. But so is much else about the story, so I'm happy to let it stand.

# About the Author

*Photo © 2018 Clifton Photographic Company*

Tim Kinsey grew up in London and read history at Bristol University. *The Beast of Littleton Woods* is the twelfth story in the Lady Hardcastle Mystery series, and he is also the author of the Dizzy Heights Mystery series. His website is at tekinsey.uk and you can follow him on: Facebook at www.facebook.com/tekinsey, Bluesky at bsky.app/profile/tekinsey.uk, Instagram at www.instagram.com/tekinseymysteries, and Threads at www.threads.net/@tekinseymysteries.

# Follow the Author on Amazon

If you enjoyed this book, follow T E Kinsey on Amazon to be notified when the author releases a new book!
To do this, please follow these instructions:

## Desktop:

1) Search for the author's name on Amazon or in the Amazon App.
2) Click on the author's name to arrive on their Amazon page.
3) Click the 'Follow' button.

## Mobile and Tablet:

1) Search for the author's name on Amazon or in the Amazon App.
2) Click on one of the author's books.
3) Click on the author's name to arrive on their Amazon page.
4) Click the 'Follow' button.

## Kindle eReader and Kindle App:

If you enjoyed this book on a Kindle eReader or in the Kindle App, you will find the author 'Follow' button after the last page.

Made in the USA
Las Vegas, NV
28 September 2021